Praying Mantis

A
Harith Athreya
Mystery

PRAYING MANTIS

RV RAMAN

A
HARITH ATHREYA
MYSTERY

Copyright © 2023 by RV Raman
Cover and jacket design by Georgia Morrissey

ISBN: 978-1-957957-00-5
eISBN: 978-1-957957-15-9
Library of Congress Control Number: Available upon request

First hardcover edition published in June 2023
By Agora Books
An imprint of Polis Books, LLC

www.PolisBooks.com
62 Ottowa Road S
Marlboro, NJ 07746

The Harith Athreya series by RV Raman

A WILL TO KILL
A DIRE ISLE
PRAYING MANTIS

DRAMATIS PERSONAE

Harith Athreya - An investigator with a vivid imagination; goes to his friend Javed's castle-turned-hotel to help solve a curious riddle

Javed Rais - An ex-police psychologist and the owner of Peter Dann Castle; Athreya's friend who tells him about the riddle

Veni Athreya - Athreya's chubby, merry and garrulous wife; always finds something to talk about

Asma Rais - Javed's twenty-three-year-old daughter

Maazin - Asma's cousin who runs Peter Dann under Javed's supervision

Dave Clarkson - An Irish-American who owns a homestay nearby Peter Dann Castle

Margot Clarkson - Dave's French wife

The five dubious guests:

1.   **Linda Mathew** - Asma's close friend and a very devout Christian

2.   **Sarosh Gulati** - An angel investor from Mumbai who seems reckless in investing

3.   **Ipshita Lahiri** - An attractive and competent interior designer from Kolkata

4.   **Purbhi Chakradhar** - A nervous freelancer from Kolkata who dabbles in technology

5.   **Dhavak Strummer** - A popular singer and a minor celebrity

Mrinal Shome - A successful young woman entrepreneur who appears very vulnerable

Kinshuk Sodhi - Mrinal's fiancé and a celebrity trainer from Mumbai

Pralay Shome - Mrinal's estranged brother

Baranwal - Staff manager at Peter Dann Castle

Ravi - A young staffer at Peter Dann Castle

Shivali Suyal - The ACP in charge; sharp, young and follows her own ideas

Sub Inspector Negi - Shivali's assistant

Chetan - An experienced trek guide; dependable

Dr Farha - The psychiatrist who treated Naira Rais for depression and associated conditions

Prologue

7 SEPTEMBER 2010
NORTH 24 PARGANAS, WEST BENGAL

The old building stood well back from the street. Built at a time when land was less precious, the owners had left generous space all around the house. The upper floor of the decades-old structure comprised a single flat where the owners lived. The ground floor was divided into two halves, both of which had been rented out. A shop occupied the front, street-facing half, while a young couple with a baby lived in the rear. Both floors had low ceilings, and the traditional wooden windows were small and not particularly conducive to good ventilation.

Dusk had fallen and a murky darkness shrouded the entire street and beyond. Low clouds, typical of the season, hung overhead oppressively. The area was in the midst of another prolonged power outage. Dim yellow light from lamps and candles flickered through most windows. The few houses that had battery-operated emergency lamps, or still had a charge in their inverter batteries, enjoyed the luxury of a brighter white light.

The dark street was deserted, but the ominous roar of rioting was not far away. One of the mobs that had been sweeping through the district, looting, breaking and burning as they went, had reached the main road at the end of the street. The acrid smell of smoke hung in the still air. Fear was palpable on both sides of locked doors.

Silent and lightless, the ground floor shop had long since

been locked and shuttered. Its doors and wooden windows were shut fast against potential rioters. The first streams of smoke escaping from under the doors and through the gaps between warped windows went unnoticed in the murky darkness. Had anyone been watching, the yellow light from the fire within might have been taken for lamplight. Only when the surging flames burst out through the windows did the neighbourhood realize that something was amiss.

But it was too late by then.

Cans, buckets and drums of paint, thinner and other combustible material that were stored in the shop had caught fire. It did not have a permit to stock flammable material. Yet, the storage area was full of it. As were the spaces under the staircase that led to the upper floor.

Once these illegally stowed incendiaries caught fire, all hope was lost for the middle-aged couple on the upper floor. With an inferno roaring up the stairwell and with all the windows barred, there was no escape.

The tenants in the rear part of the ground floor were luckier, even though they were singed and burnt by the roaring flames. But their one-year-old baby was not lucky enough. Smoke got into her little lungs as they made a dash through the leaping flames. She would succumb within forty-eight hours.

As a crowd began gathering on the street, a girl rushed out of the apartment block opposite the burning house.

'Ma!' she screamed as she ran headlong across the street. 'Baba!'

The roaring flames, fuelled by the incendiaries, singed her hair and scalded her skin as she darted towards the blazing building. She rocked back and screamed again, her eyes wide and wild.

'Ma! Baba!'

A younger boy—her brother—stared horrified and mute as the girl made another attempt to approach the burning house. A neighbour threw his arms around her waist and held her back.

'There's nothing you can do!' he yelled in Bengali. 'You'll only kill yourself!'

The girl's music teacher, who lived in the apartment block, emerged from it and hugged the girl, pulling her back across the street foot by foot. Her husband took charge of the boy and they backed away from the flames.

By then, a mob had entered the street. Seeing the rioters, the neighbours fled back to their houses. The music teacher and her husband hustled the newly orphaned girl and the boy and took them away to their flat.

The flames took little time to reduce the old building to ashes as the rioters fled the scene and residents watched from afar. By the time the fire engines arrived, the destruction was complete. The two corpses they found in the charred remnants of the house were beyond recognition, but the police eventually identified the bodies from the jewellery they were wearing.

That day would go down as one of the blacker days in West Bengal's history. Many shops had been looted and buildings gutted. The next week, the police listed the preliminary cause of the fire in the old, two-storey building as 'rioting and arson'.

Nothing could have been further from the truth.

1

Harith Athreya gazed in amusement at his friend across the table as they sat outdoors, sipping tea at the Naini Retreat, a popular hotel in Nainital. Javed Rais, a large-built, bearded man of sixty, sucked on his pipe and gazed back enquiringly. He had just invited Athreya to Peter Dann—his boutique hotel—a couple of hours drive from Nainital.

'To help solve a riddle?' Athreya asked, cocking an eyebrow. 'You want me to come to Peter Dann for that?'

'I don't see you having anything better to do,' Javed drawled in his gravelly voice, as he scratched his head through his thick greying mane. 'Your wife is soon going overseas to be with your daughter. Your son is travelling extensively as usual. What are you going to do at home all by yourself? Mope? And with no case on hand, you are not fruitfully occupied either.'

'Still... a trivial riddle, Javed?'

'I don't think it is that trivial. Don't judge before you hear what it is. Who knows, it may be the beginning of something larger. Besides, you have been promising to visit me. You've come all the way to Nainital—virtually a stone's throw from Peter Dann. Why not drive back with Asma and me?'

Asma was Javed's twenty-three-year-old daughter. She and Athreya's wife—Veni—were shopping at the local market, leaving the two old friends in each other's company.

'Fair enough.' Athreya sat back. 'Let's hear about the riddle.'

Javed glanced around the outdoor restaurant paved in an

alternating pattern of maroon and beige square stones. All
the other tables were unoccupied and the hut that was used
in the evenings for barbecue was empty. Nobody was within earshot. All around them were the Himalayan foothills.

'I was here at this very hotel in Nainital six weeks ago
for a business meeting,' he began. 'We were having lunch
at the restaurant indoors when I noticed a group of seven
people at the far corner. I happened to look in their direction several times during the fifteen minutes they were
there. I couldn't see two of them who were hidden behind
pillars, but I saw the other five quite well. I didn't think
much about it at that time, except that one of the five was
Linda, Asma's friend from her Gurgaon days.

'The group was totally engrossed in a very serious discussion. When I was halfway through my lunch, they finished their meal and left the restaurant. Apart from telling
Asma later that I had seen her friend, I dismissed the matter
from my mind.

'Until four weeks later, when the same group checked
into Peter Dann. I was in for a surprise. Each of them
arrived and checked in separately, completely independent
of the others. They came at different times and in different
vehicles. I discovered later that they had also made their
bookings individually. What really foxed me was this: they
acted as if they were strangers meeting for the first time!'

'Sure that it was the same group?' Athreya asked.

'Oh, yes! Only this time, they were five and not seven.
And one of the five was Linda. When I asked them if they
knew each other from before, they all replied in the nega-
tive. I was supposed to believe that they were meeting each
other for the very first time.'

Javed paused to relight his pipe as Athreya waited for
him to continue. Crisp mountain air blew gently across the
outdoor restaurant.

'Linda too insisted to Asma that she was meeting the
other four for the first time,' Javed resumed shortly. 'When

I casually inserted Nainital and the Naini Retreat into a conversation, they—in all seriousness—denied familiarity with the town and the hotel. Now, why would a group of young adults, most in their twenties, want to do such a thing?'

'Some sort of a practical joke?' Athreya suggested. He was amused at the riddle and wasn't taking it very seriously.

'Their denials were far too strong for that. I began wondering if there was something clandestine about their Nainital meeting. If so, was their visit to Peter Dann also fishy in some way? Or, as you say, was this all an elaborate, but innocuous, joke of some sort?'

'How long did they stay at Peter Dann?' Athreya asked, his interest rising.

'A couple of days. They were to go on a trek, but they cancelled for some reason. They cut short their stay and left. So, this is my little riddle of the five guests: a group of twenty-somethings who know each other but pretend to be strangers. What do you think of it?'

'Curious, but not worrisome.'

Athreya ran his long fingers through his uncommonly fine hair that had recently acquired its first flecks of grey. Save the silvery tuft in the front, the rest of his head was largely black. His fine-haired beard too was mostly black, except at the chin where a small patch of silver matched his forehead.

'It gets more curious,' Javed replied. 'Want to hear it?'

Athreya nodded, making the silvery tufts catch the sunlight and shine.

'The same group,' Javed continued, 'has checked into Peter Dann once again.'

'The same five?'

Javed nodded. 'Including Linda. They checked in last night.'

'But this time, they can't pretend to be strangers to each

13

other, right?'

'They can't. Not after meeting each other on their first visit.'

'And the purpose of their visit this time?' Athreya asked.

'To go on a trek... the one they missed the last time.'

'I don't see why this bothers you, Javed. Looks like a bunch of the young doing some silly thing.'

'Hang on,' Javed rumbled in his deep voice. 'There is more. A strange thing happened when the five guests made their bookings for their first visit. Peter Dann was fully booked for the dates they were to stay. Three other parties had made bookings for the same dates. Now, this is pre-season, and we almost never have a full house. But oddly enough, we were booked full to capacity. I was, of course, pleased. But two days before the five arrived, all the other parties cancelled their bookings within four hours of each other.'

'All?' Athreya asked, his eyebrows rising enquiringly.

'All,' Javed nodded. 'All except these five.'

'Maybe the other guests were a single group.'

'That's what I thought, but they weren't. The bookings were made by three different people in three different cities.'

'So?' Athreya countered.

'Remember I told you that the five have checked in again for a second time?'

'Yes. You said that they checked in last night.'

'And guess what? We had three other bookings till three nights ago. This time too, Peter Dann was fully booked. And the other three parties cancelled their bookings the day before yesterday. Just like the first time! Now, once could be a coincidence, but twice?'

'The parties who cancelled... were they from different cities this time too?'

'Yes—Bangalore, Delhi and Pune.'

Athreya paused to reflect on what Javed had said. He

had to acknowledge that there were too many coincidences here and that the modus operandi on both the occasions were too similar. That the three parties—other than the five guests—had cancelled their bookings at the last moment on both occasions, was intriguing. 'The riddle of the five guests', as he was starting to think of it now, was beginning to appeal to him.

'That is strange,' Athreya conceded. 'Anything peculiar about these five guests?'

Javed shook his head. 'They seem to be regular young people. As I said, most of them are in their twenties.'

'No sign of the other two? The group had comprised seven people in Nainital.'

'Not yet, but two people are to check in tomorrow. I don't know who they are, and I don't know if they are the other two.'

'This *is* intriguing,' Athreya admitted. 'What do you make of it?'

'You will probably disagree with me,' Javed replied, scratching his beard pensively. 'But I sense that something is amiss. I fear the five might be planning something that I'm clueless about.'

'The immediate questions to answer are these,' Athreya said. 'Who are these parties who booked and cancelled twice? Were they the same both times? Are they genuine or fake? Were those bookings orchestrated by the five guests?'

'Precisely! This is more than a mere riddle. Something strange is at play here, and I would like you with me when it plays out.'

Athreya's interest was indeed piqued. A grin spread on his face, drawing an answering smile from Javed.

'Like old times, eh?' he asked.

Large and heavy, Javed was six-foot-three and well over a hundred kilos. With a wide, ruddy face, broad shoulders, heavy biceps, large hands and a hawk nose that had been knocked askew in a fight, he looked like a prize fighter.

Nobody would have guessed that he had once been a police psychologist.

He and Athreya had served together in the police force years ago. While Athreya had been at the forefront of investigations, Javed helped in interpreting actions and words of witnesses, suspects and victims. Their discussions would often go on late into the night. On more than one occasion, Athreya's vivid imagination and Javed's understanding of the mind had combined to crack cases.

Both had taken early retirement within a few years of each other. While Athreya had continued investigating crime in a private capacity, Javed had turned a hotelier and converted his wife's family estate into a heritage hotel.

'Old times,' Athreya reminisced. 'Yes.'

'So, what say you?' Javed asked. 'Like to come?'

Before Athreya could answer, a chubby, gregarious, middle-aged woman walked up to them—Athreya's wife, Krishnaveni, who was called Veni. Her wavy hair was shot generously with grey, and her merry face hinted at garrulousness. The five-foot-two lady was, more often than not, seen talking, for she had the remarkable ability to find something to talk about in any situation. With Veni was Javed's daughter, Asma.

'Come where?' the affable Veni asked as she sat down, deftly inserting herself into the conversation.

'Javed wants me to go with him to his hotel,' Athreya replied.

'Good idea!' she exclaimed. 'Why don't you go? Asma assures me that Peter Dann is a beautiful place. You are at a loose end anyway. I would have liked to come had I not been going abroad in a few days.'

'You'll have to return to Delhi alone.' Athreya glanced at her with a trace of concern.

'No big deal,' she replied, waving her hand. 'There's a large group leaving tomorrow. I'll be fine.'

'Sure?'

'Absolutely! Go have fun at Peter Dann. I'm sure you won't miss the polluted city air when you are there.'

'Okay.' Athreya turned to Javed. 'Peter Dann, it is. When do we leave?'

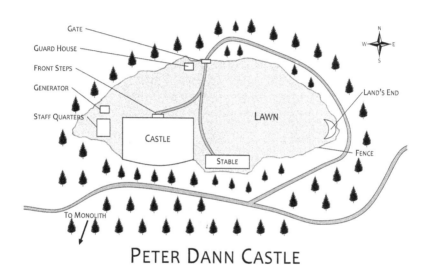

Gate

Guard House

Front Steps

Generator

Staff Quarters

Castle

Stable

Lawn

Land's End

Fence

N
W E
S

To Monolith

PETER DANN CASTLE

2

Athreya and Javed stood on Peter Dann Castle's rooftop terrace, gazing eastward as the sun began setting in the west behind them. They were awaiting one of the most spectacular sights the Himalayan foothills had to offer. The orange-red rays of the dying sun were about to illuminate the distant Nanda Devi peak and make it glow as if it were wrapped in vast sheets of gold foil. When awash with the rays of the setting sun, it was a glorious sight to behold. Craggy, snow-clad ridges undulated away on either side of the peak, adding to the distinctiveness of the view.

Standing tall and lean behind his tripod and camera, Athreya fidgeted with the remote control as he waited for the right moment to start clicking. The gleaming peak would first glow golden. And as the sun sank, it would turn coppery before surrendering to the night's embrace.

As was always the case when facing the Himalayas, Athreya was awestruck by their vast magnificence and nature's grandeur. In his mind's eye, he saw the Nanda Devi standing tall and proud like an ancient goddess watching over her domain and her people. In his vivid imagination, she seemed to be frowning at five children—representing Javed's five guests—playing hide-and-seek among the trees.

Clad in cargoes and a denim shirt, Javed lounged beside Athreya, sucking on his pipe and speaking between puffs of blue-grey smoke, which the brisk breeze whisked away. They had arrived at Peter Dann Castle half an hour ago, and had quickly adjourned to the terrace to witness the sunset.

The hundred-year-old stone edifice upon which they stood had ambitiously, if not a little immodestly, been named Peter Dann Castle by its builder. Despite lacking towers, battlements, drawbridges and other elements normally associated with castles, the name had stuck. The only thing that remotely resembled a castle was a crenellated parapet wall around the roof.

'Idyllic and utterly peaceful, isn't it?' Javed rumbled, as he scratched his salt-and-pepper beard. 'Not just the mountain range and the sunset, but everything around us.' He waved a muscular arm at the lush green slopes surrounding the estate. 'Man and nature are at peace with themselves and each other.'

'Why shouldn't they be?' Athreya asked, as he began clicking his camera using the remote control. Nanda Devi had begun gleaming golden.

'Why indeed?' Javed agreed, blowing out a cloud of smoke and watching the breeze snatch it away. 'This is as close to heaven as you can get on Earth.'

'The perfect place for an ex-policeman to retire after a lifetime of watching over sin, eh?'

'Indeed. Clean air, pure water, uncontaminated food. The only sounds that intrude upon your solitude are the chirping of birds.'

'And yet?' Athreya asked, throwing Javed a glance. The dying rays of the sun bounced off the silvery tufts on his head and chin as he turned his head, making them gleam briefly. 'There is always a "yet" or a "but" with you.'

'And yet... ' Javed favoured his friend with an indulgent smile. 'And yet, human nature is the same here too... as it is everywhere else.'

Athreya contemplated Javed's rugged profile for a couple of seconds before returning his gaze to Nanda Devi.

'Go on,' he murmured.

He knew from experience that his friend's abstract musings were often precursors to weighty discourses. He kept his eyes on the distant peak and continued snapping photographs. The sun was sinking rapidly, and Nanda Devi's golden gleam was giving way to a copper sheen. The show would end very soon.

'Even in this veritable Shangri-La,' Javed went on, 'human passions run the full range—ambition and greed, joy and grief, love and hate, desire and jealousy. Every emotion you encounter in our crowded, smelly metropolises, you will find here too. This tranquillity you see around you hides them. It's but a shroud. In the few years I've been here, I've seen it bring out the worst in some people.'

Athreya didn't respond immediately. The reflected sunshine had dimmed into a ruddy alpenglow that turned Nanda Devi and the adjacent peaks into hewn chunks of tarnished copper. Athreya hurriedly clicked to capture the last few images of the famed sight. In the dying light, the camera was taking longer and longer to capture each subsequent shot. Soon, the light had faded to an extent that it made photographing a distant peak impossible.

A short distance away from the men, Linda began talking excitedly to Asma about the spectacle that she had enjoyed immensely. Her animated voice grew louder as they joined the others. Athreya pocketed the remote control and began dismantling the tripod and the camera.

Petite, fresh-faced and wearing a red scarf around her neck that matched her lips, Asma Rais had enjoyed her favourite sight for the umpteenth time. Despite having watched it from childhood, she had not tired of it. Her little hawk nose, which she had inherited from Javed, seemed incongruous on her amicable face as she listened indulgently to her friend's excited outpouring.

A plain-faced girl of similar stature as Asma, Linda's distinguishing feature was her glossy black hair that hung gracefully down to her shoulders. She looked guileless and had an engraved silver cross hanging from a thin chain around her neck. Glancing at her, Athreya found it difficult to believe that she was one of the five involved in deception. She seemed utterly ingenuous and entirely at ease. Her open, candid face made it difficult for him to suspect her of any malintent.

Athreya placed his palms on the parapet wall and peered down from the terrace. Seventy feet below, a massive lawn, almost a hundred yards across and twice as long, stretched out across the flat tabletop that crowned the hillock on which the castle stood. The ground fell away steeply on all sides and was covered with trees and bushes. A single road snaked up the hill, wrapping possessively around it as it climbed.

Lights were just coming on at a few places on the lawn and along its periphery. Only the staff quarters, the stable and a couple of small buildings challenged the dominance of the grass.

Presiding over the east end of the lawn was a viewing deck offering an unobstructed view of rolling hills opposite and its magnificent peak. Land's End, as it was called, was now lit with soft yellow lights. A small group was gazing westward from it.

Athreya turned as a tinkle of glasses sounded behind him. A clean-shaven, amiable young man a little short of thirty, with neatly trimmed hair and a friendly smile, was approaching them with a waiter in tow.

'Some apple cider, gentlemen?' he asked, waving the waiter forward. 'Our own house stock, made from the last crop of apples from our orchard.'

'Thank you, Maazin,' Javed nodded. 'I was just thinking of calling for some.' He picked up two full glasses and handed one each to Athreya and Linda. Asma picked up a glass for herself. 'The last crop of apples was particularly good. That shows up in the cider.'

Maazin was Asma's cousin on her mother's side, whom Javed had taken under his wing a few years ago. Coming from the hinterland, Maazin had known nothing of the hospitality industry or of running establishments. He hardly spoke any English. Under Javed's tutelage, the eager young man had learnt quickly and had blossomed so well that Javed now left much of the day-to-day running of Peter Dann to him. In response to the faith reposed in him, the young man had grown in confidence as his natural friendliness became an asset in the hotel business.

'This is excellent!' Athreya exclaimed after taking a sip. A subtle blend of spices tingled his tongue. 'I haven't had such good cider in ages. There isn't much alcohol in this, right?' he asked.

'This is pretty mild,' Asma answered. 'If you'd like to try stronger stuff, you should check out Clarkson's apple brandy.'

'Clarkson's?' Athreya echoed.

'A homestay run by an Irish-American by the name of Dave Clarkson and his French wife, Margot,' Javed explained. 'It's a mile and a half away. We can go there shortly if you wish. Dave's apple brandy is famous, and for good reason, as you'll discover.'

'While you do that,' Asma chirped, 'we'll go down and mingle with the others. See you later.'

Asma, Linda and Maazin strolled away towards the staircase, chatting and laughing. Punctuated by Maazin's throaty laughs and Asma's measured voice, Linda's bubbly chatter faded away as the three went down the front stairs. The waiter placed a jug of the cider on a nearby stone table and followed the three down by the rear stairway.

A companionable silence enveloped the terrace once they were gone. Javed poured out a second round of cider and refilled his pipe as Athreya sipped, comfortable and content in the silence and the darkness that had fallen over the terrace. A match flared to life as Javed relit his pipe and puffed like a steam engine before letting out a soft sigh.

'I'm worried, Athreya,' he rumbled at length. 'Worried

about Asma going on the trek with the five guests.'

'Putting herself in danger, you think?' Athreya asked.

Javed nodded. 'She insists on going as Linda is a very close friend. Besides, she goes on the first trek every year.'

'Aren't you blowing this riddle out of proportion, Javed?' Athreya said, smiling.

'I hope I am, but I have an unease of sorts, Athreya... like a premonition.'

Athreya's smile faded.

'Subconsciously you've gathered something that bothers you?' he asked.

The psychologist in Javed was of the firm view that there was nothing psychic about premonitions. Instead, they were a natural outcome of recognizable mental processes. Premonitions, he maintained, were manifestations of unease brought about by pieces of information a person had picked up subconsciously. Sometimes, the person was aware of the information but was not conscious of its significance. When the subconscious saw the significance, it revealed itself as a premonition. Athreya shared that view.

'Yes,' Javed agreed. 'I might have picked up on something.'

Athreya studied Javed's profile in the ruddy glow of the pipe. Experience had taught him to respect Javed's premonitions. As a psychologist, he noticed more than the average person did.

'How long have you been having this... premonition?' he asked.

'For over a month. From when the five checked in the first time. What if they are planning something nefarious during the trek? Asma disagrees—she believes that their pretence is some sort of a practical joke.'

'Well, if you can't stop her, do the next best thing—send an escort.'

'Yes. I'm sending Maazin and another man, Chetan. Chetan is an experienced tourist guide and a very dependable fellow. He knows the foothills like the back of his hand. He will come in handy if trouble strikes. And I know that Maazin will give his life for his cousin.'

'Will they be armed?'

'Maazin will carry my automatic. Chetan always has knives on his person.'

Athreya looked away and stared unseeingly into the darkness that had enveloped Peter Dann. The puzzle, which had begun as a riddle, seemed to be deepening. His gut was beginning to suggest that it might not be an innocuous prank after all. He decided to find out more about the guests who had cancelled their bookings at the eleventh hour.

* * *

Ten minutes later, they were in Javed's office downstairs. Javed pulled up the details of the three guests who had made reservations for two weeks ago and cancelled them at the last moment. Athreya sat beside him with his hand on the desk telephone, picked up the handset and dialled the first number.

'Good evening,' he said when the call was answered. 'I am calling from Peter Dann Hotel. Can I speak to Mr Vinod Kumar please?'

'Wrong number!' the woman at the other end snapped and cut the call.

Unfazed, Athreya called again.

'I'm sorry to bother you again, ma'am,' he said when she answered again, 'but one Mr Vinod Kumar had made a reservation with us and gave this as his contact number. Is your address in Koramangala, Bangalore?'

'No, this is Indira Nagar,' the woman replied. 'There is no Vinod Kumar here.'

'Did anyone else from this number make a booking at Peter Dann Hotel, ma'am? Maybe in some other name?'

'Can't be. Only my daughter and I live here, and there is

no Vinod Kumar or any other man here. Now, will you stop pestering me, please?'

'Thank you, ma'am,' Athreya said. 'I'm sorry to have bothered you.'

'Fake number?' Javed asked as Athreya hung up.

'So it seems. Let's try the next one. It's a mobile.'

Athreya dialled the number and waited for the beep-beep-beep sound to play out until a connection was made. But instead a recorded message sounded: 'The number you dialled does not exist.'

Athreya tried once more, with the same result.

'Another fake,' Javed growled. 'Try the third.'

The third number did not exist either. All the three parties that had made reservations for two weeks ago were bogus.

'Now,' Athreya said, 'let's try the parties that had made bookings to coincide with the *second* visit of the five guests and had cancelled their bookings.'

Two calls went to addresses that didn't match with the ones provided by the guests. Nor was there anyone of the name in which the reservation had been made. The last number didn't exist.

'I don't like this,' Athreya growled, as he leaned forward with his elbows on the desk. 'Someone has gone to great lengths to ensure that there are no other guests around when the five stay here.'

'Indeed. They booked out the hotel to prevent a random guest from arriving.'

'I'd love to check the credit card numbers, but we can't do that without involving the police.'

'Something dark is at work here,' Javed grunted with a worried frown. 'Why else would five young people go to such lengths to keep out other guests? This can't be a mere practical joke.'

'These are but preparations, Javed,' Athreya mused. His vivid imagination was already seeing nasty possibilities.

'More might be in store. Could be something unpleasant.'

'I can't believe that Linda could be a part of this duplicity. She's a simple, God-fearing girl.'

'It's too early to tell who is orchestrating this. Let's keep this discovery to ourselves for now. I'll meet the five guests and see what I can glean from each. If they are surprised to learn that I too am a guest, it would suggest that they are involved in this deceit.'

3

Javed's blue Jeep Compass purred down the road from Peter Dann with Javed's driver at the wheel. The woods on both sides were swathed in darkness that was mitigated only by the solar lamps set about a hundred feet apart, while red reflectors marked the edge of safety every twenty feet or so. The white light of the vehicle's headlamps followed the road that wrapped itself around Peter Dann's hillock like a covetous python.

'We could have ridden to Clarkson's on horseback,' Javed said. 'But that's not a safe thing to do after dark. We'll ride out tomorrow or the day after if you like. We can check out the valley and the slopes.'

'I'd like that,' Athreya replied. 'I need to brush up my riding skills anyway. Maybe after breakfast?'

'That'll be a good time. Think you can spend a few hours on horseback?'

'Come on, I'm not *that* old! At least, not yet.'

The ten-minute drive passed quickly as they chatted about trivial matters. There was nothing to be seen in the velvety darkness surrounding them, save what their headlamps illuminated. No man or beast, no other vehicle either. The narrow road curved frequently as it went down one hill and up another. Sounds of crickets and nocturnal birds reached their ears through the open windows, as did the occasional rustle of leaves and branches.

Soon, they pulled up in front of the only patch of light they had seen since leaving Peter Dann.

Clarkson's turned out to be a low, horseshoe-shaped building on the slope of an adjacent hill. It had a sloping, red-tiled roof and used timber and brick in equal measure for its walls. The two arms of the horseshoe ran down the hill enclosing a tidy lawn that served as an outdoor dining area when the weather permitted it. The last two rooms at the far ends of each arm were the guest rooms—four rooms in all, while the other rooms were common facilities and the owners' abode.

Dave Clarkson—a loud man with a red, bewhiskered face—welcomed Javed with a guffaw and a slap on the back as they entered through a wide doorway. His wife—a short and busy Frenchwoman—hurried forward to shake Javed and Athreya by the hand.

The Clarksons made an odd couple in many ways—height, complexion and demeanour. Margot Clarkson was at least a foot shorter than her husband and possessed less than half his girth. She also sounded far more soft-spoken.

'Dinner tonight, Javed?' Margot asked, once introductions had been made and they had settled down at a large, circular table. Athreya sat facing the doorway through which they had entered. 'I can make some nice coq au vin and ratatouille.'

'Not tonight, Margot,' Javed replied. 'We came down for Athreya to try Dave's apple brandy and your liqueurs.'

'That's wonderful!' she beamed. 'Would you like to start with some apple brandy?'

'Hey, that's my department!' Dave bellowed, waving his wife back to her chair. But she rose anyway and went into the kitchen. 'First time here, Mr Athreya?' he asked.

'Yes,' Athreya replied with a nod and a smile. 'Lovely place you have, Mr Clarkson.'

'Dave, if you please,' boomed their florid host. 'That's what everyone calls me. "Mr Clarkson" is bit of a mouthful, especially after a couple of brandies. How are you with brandies? A connoisseur like Javed?'

29

'I'm afraid not!' Athreya laughed. 'I'm a bit of an igno-
ramus, actually.'

'That can't be true! Javed's friends cannot be rookies
when it comes to spirits. Tell you what! I'll give you three
samples—small shots first. Tell me which you fancy, and
you can have more of that.'

'Wonderful! That's kind of you, Dave.'

Dave lumbered away and returned with several small
shot glasses and three bottles that bore no labels. The
liquors were of different shades of brown. Meanwhile, Margot had brought some cheese wedges, pineapple slices and
olives. The four of them sat down to sip brandies.

Soon, Athreya was in the midst of a veritable feast. Each
variety of apple brandy was better than the previous one.
Several flavours and aromas—some subtle, some sharp—
took his taste buds on an enjoyable ride. He began feeling
entirely at ease.

Javed too had relaxed visibly as merry chatter, punctuated by Dave's guffaws and Margot's tinkling laughter,
livened the pub. Athreya learnt that brandy was Dave's
speciality while liqueurs and wine were Margot's. While
they had a local cook who rustled up meals for the guests
staying with them and the occasional visitor who dropped
by, special dishes—French, European and Indian—were
Margot's prerogative.

When she politely enquired about Athreya's background
and learned that he had been a police investigator, Dave
rose abruptly.

'Investigator?' he asked gruffly. 'Let me show you
something.'

He went to a window at the back of the room and pointed to a glass pane. On the outside was a vivid mark: a print
of a hand that was maroon-brown in colour.

The colour of dried blood.

The bony hand had long knobby fingers and a narrow
palm. Someone had dipped his left hand in a viscous, ma-

roonish liquid and pressed it against the windowpane.

It was meant to be a bloodied hand. A shiver ran down Athreya's spine even as he heard Javed draw in his breath sharply. Coming on the heels of the riddle at Peter Dann, the bloody handprint felt ominous.

'When did this happen?' Javed asked with an edge in his voice.

Athreya glanced at his friend. There was an uncharacteristic tautness to his face.

'Sometime last night. We discovered it this morning. It's straight out of horror movie. Gave Margot the willies.'

Athreya stared at it. He imagined a dark figure skulking outside Dave's windows at night, peering in. The figure lifted its bony hand and pressed it against the pane, leaving a bloody mark. It felt grotesquely out of place in these lovely foothills. His gut told him that this was no idle prank. People didn't wander about at night leaving bloody handprints on windows. He wondered if this had any connection with the five guests at Peter Dann.

'Are there more marks?' Javed interrupted his thoughts. His voice was tight.

'Several. Two handprints on the guest room windows and at least three more on the walls.'

'Show me one on a wall.'

Dave lumbered to the front of the building. He stopped a few feet beyond the door and pointed to a newly white-washed pillar. On it was the same bloody handprint, standing out starkly against the whiteness.

Javed touched the mark with his fingers and scratched it with his fingernail. It was dry and a red powder fell away under his fingernail.

'Redstone powder,' he growled, rubbing it between his thumb and middle finger. 'Used by locals to colour their walls and floors. Also used as a red-brown paste for drawing rangoli designs.'

'What do you make of it?' Dave asked.

'I don't know,' Javed muttered with a frown. 'Just some tomfoolery, I hope. Has it happened before?' His tone and words, Athreya thought, were not mutually consistent.

'Never. First time.'

They returned to the pub and resumed their seats beside a worried-looking Margot. All sat in silence for a minute. Dave poured out some more apple brandy. Slowly, Javed stirred.

'Nothing more than a prank, I suspect,' he assured Margot with affected lightness. He changed the topic quickly. 'Do you have any guests now?'

Athreya wasn't fooled. Watching his old friend, he knew that the big man was worried and was trying to keep it from showing. Athreya himself was troubled, but if he read Javed correctly, the big man was seriously worried.

It turned out that the Clarksons had two guests staying with them. A man and a woman had come together and were staying in adjacent rooms. Javed's eyes flickered towards Athreya when he heard this. Were these the last two of group he had seen in Nainital?

But Javed didn't pursue the matter and began talking about all manner of things. Fifteen minutes passed quickly, and once Athreya began sampling Margot's liqueurs, he began feeling light-headed from the accumulating alcohol. The bloody handprint receded to the back of his mind.

They were in the midst of an animated conversation when a petite, fresh-faced young woman walked in through the wide-open doors. Athreya estimated that the pleasant-looking woman was about twenty-five years old, and she was of Asma's height and build but had larger eyes that were bright and clear. She had a small chin and mouth, and wore her black hair in a ponytail.

'Oh, hello,' she said, as she stopped hesitantly after taking a couple of steps into the room. 'I didn't know you had company.'

'Come on in, my dear,' Margot twittered in response as

she bounced up from her chair and invited the newcomer to join them. 'Our neighbours stopped by for a drop of brandy. Come join us.'

'Sure?' A hesitant smile brightened the woman's agreeable face.

'Of course!'

The first impression Athreya got on seeing and hearing the newcomer was that she was very tentative. For some reason, she seemed vulnerable too. Her hesitation and timidity seemed to convey a picture of someone who was out in the world on her own with little help or protection. Why he got such an impression, Athreya didn't know. Was it seeing her petite figure framed against the large doorway and dark night beyond? Was it the cautious look on her face, or the way she carried herself or something else in her body language? Or was it merely his overactive imagination that acted up from time to time? He didn't know. Regardless, he got the feeling that she might be battling life out on her own. At once, he felt sorry for her. In response, he sensed an avuncular feeling developing towards her.

Unsure of what that might mean, he watched her as she walked up to their table taking small steps. While she was pleasing in appearance, she was not glamorous. She was simply but neatly dressed in black slacks and a light top. He noticed physical similarities with Asma, but the latter was much the more assured of the two. As the woman's cautious eyes rested on him for a moment, he wondered if she was trying to hide her anxiety or if she was feeling intimidated in some way.

'Have you found out anything about those awful hand marks on the windows and walls?' she asked Dave, breaking into Athreya's thoughts. She sounded frightened.

'Nah!' Dave dismissed it with an over-casual wave of his arm. 'Don't you worry about it. Just some silly prank.'

'Introduce yourself, my dear,' Margot interrupted, changing the topic. 'I'm not very good at remembering names that are new to me.'

'I'm Mrinal,' the woman said simply and stood there smiling. As an afterthought, she added, 'Oh! I'm staying here.'

'First time in these parts?' Javed asked after they had introduced themselves and Mrinal had sat down.

'Yes, my first time here.' Her voice was soft and low and didn't carry very far. 'I'd been told that it is beautiful here and have always wanted to come. But... you know... '

She left the sentence unfinished and smiled apologetically.

'Did you watch the sunset? Javed asked. 'It was an unusually clear day today.'

'Sunset?' She seemed confused. 'No... should I have?'

'It's one of the popular sights here. The setting sun illuminates the Nanda Devi peak and makes it glow golden.'

'Oh, really?' Mrinal's eyes opened a trifle wider. 'I should try and remember tomorrow.'

'Where are you from?' Athreya asked.

'Mumbai. I came the day before yesterday.'

'Drove from Nainital?'

'Nainital?' A crease appeared on her brow. 'No, I don't think I've ever been there. I came from Delhi and hope to be hereabouts for a few more days.'

'Hereabouts?' Athreya echoed.

'I'll be moving to Peter Dann Castle the day after tomorrow. I'm going on a trek from there.'

'Ah!' Javed exclaimed and raised his glass in toast. 'We'll see more of you, then.'

A look of apprehension came into her eyes as she missed the import of Javed's comment.

'Javed is the owner of the blessed Peter Dann Castle,' Dave explained.

'Oh! I'm so sorry!' Mrinal apologized, reddening in embarrassment. 'I didn't know. Please forgive me.'

'Please don't apologize!' Javed brushed it off with a

wave of his large hand. 'We'd love to have you over. Staying for long?'

'A couple of days after the trek. Is it true that the castle is a hundred years old?'

'A little older, actually. It has a bit of history.'

'Really?' Mrinal's smile widened. 'I'd love to hear it.'

'It would be my pleasure to hold forth.' Javed inclined his head a shade. 'Perhaps the first evening when you are staying with us?'

'That would be lovely, thank you.' She turned to Dave. 'Blessed?' she asked. 'Did you say the castle is blessed?'

Dave nodded vigorously, making his jowls quiver. 'Didn't you know? Nothing bad ever happens there. Everything that happens at Peter Dann happens for the good. It's a sort of lucky charm for us folks here.'

'Wow! How did that come to be?'

'There's this story about a Christian bishop and Tibetan monk who took refuge there during a very bad night. Pursued by bandits and wild animals, they were at their wits' end. The castle, with its stout doors and heavy iron grills, protected them for two days and two nights until British soldiers rescued them. Before they left the castle, the bishop and the monk blessed it.'

'Nothing bad happens there?' Athreya queried. 'Surely, a hundred years would have seen deaths.'

'Death is not necessarily a bad thing,' Margot countered. 'For the aged or the gravely ill, it is a relief.'

'And for their loved one too,' Dave added. 'Seeing someone suffer from an incurable illness can be heart-wrenching. Locals believe that anything that happens at Peter Dann happens for the good.'

Athreya didn't pursue it further. He was acutely aware that Javed had fallen silent. His late wife, Naira, had died at Peter Dann a few years ago. Athreya knew no details, but he wondered how it could have been a good thing for Javed or Asma. Especially when Naira had only been in her late forties and Asma a teenager. It was curious that Dave and Margot, who were good friends with Javed and a very sensible couple, had so openly spoken about Peter Dann being blessed. That too in Javed's presence. Mrinal, who seemed to be a perceptive young woman, had sensed something and fallen silent with a puzzled expression on her face.

Thankfully, they were interrupted by the entry of a man who had apparently been out for a run. His T-shirt, which was two sizes too small for him, was clinging to his well-muscled torso. He was wearing high-end running shoes and must be in his early thirties. He was the second person staying at Clarkson's.

'Howdy, Margot, Dave,' he said breezily with an acquired Western accent. 'Wonderful evening for a run. I must have done at least five miles.'

Dave beamed back at him as if the salubrious evening was of his making.

'That's a lot in such hilly terrain,' he said. 'I'm impressed that you did five miles!'

The newcomer shrugged and went on, 'I can do more. By the way, you really must install a gym, you know. I crave some upper-body exercise. Running only exercises the legs.'

Dave's smile vanished but he said nothing.

'This is Kinshuk,' Mrinal cut in, turning to Athreya and Javed. 'My fiancé. He's a celebrity trainer, you know. I don't think I know a fitter person in all of Mumbai.'

Athreya's eyes followed Kinshuk as he pulled out a mobile phone and clicked a couple of selfies of himself with the others at the table as the background. He inspected the photographs critically and decided to take two more from another angle.

He went over to a table and poured himself a large glass of water. He had short hair and was clean-shaven and friendly-looking, but the touch of hubris couldn't be hidden. His well-toned body corroborated Mrinal's opinion about his fitness.

'I'm sorry if I offended you, Dave,' Kinshuk said as he set down the empty glass. 'Mrinal will tell you that I am a bit of an exercise freak. I go wonky when I don't get my full quota. I realize that people who live in the hills don't need a gym. They probably get their exercise just going about their work every day. My apologies.'

The smile that had vanished from Dave's face, returned. Javed glanced at his watch. 'We should be going shortly,' he said.

'One for the road, gentlemen?' Dave asked. 'I see that you are not driving.'

'Thank you. I *always* bring a driver when I come here. I don't fancy negotiating those bends after imbibing your brandy.'

As they were talking, Kinshuk put a protective arm around Mrinal and clicked another selfie of himself and his fiancée. Mrinal wrinkled her nose and pushed him away, telling him to go and bathe. With a grin, Kinshuk left.

'We'll come over to Peter Dann sometime in the early evening the day after tomorrow,' Mrinal said to Javed. 'Mrs Clarkson is cooking us a special French lunch tomorrow. I want to enjoy more of her cooking before we go over to the castle.'

Margot rose and excused herself. 'I better ensure that dinner gets ready in time,' she said. 'Goodbye, Javed. Bye, Mr Athreya. Come back soon.'

As Margot turned, Mrinal also rose.

'Let me help you, Mrs Clarkson,' she said. 'Goodbye, gentlemen. I'll see you in two days at Peter Dann.'

Dave waited till she was out of earshot before leaning forward.

'A nice, sweet girl,' he whispered conspiratorially. 'Can't, for the life of me, understand why she went and hooked up with a pseudo like Kinshuk. Must have fallen for his looks and muscled body, I suppose.'

'What's wrong with Kinshuk?' Athreya asked.

'He strikes me as a bit of a narcissist and a faker who is interested only in himself. Do you know how many selfies he has taken here alone? Dozens every day! He's the kind of man who will get attracted to the next shiny thing that come along. I fear it's only a matter of time before his attention wanders from Mrinal. I'm afraid the poor girl is in for a heartbreak.'

'Feel sorry for her, Dave?' Athreya asked, wondering if Mrinal had evoked the same kind of response in Dave as she had in him.

'Don't you?' His voice dropped a notch. 'I get the impression that she doesn't have much of a family. Maybe, she has nobody to guide her on how to judge people. She seems to trust her fiancé quite implicitly.'

He shook his head and sat back in his chair. As Javed picked up his glass to finish his last drink, Athreya's gaze wandered towards the dark lawn outside the wide-open doors. Of the three at the table, only he was facing the doorway, and he saw a tall, hirsute man outside. His long hair was thick and unkempt. He was heavily bearded and was dressed like a hippie in faded jeans and a heavy pullover.

As Athreya watched, the grim-faced man came to the doorway and peered in as if he was looking for someone. Dismissing the three men, he scanned the rest of the room with his flinty eyes. Finding no one else, the hirsute stranger turned and vanished before Athreya could say anything or alert the others.

4

The next morning found Javed and Athreya at breakfast on the lawns of Peter Dann. Soaking in the morning sun, Athreya glanced at his friend filling his pipe.

'So,' he asked, 'did Mrinal or Kinshuk look familiar?'

Javed shook his head as he puffed on his pipe to get it going.

'No,' he said at length. 'As I said, the two I didn't see at the Nainital restaurant were obscured by pillars. It's possible that they were Mrinal and Kinshuk, but it's equally possible that they weren't. I can't tell one way or the other. But I wanted to ask you about something—what did you make of the bloodied hand marks?'

'It could be a prank, but they made me uncomfortable,' Athreya replied. 'My gut tells me that there must be a reason behind them. But on the other hand, your five guests are here while the marks appeared at Clarkson's. Maybe there is no connection.'

'It's not a prank, Athreya.' Javed's voice was low and serious.

Athreya studied his friend for a moment, his interest heightened by the sombre tone. He remembered how Javed had brushed it aside as some antic at Clarkson's.

'Why do you say that?' he asked quietly.

Javed didn't reply. Instead, he pulled out his phone and navigated to the photo gallery. He touched one and passed the phone to Athreya. It was a snap of a bloody handprint. Only, this was a right hand. The ones at Clarkson's were a left hand. In the photo gallery were several such snaps.

'These are not from Clarkson's!' Athreya exclaimed softly.

'They aren't,' Javed confirmed in his gravelly voice. 'They are from Peter Dann.'

'*Here?*' Athreya's eyebrows shot up. 'When?'

'Two weeks ago. When the five guests checked in the first time. Then too, the marks appeared at night... the first night the five spent here. We saw them the next morning. I had them washed off immediately.'

Athreya studied the photographs with fresh interest. One was on a stone wall and another on a glass pane.

'Where did you find these marks?' he asked.

'On the rooftop terrace and on two of the windows facing south. The ones on the windowpanes were made on the *outside* of the glass.'

'*Outside?*' Athreya echoed in surprise. His eyes snapped to Javed's. 'On the windows facing *south*? Were the windows shut?'

Javed nodded.

'How is that possible?' Athreya persisted. 'It's a two-hundred-and-fifty-foot drop out there. Unless someone flew up or scaled the southern wall... '

'Precisely. So, you see why it can't be a silly joke? No prankster would risk his life to leave a mark two-hundred-and-fifty feet above the ground. This is no longer an innocuous deception, Athreya—the riddle and these marks. This is deadly serious. There's a dark design behind all this.' His head snapped around at a sound. 'Good lord!'

The sound of hoofs had interrupted him. A horse had just run up the road and thundered in through the gate. It was a young one, little more than a pony. Perched precariously in the saddle and swaying dangerously, was a young woman clad in a brown leather jacket and fawn-coloured jeans. She was clutching her left arm with her right hand as a grimace contorted her face. A maroon ooze had seeped through the fingers and dripped on to her jeans, which had turned red.

She was clearly in pain.

'Asma!'

With a hoarse shout, Javed leapt up and ran to his daughter even as the horse slowed. A stable boy who was closer reached her first and began calming the panting and frantic horse. Just as Asma looked like she would fall off, Javed reached her and lowered her gently to the ground. Athreya came up a few paces behind him.

A long, clean cut ran across the upper part of the leather jacket sleeve, dripping red. Another red cut split the arm below the elbow. Asma's face was pale from loss of blood and fright and her legs began to buckle as soon as she was off the horse.

With a policeman's instinct, Javed didn't ask her questions. Instead, he picked her up as if she were a child and hastened to the castle. Maazin shot out of the front door and met him halfway. Together, they sat Asma on a sofa and began removing her jacket. The same look of despair mingled with anger showed on Javed's and Maazin's faces, but the younger man seemed close to tears.

'Slowly, Dad! Slowly!' Asma hissed in pain. 'My shirt is stuck to the wound. Dried blood.'

'Warm water and first-aid kit!' Javed snapped to Maazin. 'Cotton, Betadine, cloth and bandages.'

Maazin sprinted away and Javed slid slowly the jacket off the uninjured arm.

'Hold up her injured arm up, Athreya. I'll take the jacket off.'

'Slowly, please! Carefully!' Asma gasped.

Athreya gently raised the arm and Javed peeled off the jacket inch-by-inch to reveal her shirt was soaked in blood.

'Dear God!' Javed breathed as he took in the gory sight.

'Take her to her bedroom,' Athreya whispered. 'You need to remove her shirt too. I'll get one of the girls from the kitchen.'

He didn't have to. With good presence of mind, a

white-faced Maazin returned with two female staffers and the items Javed had asked for. Athreya mutely pointed to Asma's bedroom door. The young women went in with the first-aid kit as an agitated Maazin joined Athreya outside. Deep anxiety was etched on his young face, so Athreya put his arm around him. There was little to say. Minutes passed.

Shortly, a grim-faced Javed came out of Asma's room and walked up to them.

'Thank God, it isn't as bad as it looks,' he said. 'Fortunately, she was wearing her thick leather jacket—always a good idea when you are out training a young horse. Otherwise she would have been cut to the bone.'

'Knife?' Athreya asked softly.

'Knife,' Javed confirmed, glancing at him with troubled eyes.

A series of images flashed through Athreya's mind—the riddle, a bloodied hand and the vision of a bleeding Asma riding in. Matters were taking a turn for the worse.

'What happened, Uncle?' Maazin cut in. 'I saw a deep cut in the saddle too.'

Javed reached out and grasped his hands.

'Someone tried to kill Asma, Maazin.'

* * *

'Slow down, Maazin,' Javed growled, as the young man took a bend at a high speed. 'I'd rather get there five minutes late than never.'

They were on their way to Ranikhet, a nearby town with a large hospital. An agitated Maazin was at the wheel with Athreya beside him. Asma sat in the rear seat, her left arm swathed in bandages, with her father. Maazin slowed the car a little but didn't say anything.

'She'll be fine,' Athreya assured the young man, patting him on the shoulder. 'The wounds are not as deep as they seemed at first. The leather jacket acted as a sort of armour.

We are going to a hospital only as a precaution.'

'Ease up, Maaz,' Asma added from behind. 'I'm already much better. It was a bit of a shock then, but I've recovered now. Don't worry, Maaz. The cuts will heal quickly.'

'Do you feel capable of telling us what happened, Asma?' Athreya asked as Maazin nodded mutely.

'Yes, Uncle. Nothing much to tell, actually. It all happened so quickly! I had taken Daisy out for a ride—'

'Daisy?'

'The young mare I was riding. I'm training her. I've gone out several times on her. The spirited girl is learning quickly. Anyway, I was returning home after a nice little workout at Pottersfield when a man jumped out from the forest and ran up to me. I was taken by surprise.

'Before I realized what he was doing, he slashed at me with a knife. Instinctively, I had bent my arm and raised it in defence. The blade cut me in two places—above and below the elbow. Daisy, being the frisky girl she is, must have pranced sideways, away from the man. That reduced the impact of the knife.

'He came at me again and slashed the knife downward. With Daisy moving about, he missed me but hit the saddle. As soon as he did, she bolted forward. I was beginning to feel dizzy with the pain but managed to hang on as Daisy ran. Without my directing her, she came straight home. She's turning out to be a great little horse.'

'The man nicked Daisy, Asma,' Maazin said, his eyes fixed on the road ahead. 'His second slash was downward, right? After cutting the saddle, the knife must have nicked Daisy. That's probably why she bolted. There's a vertical cut on her left side.'

'Poor Daisy! Is it serious, Maaz?'

'No. A shallow cut.'

'Did you get a good look at the man?' Javed cut in.

'Well… yes and no. He looked like a Cochha but was wearing town clothes. He had wrapped a thin towel around his head and ears like a mini-turban... just like how the labourers sometimes wear.'

'Cochha?' Athreya asked. 'What's that?'

'A local tribe,' Javed explained. 'Excellent climbers. They can climb almost anything.'

'Including the castle's southern wall?'

'That's why we keep the doors of the rooftop terrace locked.'

Athreya blinked. A Cochha had attacked Asma. Had he scaled the wall and made the bloodied hand mark as well?

Javed rumbled on, interrupting Athreya's thoughts.

'... they usually keep to themselves. They are not known to be aggressive. I am surprised that a Cochha attacked her. Are you sure, Asma?'

'I think so but I can't be sure. It all happened so quickly. Plus, he was wearing a turban of sorts. But his build was that of a Cochha—tall and wiry with bony hands. His skin had their typical reddish tinge too.'

'He slashed at you both times?' Athreya asked. 'He didn't stab?'

'No, he didn't stab.'

'He didn't try to pull you off the horse either?'

'No.'

'What's on your mind, Athreya?' Javed asked.

'Just wondering. It would have been so much easier for him to attack—even kill—her if he had pulled her off the horse first. That wouldn't have been difficult for a tall man. She would have been completely at his mercy.' He turned to the back to Asma. 'What happened to him after the second slash?'

'I don't know. I didn't look back. I was scared that the movement might make me slip off the saddle.'

'Something mighty strange is going on,' Javed growled. 'We've lived here for decades. Never has one of us been shouted at, let alone be attacked.'

They fell silent, each with their own thoughts. Athreya

was thinking about how quickly things had happened. He had come to Peter Dann only last evening. The innocuous-seeming riddle of the five guests had darkened disconcertingly. A few minutes later, Javed broke the silence.

'Why would a Cochha want to attack Asma?' he asked. 'We are on excellent terms with them; we contribute for their festivals and provide medical help. They know Asma... she and Maazin join some of their celebrations.'

'Best to take precautions, I guess,' Athreya suggested.

'Double the guard, Maazin. Tell the watchmen to patrol the perimeter fence and keep an eye on the slopes outside it. Make sure that the terrace doors are secured every night. A Cochha can climb in from anywhere.'

* * *

When they returned to Peter Dann a few hours later, Asma's arm was in a neat sling that hid the bandages. Her colour had returned and she was cheerful, showing no signs of the ordeal she had endured. It was probably a bit of a put-on, but it didn't matter to Athreya. Maazin, who had said little during the journey, seemed a little more at ease after hearing the doctor at Ranikhet say that the injuries were not serious, who had continued cheerfully, that Asma should be able to go on her trek as planned. Maazin's spirits had recovered after that, but Javed's had plummeted. He, Athreya knew, was even more opposed to Asma going on the trek now.

Athreya went up to his room to rest a bit and take a shower before dinner. Javed had given him the best room in his hotel: Room 8. Its windows opened out to the Himalayas that dominated the entire horizon from the north to the east. The majestic vastness of the mountain range rolled away for as far as the eye could see. Athreya liked the sight so much that he had decided he would sketch it sometime.

The oversized room was filled with heavy, exquisitely

carved furniture. The bed seemed larger than the typical king-size bed. The rest of the room, which could have easily accommodated half a dozen more people, was furnished with luxurious sofas and antique-looking chairs and tables.

The lounge outside his room had been empty and silent when Athreya had come up. Now after a rest, a shower and donning a warm pullover, he expected it to be much the same. But as he gripped the doorknob to open his door, he heard an unfamiliar female voice outside.

'You *must* go through with it!' the voice hissed in an intense but hushed tone. 'You have come so far! You made the decision after months of going back and forth. You *can't* back out now!'

'But—' pleaded female rasping voice, only to be cut off.

'You owe it to yourself!' the first voice continued to goad. 'Everything is in place and you've finally summoned up your courage. It's now or never.'

'I'm afraid!' the low harsh second voice protested. 'What if I can't go through with it?'

'You can and you will! I'm with you. I'll back you up. This is the only way you'll find peace!'

Apparently secure in the belief that they were alone, the two women were having a quick talk where they couldn't be heard. Or so they thought.

'What if someone finds out?' the rasping voice asked in a whisper.

'Nobody will,' said the answering whisper from the first woman. 'Come, let's go down for dinner.'

The two voices began moving away.

'This will be the hardest thing I've ever done!'

'Don't worry.' Athreya heard a tread on the nearby wooden staircase as the two women went down the stairs. 'It won't be that hard when the time comes. You'll see.'

Athreya stood still for a moment. His hand clutched the doorknob, but didn't turn it. He was torn between two impulses. If he didn't open the door and peer down the staircase, he would not know who the two speakers were. But if he did rush out, the women would know that he had overheard them.

Considering what had been said during the conversation and the deception the five guests were engaged in, Athreya decided to retain the advantage of surprise. It was best that the women did not know that he had overheard their private conversation.

He waited for a full minute before opening the door. When he did, the lounge was empty. He went down the staircase, his eyes scanning the ground floor for the women who had just preceded him.

He couldn't see them. Only Javed stood in the hall, waiting for Athreya. With him was a lanky young man looking rather odd.

5

The first thing about the tall young man that caught Athreya's eye was his head. The hair on the sides was trimmed very short, lending the area above his ears the look of freshly mowed lawn. However, the top and back were the opposite. A thatch of long, wavy hair had been carefully gelled and brushed back into a luxurious cover from his forehead to the nape of his neck. Here and there, strands of black hair had been dyed brown, and a few were even blond.

The beard too had been trimmed short to match the style at the sides of his head, except the chin, where a rectangular wad of longer growth, a couple of inches wide and adorned with brown and blond streaks, provided contrast. But the thing that stood out the most was his jet-black moustache. It was of the kind that would have made a medieval English gentleman proud. This grand feature, also carefully gelled and styled, curved proudly upwards at the ends.

From one ear hung a large silver ring, an inch and a half wide, while the other ear sported a shiny bronze ring half that size. The tight-fitting jeans looked expensive and custom-made. His lean upper body was covered in a short, branded jersey that ended precisely at his belt. His left wrist sported an oversized metal watch of a silver-bronze colour that Athreya had not seen before. The entire watch, from the large casing to the thick metal strap, was of the same shiny material. Athreya wondered if it was a limited-edition piece.

'Meet Sarosh Gulati,' Javed introduced the young man

whose intense eyes turned to Athreya. 'He's from Mumbai.'

'Good evening,' Sarosh said smoothly in a confident voice. A lean arm reached out towards Athreya to shake his hand. 'Pleasure to meet you. Are you a guest here?' He asked it as if he were not expecting Athreya to be staying at Peter Dann.

'I am,' Athreya confirmed, bringing a flicker of surprise to Sarosh's face. 'I came yesterday.'

So, this was one of the five guests. He had not expected Athreya to be a guest at Peter Dann too.

'Lovely place, isn't it?' Sarosh continued, recovering quickly. 'Far away from the concrete jungles we live in, blessed with a divine climate and situated bang in nature's lap. Did you watch the sunset? What a fantastic sight!'

Sarosh barrelled ahead, not waiting for Athreya to respond.

'I've been telling Javed that he should convert this to an exclusive luxury property. Five-star or even seven-star. This is the perfect place for celebrities to get away from their pestering fans; an ideal hideaway that's not too difficult to get to. He can charge five times the rates he currently does.'

'Upgrading Peter Dann to a luxury destination would require considerable investment,' Athreya began. 'Where—'

'Of course, it would!' Sarosh interrupted. The tips of his moustache quivered. 'That's where I can help. I was just telling Javed that I would be happy to invest in this property. I believe it has tremendous potential—it's so unique!'

'Invest?' Athreya asked. 'Are you a banker, Mr Gulati?'

'Better that that!' The lean young man smiled. 'I'm an angel investor. I invest in ventures that show promise. Unlike a bank loan that comes with a bunch of conditions and repayment obligations, my investments come with no strings attached. I'll put in the money as equity and Javed can run the place. I won't interfere—all I am looking for is returns on my investment. By the way, call me Sarosh.'

Athreya judged Sarosh to be in his late twenties. It was

unlikely that he could have made so much money on his own that he could afford to be an angel investor. In all likelihood, he was a scion, flaunting his wealthy family's money.

'One of the reasons I came here was to scout for properties to invest in,' Sarosh went on. 'As far as I know, there is nothing like Peter Dann for light years around. This place has *everything* going for it—it's a short distance from the main road, it's a genuine British-era castle, the rooms are palatial, and I'm told it has some interesting stories under its belt too. Did you hear the story about the bishop and the monk? Apparently, they blessed this place. This is *exactly* the kind of resort celebrities would like to stay at and brag about later.'

Athreya watched the younger man holding forth. Why was he talking so much? Investors seldom exposed their hand to strangers or potential clients. They played their cards close to their chests and tried to secure the best possible deal. It was almost as if Sarosh couldn't help speaking. Was he covering up something that he feared would be exposed by silence?

Abruptly, realization dawned. Under his incessant chatter, Sarosh was edgy. It was apparent from his eyes. The breezy conversation was a cover.

Losing interest in Athreya abruptly, Sarosh turned to Javed.

'Think about my offer,' he said. 'We can work out the details to your satisfaction. Shall we go in for dinner?'

The three men went to the dining hall, and the conversation moved on to trivial matters. This was Athreya's first visit there as he had eaten a quiet dinner in his room after returning from Clarkson's the previous night. Unlike most hotels, which set up several small tables, Peter Dann had a single long table occupying the centre of the room. 'To create a family-like atmosphere,' Javed had explained. As with much of the furniture in the castle, the solid wood table had an antique look to it. Athreya judged its seating capacity to be about twenty.

At the far end of the table were four young women— Asma and Linda with two who were strangers to Athreya and around Asma's age. These must be the third and fourth guests after Linda and Sarosh. They were looking at Asma with horrified expressions on their faces, so she must have just been describing her injuries.

One was slim and had short curly hair, and was dressed in a way that accentuated her femininity. Her large brown eyes, clear and bright, blinked often as she looked at the three men with a slightly bewildered gaze. From the way she blinked, Athreya figured that she wore contact lenses.

The other woman was angular and taller by at least three inches. She was slightly ferret-faced and wore her straight black hair in a high ponytail that seemed to sprout from a spot closer to the top of her head than to the back. Her jet-black eyes, peering through the black, large-framed glasses that were currently in vogue, darted from one woman to another. Her nose jutted forward from an angular face and her mouth was pursed as if she were distracted and tense. Unlike the curly-haired woman who was neatly turned out, this one was dressed shabbily in a pair of jeans and a denim jacket, both of which looked as if they needed a wash.

They all stopped talking and turned to the men entering the room.

'Ipshita Lahiri,' Asma told Athreya, gesturing to the pretty, curly-haired woman. Asma seemed cheerful despite having her arm in a sling. She then indicated the bespecta-cled woman and continued, 'And this is Purbhi Chakrad-har.'

'Good evening,' Athreya said with a smile and a nod.

'Good evening,' Ipshita responded with a pleasing smile.

Purbhi stared at Athreya noncommittally with her narrow eyes. Her pursed lips complemented the unfriend-ly lines on her face. Clutched tightly in her hand was her mobile phone.

'This is Mr Athreya, my father's old friend,' Asma went on, completing the introductions. 'He's staying with us for a few days.'

Surprise flared on their faces and their gazes flickered to Sarosh. Clearly, they too hadn't expected Athreya to be staying on as a guest at Peter Dann.

Asma drew out a chair with her good hand and sat down. Maazin, who had just entered the room, took the chair beside her and began enquiring about her arm.

'Are you also coming on the trek?' Ipshita asked amiably, as Athreya took a seat opposite her.

'No, no,' he laughed. 'This is an unplanned trip. I'm going to spend a few days here, doing nothing other than laze around. In any case, hiking is not my cup of tea.'

What he didn't say was that an injury had made it difficult for him. One of his legs was reinforced with a metal rod after a bullet had shattered a bone. A few years ago, he had tracked a sandalwood smuggler to her jungle lodge in the forests of Karnataka, where she had been hiding. Unfortunately, he had reached the lodge a minute ahead of the police, and had become an immediate target. He would have been more careful had he not underestimated the woman. Whether she had chosen to shoot him in the leg or had missed his chest, he never found out. The sound of her shot drew the police to her. A couple of minutes later, she lay dying with two bullets in her chest.

Now, as Athreya spoke, he tried to recall the two voices he had overheard through the closed door of his room. Was Ipshita's soft voice one of them? He was not sure—they had been whispering.

'Where are you from?' Athreya asked, trying to extend the conversation so that he could make up his mind whether Ipshita's voice was one of the voices he had overheard.

'Kolkata.'

'And you, Purbhi?' Athreya asked, eager to hear her

voice.

'She too is from Kolkata,' Ipshita offered, as Purbhi continued clutching her mobile phone as if it was the centre of her existence. 'We've been friends from school. We came here together.'

Yet they had arrived separately during their first visit to Peter Dann, Athreya mused.

A waiter interrupted to ask Athreya if he preferred the vegetarian soup or the non-vegetarian one. By the time Athreya finished with him and turned to resume the conversation, he found that Purbhi had was peering into her mobile phone. Her thumbs were flying over the touchscreen at a speed that fascinated him. Clearly, she didn't want to talk. For the second time in as many minutes, Athreya thought he sensed an air of distracted anxiety around her.

Meanwhile, Ipshita had struck up a conversation with Sarosh, who seemed intent on monopolizing the attractive woman. Athreya turned to Linda on his other side.

'Excited about your trek, Linda?' he asked.

'Oh, yes!' she gushed. 'I've never been on one before. This is a great opportunity, thanks to Asma.' She threw a grateful glance at her friend, who was deep in conversation with Maazin. 'It's so good of her to invite me to Peter Dann.'

'I believe you and Asma were colleagues in Gurgaon.'

Linda nodded briskly. 'For three years. We worked at a firm to which international hotel chains outsource billing and client management work. We had a wonderful time.'

Athreya leaned towards Linda to make way for the waiter to place his soup.

'We have a lot in common, you know, Asma and I,' Linda went on. 'We hit it off *really* well together and became very close friends. I'm *so* happy that I met her. She's *such* a wonderful person. I'm so sorry to see that she was hurt.'

'I'm glad that she found a good friend in you,' Athreya said, his voice dropping a notch. 'She must have been lonely and devastated after her mother died. Isn't that when she went to Gurgaon?'

'Yes.' Linda's voice also dropped to match his. 'Poor Asma, she was overcome with grief. Completely broken. She would cry *every single day*. She hadn't wanted to leave her father alone so soon after her mother's death, but he insisted that nothing should interrupt her training. He assured her that he would be fine and sent her to Gurgaon. He would visit her every month. What a marvellous man he is! So *strong*!'

'Your being with her must have been a huge comfort to Asma,' Athreya murmured. 'It must have helped immensely in getting over a difficult patch.'

'I think so… it was mutual.' Linda put down her soup spoon and bowed her head a little. When she resumed talking, her voice trembled ever so slightly. 'It was mutual, you know,' she repeated. 'I had just lost my brother. We found comfort in each other's company. United in grief, so to speak.'

She offered him a wan smile.

'Oh, I'm so sorry to hear that,' Athreya whispered back. 'He couldn't have been very old even if he was your elder brother.'

Linda nodded and swallowed. 'Twenty-seven,' she whispered. Her hand went to the cross that hung from her neck.

'Good lord! I'm so sorry, Linda. I shouldn't have brought this up.'

'No, no, Mr Athreya. Please don't apologize. This helps me get it out of my system. It just festers if it stays inside and finds no expression. My mother says that I should talk about it often.' She threw him a quick glance. 'I already feel better for having spoken to you. You are… you are a kind person. Just as Asma said.'

Athreya reached out and patted her hand. No words were necessary.

'You must have witnessed a lot of grief in your life,'

Linda went on. 'Asma has told me about your work as an investigator and a crime-fighter.'

'Yes,' Athreya replied. 'Both Javed and I have seen more of humanity's dark side than we care to remember. Fortunately, people have the ability to overcome grief and get on with life. Reconciliation is the only way forward.'

'Solving the crime helps with reconciliation, doesn't it?'

'Unquestionably. It goes a very long way in healing the wounds. If a crime remains unsolved, it can have very nasty side effects.'

'Did you solve a lot of crimes, Mr Athreya?'

'When you've been at it for decades, Linda, you do end up solving quite a few. Criminals are seldom as smart as they think they are.'

'What are you guys whispering about?' Sarosh's voice intruded upon their conversation, making Linda jerk her head up. 'Let us into the secret too.'

Athreya looked over to see a grinning Sarosh and a curious Ipshita staring at him and Linda. At Sarosh's comment, Asma had broken off her conversation with Maazin and both of them turned their faces towards Linda.

'Oh, nothing really,' Linda responded smoothly. 'Mr Athreya was just saying that criminals are often not as clever as they think they are.'

'If that's so, why are so few criminals are brought to book?' Sarosh demanded.

'It's a question of manpower,' Javed cut in. 'Dozens of major crimes take place every day in every city. We don't have nearly enough manpower to go after all of them. When you can't deploy enough people on a case, the perpetrator remains free.'

'Perhaps,' Athreya interposed with a smile, 'if the police force employed more psychologists, their success rates might be higher. To me, Javed's perspectives were invaluable. They helped me investigate more intelligently.'

'Did you have any unsolved cases, Mr Athreya?' Linda

asked.

'Oh, yes,' Athreya replied with a rueful smile. 'If an investigator tells you that he cracked every case that came his way, he is lying.'

'Doesn't that make you feel awful? I mean, letting a criminal go scot-free?'

'It does. But you learn to live with it.'

'Must have been really awful,' Asma echoed. 'Dad says that you sometimes know who the criminal is, but you don't have the evidence to prosecute him. Or her.'

'Indeed. You feel so impotent when that happens. But it goes with the territory.' Athreya set aside the breadstick he had picked up. It was as if he had suddenly lost his appetite. 'But for me,' he went on in a softer voice, 'that wasn't the worst I experienced.'

'Really? Is there something worse than letting a criminal go scot-free?' Linda seemed indignant.

Athreya abandoned his half-finished soup and pushed the bowl away.

'Among the most difficult things to live down,' he said, staring unseeingly at the bamboo place mat in front of him, 'is the knowledge that you sent an undeserving man to the gallows.'

'Undeserving?' Asma echoed with a furrowed brow. 'When did that happen to you? Dad says that you caught far, far more criminals than anyone else in the police force. And that you were always right.'

'This particular man was guilty, Asma,' Athreya replied, his tone sombre and reminiscent. 'Guilty of wilful murder, no less. But he didn't deserve to hang.'

'After committing *murder*?' Linda demanded. Her indignation had turned to outrage.

Athreya looked up and ran his eye around the table. All of them except Javed were staring at him. Under lowered eyebrows, Sarosh's intense eyes bored into his. Ipshita's eyes had grown large. Purbhi had stopped fidgeting with her phone and was watching Athreya like a cat. Asma's brow was still creased, and Linda seemed positively distressed. Maazin was staring at Athreya with a puzzled expression on his face.

'There are times when the murderer does the world a service by killing someone,' Athreya said, choosing his words with care. 'This was one such case. The person he killed was a monster. By his act, the killer made the world a better place.'

'How so?'

'Javed can speak in great detail about personality disorders, about how some people completely lack empathy and are unable to care about others. He can draw psychological profiles of such people, as he used to draw them for me. Shorn of terminology and jargon, it is actually very simple.

'Sometimes men become so vile, so warped in their minds and so wrapped up in their own desires, that they lose sight of the pain and misery they inflict upon others, especially their loved ones.' A trace of bitterness crept into his voice. 'In extreme cases, such men need to be put away. Only then does peace and justice return. Only then is reconciliation possible.'

Astonished faces stared at him silence. This was not what they had expected to hear from a celebrated crime-fighter. Perhaps, they had expected an ex-policeman to hold the law inviolate and above everything else.

But Javed seemed to know exactly what Athreya was talking about.

'I remember the case,' he said in his gravelly voice, pushing away his soup bowl. 'It had happened a few months before I left the force. It had bothered you no end, I remember. Kept you up for many nights.'

Athreya sighed softly.

'Sometimes, law and justice are two different things,' he said, glancing at Asma. 'As police officers, we were required to serve the law. Not justice.'

'Was that the final straw that made you leave the force?' Javed's deep voice had softened.

Athreya nodded. 'As a part of the force, you are bound by its rules. Everything *must* be reported. *Everything.* You have no discretion. Even if it goes against natural justice.'

'Is it different when you are a private investigator?' Javed asked.

'It can be... if you want it to be so. You are at liberty to follow your conscience. You can leave some things unsaid... small things that the official investigators often miss. It can lead to a better outcome... and less guilt.'

'And you can also refuse a commission or resign it,' Javed added. 'Something you can't do in the force.'

A silence fell over the table. It lasted a few long moments before it was broken by a voice from an unexpected source.

'But after striving for justice all your life, can you *really* walk away from murder? Without exposing the murderer?'

Athreya's eyes snapped to the speaker. It was Purbhi. He recognized the distinctive voice—it was low and rasping. It was one of the two voices he had overheard through his bedroom door.

'Maybe,' he replied distractedly, with half his mind processing what he had just learnt. 'Maybe I can. If the occasion demands it.'

6

Hardly had Athreya stepped out of the castle and onto the huge lawn than was he accosted. Striding purposefully, Sarosh came from behind him and fell in step beside him. He had hurried through his dinner and waited for the older man to rise from the table.

'I didn't know that you are a private detective,' Sarosh began without preamble.

'I am not,' Athreya responded. 'At least, that is not what I call myself. In today's world, "private detective" has connotations that I don't care much for.'

'Come on! Sherlock—'

'Sherlock Holmes and Hercule Poirot exist only in the realm of fiction,' Athreya cut in smoothly. 'A real-life private detective today handles more divorce cases than anything else. He probably spends much of his time tailing unfaithful spouses.'

'There's money in it,' Sarosh protested, the tips of his spectacular moustache trembling. 'Especially if you can get a share of the settlement proceeds. The wealthy pay heavily for actionable evidence.'

'Indeed! The "action" they take after a detective gathers the evidence is often blackmail. That aside, did you have something specific you wanted to talk about?'

'I have a proposition for you.'

'Proposition?' Athreya cast him a quick glance as they ambled towards Land's End.

'As I told you, I invest in different businesses. I have

been considering setting up a private detective agency.'

'Really?' Athreya asked, suppressing a smile. 'Who would run the agency?'

'Oh, not me, for sure. We'll need an experienced detective for that... someone like you.' Sarosh stopped and turned to Athreya. His mismatched earrings swayed crazily at the sudden movement. 'You can have an equal share in the profits. If you don't like tailing targets, you can hire younger people and invest in technology and gadgets. You'd need money for that, and that's where I come in. I provide the money and you bring in the expertise. For a fifty-fifty split of profits.'

Athreya was amused. This misguided scion was prepared to put in money without taking the effort to understand even the basics of a business. Athreya could think of a dozen ways to siphon off funds from the detective agency that Sarosh wanted him to set up. It wouldn't be very difficult to chisel money off this rich young man. He wondered how much money Sarosh had already lost.

'No,' Athreya said, as he resumed sauntering towards Land's End. Sarosh continued beside him. 'I am not the person you want. I have no interest in this. But I'll offer a piece of unsolicited advice, if you don't mind. Don't invest in a business without first understanding it. You'll get ripped off.'

'Well... you may be right,' Sarosh replied, stroking his moustache. 'Actually, we already have a client who needs a private detective. He has been shafted by someone he trusted. Maybe, you can help him? He's willing to pay well.'

'Was it in a business deal?'

'Yes.'

'Then, I'm not the right person for it. He probably needs a lawyer.'

'Don't turn it down without hearing the details.'

'It must be confiden—'

'Don't worry,' Sarosh went on. 'Yes, it is confidential, but I won't tell you who the client is, or give you any specifics. Let's call him… Amit. Just to give him a name. Three years ago, Amit entered into a pretty big deal with someone called… Rahul. That's not particularly creative, but that name will serve our purpose.

'So, Amit entered into a deal with Rahul. It was worth about twenty crores. But within two years, Amit realized that he had been cheated. Duped. Some of the things that Rahul had said were not really true and some were outright lies. Unfortunately, many of the things the two had agreed upon were not put in writing.

'As a result, Amit stands to his lose twenty crores, unless he can prove that Rahul had deliberately deceived him. He can then claim the twenty crores from Rahul's other assets. He is willing to give twenty per cent of that—four crores—to anyone who can prove that Rahul cheated.'

Sarosh stopped speaking and glanced enquiringly at Athreya, who remained silent. The sound of someone singing in the distance was the only sound to be heard. Accompanying it were precise musical notes from a guitar.

After a few moments, Sarosh asked, 'So, what do you say, Mr Athreya?'

'Well,' Athreya replied, shaking his head. He had heard Sarosh out. 'This is not up my street—'

'Don't decide now,' Sarosh cut in hurriedly. 'Mull over it when I'm away on the trek. We'll talk about this after I return. Okay? Goodnight.'

He smiled affably, shook Athreya's hand and headed back towards the castle. As he did, an attractive figure with short hair, who had been strolling on the lawn a hundred feet away, turned and hurried towards Athreya.

Ipshita had been waiting for him to be alone.

At dinner, he had seen her only briefly before she sat down at the dining table. Now as she approached him, he noticed that she was a little taller than Asma and Linda. Slim and erect, Ipshita walked with natural grace. The dark trousers and the light-coloured top she wore enhanced her looks.

'Good evening,' she said with a pleasant smile as she reached Athreya. 'Can I walk with you?'

'Of course.' He smiled and nodded in the semi-darkness that was punctuated by solar LED lamps set far apart. 'Tell me, who is that playing the guitar?'

The mellifluous notes were coming from Land's End at the far end of the lawn. Accompanying it was a rich male voice singing 'Hotel California' surprisingly effortlessly. The pleasant voice carried clearly in the cool night air.

Gazing towards Land's End, Athreya saw a tall figure on the platform with one foot on a chair. The guitar was resting on his raised leg as he strummed it. Beside him was Maazin, who was moving his torso in time with the music. Next to Maazin was a thin woman whom Athreya had no difficulty recognizing by her distinctive high ponytail: Purbhi. Asma and Linda were a little distance away, enjoying to the music.

'That's Dhavak,' Ipshita said, replying to Athreya's question. She too turned to face Land's End. 'Haven't you met him? He's staying here as well.'

Then, Athreya surmised, he must be the last of the five guests.

'He wasn't at dinner tonight,' he remarked.

'He eats when he feels like it,' Ipshita explained. 'Never sticks to timings. Does his own thing.'

'He sings very well,' Athreya said, gazing towards the source of the music. 'A seasoned singer, I must say.'

'He is popular. Haven't you heard of him? Dhavak Strummer is his name.'

'*Strummer?*' Athreya threw a quick glance at her. 'Is that his professional pseudonym? Like a stage name some performers adopt?'

'I'm not sure, but I don't think so. Why would he want a stage name? He released an album last month as Dhavak

Strummer.'

'Really? Clearly, I'm not as familiar with contemporary music as I should be.'

'He has a lovely voice, doesn't he?' Her voice was wistful. 'Must be wonderful to be able to sing so well.'

'Do you sing, Ipshita?'

'Me?' Her laugh tinkled in the night. 'Who doesn't dabble in casual singing? I did learn classical music when I was a kid. Didn't take it forward, though. Fate had other plans for me.'

'You have a clear voice,' Athreya pointed out. 'Not all singers do.'

'That's what my music teacher used to say. My voice is okay, but my problem is breath control. It's not good enough to sing difficult songs. Casual singing is fine, but I can't do the real stuff. I also struggle with high notes—I don't have the voice range, I suppose. My singing is *nowhere* near Dhavak's.'

'Maybe you and Dhavak can give us a few duets tomorrow night. I believe Maazin is organizing a little party.'

'You think so?' Ipshita's eyes seemed to shine.

'I'm serious,' Athreya affirmed.

'Then, can you… can you suggest it to Dhavak? I can't summon the courage to ask him. He's such a wonderful singer and I am just an amateur. He might be insulted if I ask.'

'Sure, I'll ask him once we are introduced to each other. For now, I don't want to interrupt him. Let's enjoy the singing from here.'

They stood side by side and listened as Dhavak picked John Denver's 'Take Me Home, Country Roads' as his next song. Athreya wondered why Ipshita wanted to talk to him alone. He waited for her make the first move. As Dhavak completed the second stanza, she spoke softly.

'I've been thinking about what you said at dinner,' she said. 'It must be terrible, not having the proof to nail the murderer when you *know* that he committed the murder.'

'Well, yes and no. As investigators, we—'

'Oh! I don't mean for you as the investigator. I was thinking of the victim's family—they know who the murderer is. Imagine, they see him *every* day, going in and out. Going about free as a bird and totally unpunished. How can they bear it? Day after day, month after month. For years, maybe! They *know* that he killed their loved one, but they can't do anything about it.'

'In such situations,' Athreya said in an undertone, 'the scars *never* heal. Unless the murderer is somehow brought to book.'

'Or God strikes him down.'

Athreya snapped his head around to her. Her profile under the curly mane was striking. She continued to gaze towards Land's End, not willing to meet his eyes. He wondered if she knew of an unpunished murderer.

'You mean that?' he whispered. 'Wouldn't that be a second murder? God has no hands; He works through the hands of men.'

'Maybe,' she whispered in return. 'Maybe. How is it different from what you said at dinner? Wouldn't the second murderer be doing the world a service by killing the first murderer? Doing the family a *great* service?' She drew a deep breath and quoted in a whisper: '"*Only then does peace and justice return. Only then is reconciliation possible.*"' She turned to face him. 'Those are *your* words, Mr Athreya; not mine.'

'Fair enough,' Athreya conceded, feeling that the conversation was getting into dangerous territory. He decided to change the topic. 'What do you do in Kolkata, Ipshita? Do you work, or are you a student?'

'I'm an interior designer.' Her voice lost some of its tension. 'I set up my own little shop last year.'

'Yet another budding entrepreneur!' Athreya exclaimed softly. 'Peter Dann seems to have attracted quite a few. Is interior designing a lucrative business?'

'Once you establish your name, yes. Till such time, it's hand to mouth. But on the flip side, you need just one break. If you pull it off, you are on the road to success.'

'Are you alone right now?'

'Yup! It's a one-woman shop. I've managed to get half a dozen clients. Small jobs, but they help pay the bills and build credentials.'

'What does your friend, Purbhi, do? She hardly spoke at dinner.'

'Except when you shocked her out of her silence!' Ipshita laughed.

'Is she always so quiet?'

'Ha! I wish! Sometimes, she just can't stop talking.' Her voice dropped a notch. 'It's just that she's a little off colour today.'

'Why? Anything I—or someone—said?'

'No, no! It's just that she doesn't want to... er... she's a little anxious about the trek. She's never been on one before.'

'Have you been on one?' Athreya asked.

'No, but I take things as they come. I don't anticipate the future and get tense about it.'

'That's a sensible way to live life. Why is Purbhi anxious?'

'Let it be. Shall we, please?'

'Certainly.' Athreya was surprised at the abrupt shift. 'You were about to tell me what Purbhi does.'

'Well, I am not sure how to put it... she does a basket of things. But what is common among everything is that they are all about the internet and mobile phones.'

'Is she an entrepreneur too?'

'Sort of. She's freelance. She does Search Engine Optimization—SEO for short, writes bots for mining websites for information, develops apps for mobile, dabbles in mobile-based advertising, et cetera. She's very good with that kind of stuff.'

'Come,' Athreya said, taking a step forward. 'Let's go to

Land's End.'

They strolled down the lawn towards the raised platform. Dhavak had moved the chair on which he had his foot, so that now he had his back to them as they approached. Purbhi and Maazin were standing a few paces away to his right, while Asma and Linda stood a few feet beyond.

On reaching Land's End, Athreya stopped short of the platform and waited for Dhavak to finish singing an unfamiliar song. Despite not knowing it, Athreya had no trouble appreciating the consummate ease with which he sang the tune. As he gazed at the tall singer's broad back, he thought there was something vaguely familiar about him. Something he couldn't put his finger on.

Presently, Dhavak completed the song, strummed his guitar vigorously and stood erect. Led by Maazin, the group erupted in applause, which Athreya joined, and Asma slapped her thigh. Dhavak nodded in acknowledgement and lit a cigarette as he leaned his guitar against the chair. With the glowing cigarette dangling from his lips, he poured a generous amount of whisky from a bottle into a glass.

'That was outstanding!' Linda gushed as the applause subsided. 'Simply marvellous! You *must* give us more numbers tomorrow.'

Athreya couldn't hear Dhavak's response as he still had his back to him. But as Linda had just spoken about Dhavak singing at the next day's party, Athreya stepped forward to steer the conversation towards him doing duets with Ipshita. Seeing Athreya come towards them, Asma made the introduction.

'Dhavak,' she said, 'meet Mr Athreya, my father's very close friend. He is staying here too.'

Although Athreya could still only see Dhavak's back, he sensed the singer stiffen. He seemed to freeze for a brief moment. Then, with the cigarette in his right hand and his whisky glass in his left, he swivelled unhurriedly around to face Athreya. With his greater height and the benefit from another two feet of the platform, Dhavak stared down at Athreya.

Below him, Athreya had begun lifting his arm to offer his hand to the singer. But when his arm was half-raised, Athreya froze. He had just realized why Dhavak had seemed vaguely familiar. This was the hirsute stranger he had seen briefly at Clarkson's, the man who had peeped into the pub before disappearing into the darkness.

Dhavak made no move to greet Athreya. Instead, he lifted his glass, which was half-full of undiluted whisky, and drank deeply, staring at Athreya through flinty eyes. Their eyes locked for a few seconds as the others at Land's End fell silent. Dhavak took a pull at his cigarette and then drained his glass. He had it in just two gulps.

Without a word, Dhavak turned and stubbed out his cigarette as he placed the empty glass on a wrought-iron table. He unhurriedly hoisted his guitar by its strap and slung it across his body. He picked up the half-full whisky bottle with his large hand and turned to face Athreya, who had dropped his arm and was watching silently. Dhavak's long, unkempt locks fell over his eyes. His large hand with long fingers came up and pushed them back.

'Athreya,' Dhavak growled with a patently unfriendly air. His voice was gruff and low. 'You're a cop.'

It was an accusation, not a question. Athreya remained silent, watching the big man as he tried in vain to keep his hair from falling back over his eyes. A distressed Maazin had taken a couple of uncertain steps towards Dhavak.

'Mr Athreya has retired,' Asma said in an embarrassed voice. 'Just like my father.'

'Your dad was a psychologist,' Dhavak countered without taking his hard eyes off Athreya. 'But this man was a cop. Big difference between the two.'

He stepped off Land's End onto the lawn and stood a couple of yards from Athreya. A strong smell of whisky and tobacco came from him. Athreya thought that he detected a whiff of marijuana too. The full-sized whisky bottle seemed small in his hand.

'Nothing personal, Mister Policeman,' Dhavak growled. 'It's just that I can't stand cops. I'm allergic to them. I'll stay out of your way, and you stay out of mine.'

With that, he brushed past Athreya and strode away towards the castle without a backward glance.

7

Athreya woke up late the next morning. He had lain awake in bed for a long while, reviewing the events of the previous days in his mind. From Javed's riddle to the ominous handprints at Clarkson's. From the peculiar declaration that whatever happened at Peter Dann happened for the best to the strange conversations at dinner. And finally, from the intriguing chats on the lawn to Dhavak's rudeness.

He was not offended by the singer's behaviour. Rather, he was intrigued. What would cause a man to hate all cops, even those he had never met? Had he run afoul of the police in the past? What had happened to leave him bitter enough to be so nasty to a stranger? It couldn't have been very long ago, as he seemed to be in his mid-thirties.

Eventually, Athreya had drifted off to sleep, and when he woke up, it was well past his usual waking time. He rose and called Veni to check how her preparations for going overseas were coming along.

'All well,' she said. 'I'm quite looking forward to the trip. By the way, your Nanda Devi photos from the day before yesterday are brilliant! What do you plan to do today?'

'Going riding with Javed shortly,' he said.

'Horse riding?' Concern tinged her voice. 'Be careful, Hari. Your leg might act up. You haven't ridden since the metal rod was inserted in your leg.'

'I won't do anything rash, don't worry. I think the leg shouldn't trouble me. I haven't felt the rod for the past couple of years.'

After ringing off, he got ready for a lengthy horseback ride after breakfast. He took out a cotton scarf, dark glasses and an assortment of little things, which he stuffed into his leather sling bag. He picked up the broad-brimmed hat Javed had lent him. Finally, he plugged in his high-capacity power bank to charge and went downstairs for breakfast. It would be fully charged by the time he returned in the afternoon.

None of the five guests was around when he went down. They were probably still in bed. When he and Javed went to the stables after a slow breakfast, they found that the horses were saddled and ready. Athreya noted with relief that his horse was not very tall, certainly not as large as the ones he had ridden when he was in the police force. Though they were bigger than the mountain ponies that tourists usually used in the Himalayan foothills, he didn't anticipate much difficulty in climbing into the saddle and getting off.

The mount that had been picked for him was a dun, and it seemed to be a mild-mannered creature. He went up to it and slowly stroked its neck as the stable boy held the reins. When the horse didn't object, he stepped closer and spoke softly to it as he rubbed its neck and shoulder. Apparently, the dun was accustomed to strangers riding it. Asma, who was stroking Daisy with her good arm, turned to watch Athreya.

'Ride him around the lawn for a few minutes, sir,' Maazin suggested. 'That way, you'll get used to him and he to you. Gutsy is a sweet-tempered boy, no worries.'

Athreya spoke the horse's name a couple of times and mounted the saddle with far less difficulty than he had anticipated. The rod in his leg made no protest.

'Not bad!' Javed called out from where he was checking his large black horse. 'Into the saddle in the first try. Doesn't look like you are out of practice, Athreya.'

Athreya sent the dun forward and rode slowly along the periphery of the large lawn. As muscle memory returned, he found himself settling into the saddle, unconsciously moving in tandem with the horse like a practised rider.

Within five minutes, he had become comfortable with Gutsy and the horse was accepting his commands. He sent it into a fast trot on the second circuit around the lawn. Pleased with himself, he returned to the stable where Javed was in the saddle. His large black horse seemed to be capable of carrying Javed's considerable weight.

'Your water bottles and snacks are here,' Maazin said, patting the jute pouches hanging behind their saddles. 'Mr Rais has sunscreen and first aid. Enjoy your ride!'

He turned to Javed and continued softly, 'Taken your automatic, Uncle?'

Javed patted a bulge under his left arm, indicating a concealed holster. The front zip of his jacket was undone, providing quick access.

'You bet!' he growled menacingly. 'If the man comes at us, I promise you that he'll get it. Self-defence.'

They rode out of the gate and down the private road that wound around the hillock until it met the public road. Javed was watchful, scanning the trees on both sides for strangers. Athreya too grew vigilant and moved his horse to the middle of the road.

'So,' Javed asked softly, as they made their way east along the public road, 'what do you think of my five guests?' His eyes were restless, darting from side to side, scanning the forest around them.

'A curious bunch,' Athreya replied equally softly. 'But I don't see anything amiss. I have no idea why they pretended to be strangers or why they faked bookings. How is the premonition?'

'Alive and kicking. I have a bad feeling about this, Athreya.'

'Are you sure you aren't mistaken? You thought you recognized Linda in Nainital, but she denied being there. And all the others were strangers to you. What if you are mistaken?'

'Not unless the girl I saw was Linda's twin sister,' Javed rumbled. 'I have met her many times when she and Asma were together in Gurgaon. I am sure.'

'What about the others?' Athreya persisted.

'Let's take them one by one. How easy or difficult is it to confuse Sarosh with someone else? What with his weird hairstyle, moustache, mismatched earrings and the way he dresses?'

'I agree. He is quite a unique character. I haven't seen another like him.'

'How about Dhavak? Tall, hirsute, unkempt? And his hippie-like clothes? He sat facing me in Nainital. I looked at him several times and wondered why he was so frowzy.'

'Hmm.'

'And Purbhi? How many girls wear their ponytail so high on the head? Yes, many do favour a high ponytail. But so high? It almost springs out of the top of her head.'

'That leaves Ipshita. She's very pretty and knows how to dress well. Her short, curly hair and well-fitting clothes make her stand out, especially in Nainital. She is difficult to mistake for someone else.'

Athreya nodded. Javed's explanations seemed to hold water.

'The remaining two whom you didn't see,' Athreya asked. 'Were they men or women?'

'Don't know. I didn't see any part of them other than their feet sticking out under the table. Their faces and torsos were hidden. All I remember was that both were wearing jeans and sneakers. They could have been male or female. All I can say is that one of them was probably a little shorter than the other. I am going by how far their legs were sticking out. I can't say if they were Mrinal and Kinshuk.'

* * *

They headed east on the road and passed Clarkson's fifteen minutes later. Margot was in the front garden, watering her plants while Dave was peering into the hood of his 4x4. Kinshuk was breaking his fast alone at a table on the lawn, looking preoccupied as he gazed forward fixedly. Mrinal was nowhere to be seen.

The two riders speeded up to a trot and continued on the road. Fifteen minutes later, they came to a large, grassy plain between two hills. Single trees and small groves dotted the dale. At the far end, a thin ribbon of water reflected the sunshine. Nothing man-made could be seen.

'This is where we get off the road,' Javed said, and rode onto the grass. 'We will turn north at the end of this plain and make our way between those two hills.'

'So pristine!' Athreya remarked, gazing with pleasure at the unspoilt beauty before him. 'Simply outstanding.'

'Pottersfield—that's what it is called. Asma loves this place. We used to come here so often when she was a child.' He paused for the briefest moment and continued, 'Naira too loved it. She and Asma would camp here for at least one night, even if they were visiting Peter Dann just for a couple of days. It was one of those mother–daughter things. Asma still comes here as often as she can.'

'Isn't this where she rode Daisy to yesterday?' Athreya asked.

'That's right.'

They rode in silence, enjoying the wide vale and the rolling hills enclosing it. The ribbon of water gradually widened as they neared it. When they were about a hundred yards away, they spotted someone sitting on a rock by the stream. Javed slid his hand into his jacket and loosened the automatic in its holster. He then rested his hand on the saddle so that he could reach the gun quickly.

But as they neared, they saw that it was a woman. Javed relaxed and his hand fell away. The woman had her back to them, and was gazing into a small fire in front of her. It had burnt itself down to embers. Beyond the fire was the stream. Athreya wondered what a lone woman would be doing with a fire at the far side of Pottersfield.

Hearing the horses, the woman turned around and looked at them. It was Mrinal. Her face was wet.

She quickly opened a bottle of water and poured half on the embers, extinguishing them. She then stamped the wet ash a few times, crumbling it to powder. She took more water from the bottle and splashed her face with it. Twice more, she rubbed her face and splashed it with water. When she turned back to face them, her face was glistening with moisture.

'Good morning,' she greeted them with a wan smile that didn't quite reach her red-tinged eyes.

It was apparent that she had been crying and had used the water to erase the signs of tears. Her eyes darted to the small fire she had just put out.

'Good morning,' the men replied in unison.

'You are quite some distance from Clarkson's,' Javed continued. 'Did you walk here?'

'Yes. It's a lovely morning, and I decided to check out Pottersfield. Mrs Clarkson told me about this place and said that it was lovely. It *is* beautiful.'

'You came alone?'

Mrinal shrugged. 'I find solitude therapeutic. Takes me away from the cares of the everyday world. And heaven knows that we all have more worries than we want.' She waved her hand breezily as if to dismiss what she had just said and tried to widen her smile. 'Where are you headed to? I didn't know Peter Dann had horses. Clarkson's has a couple of ponies.'

'Yes, we have a stable,' Javed replied. 'We thought we'd check out the foothills before the trekking season begins. Also just wanted to do some riding. You will be passing through here tomorrow on your trip.'

'Will we?' She turned to go, but not before she threw

another quick glance at the doused embers. 'I'll return to Clarkson's now. I'll see you in the evening.'

'We are organizing a party this evening. You'll meet your fellow trekkers. Are you returning alone to Clarkson's?'

'Yes. Why?'

'There's a crazy man around with a knife. He attacked my daughter.'

Mrinal's eyes went wide. 'When?'

'Yesterday. It's best that you don't go alone. I'll call Dave and have you picked up.'

He pulled out his mobile and called Dave, who arrived on a motorbike ten minutes later. Mrinal waved to them and mounted the bike.

'Goodbye and thank you.'

They parted company.

'They've had a fight,' Javed said, as they watched the motorbike disappearing across Pottersfield towards the road. 'She and her fiancé. He was brooding over breakfast and she came here to get away from him.'

Athreya didn't respond. He was looking at the grey embers on the ground and wondering why Mrinal had lit the fire in the middle of nowhere, and why she had stamped the ashes after extinguishing it. Had she been trying to destroy something? What was she hiding?

* * *

It was late afternoon when the two riders returned to Peter Dann. Athreya saw at once that the number of guards patrolling the property had increased. Javed too noticed it and nodded approvingly.

After spending several hours in the saddle, Athreya was sore all over, but he had thoroughly enjoyed riding after all these years. He was pleased that his leg hadn't troubled him. In fact, he had forgotten all about it! He ate a snack and took a hot bath to ease his aching muscles. Drowsy after the unaccustomed activity and from the hot water therapy, he dozed off until he was woken up by noise and voices outside his door. The preparations for the evening party had begun.

He sat up and looked around the room. A minute later, he felt that something was missing, something he hadn't realized on his return. For a few moments, he couldn't identify what it was. He looked around a couple of times before it struck him—the power bank was not on the table where he had left it. He rose from the bed and went to the table. The charger was there, still plugged into the wall socket, with its wire snaking across the table. But the dark blue gadget itself was nowhere in sight. He looked for it under the table and around the room. Ten minutes later, it was clear that the power bank was missing.

He checked the rest of his belongings, but his clothes and toiletries were all as he had left them and his suitcase was locked. Nothing else was missing. At Maazin's suggestion, he had left his room unlocked when he had gone riding so that it could be cleaned. There was nothing to fear, Maazin had said; every member of the staff was entirely trustworthy. Athreya made a mental note to speak to him about the missing power bank.

When Athreya joined the party an hour and a half later, most of the guests were already in the lounge. It was a huge rectangular space running east-west along the northern wall of the castle. The door to Athreya's room was at the east end, while a similar oversized room at the west end was vacant. The other guest rooms, Room 3 to Room 7, were on the southern wall of the castle.

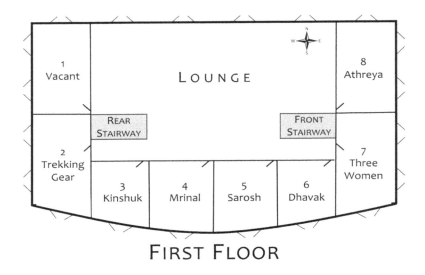

FIRST FLOOR

Both the stairways that opened into the lounge provided access to the ground floor as well as to the rooftop terrace. The stairway closer to Athreya's room—the 'front' stairway, as it was called—was the one that the guests usually used. The castle's staff mostly used the 'rear' stairway, which was near the far end of the lounge. Four large windows, which opened to the lawn to the north, provided ample ventilation in the lounge.

Several clusters of sofas and chairs ensured that sitting space was never in short supply. The furniture at the west and east ends of the northern wall had been moved to accommodate two food counters and a bar, respectively. Paintings, tapestries and framed sketches hung on the walls of the lounge.

The four women—Asma, Linda, Ipshita and Purbhi—stood together beside one of the windows in the northern wall, chatting with each other. Asma was wearing a dark skirt and a light shirt, and had let her hair loose. Except for her sling, there was no sign of her recent ordeal. Linda, her hair tied in a neat ponytail, was clad in light-coloured trousers and a dark sweater.

Ipshita, very neatly turned out again, wore baggy trousers that were snug at the waist and hips and then flared out. Not as much as a palazzo but more like harem pants without the narrowing at the ankles. They were beige with a large floral print in maroon. Above, she wore a plain black top. Javed was right—with her elegant dressing, striking curly hair and pretty face, she was difficult to confuse with someone else.

Purbhi was all-blue in a pair of loose jeans and an oversized denim jacket, both of which looked exactly like what she had worn the previous evening at dinner. As had been the case then, she looked shabby. Her distinctive high ponytail seemed to be sprouting close to the top of her head. Now too, she was clutching her mobile phone.

As soon as Athreya entered the lounge, Ipshita and Purbhi, who were facing his direction, turned their gazes to him. Purbhi's ferret-face was inscrutable as she stared unblinkingly at him through her large black spectacles. Her anxiety, which Athreya had noticed the previous evening, was more apparent now.

Ipshita blinked in a way that reminded him that she wore contact lenses. There was something more in her face that Athreya couldn't place; some sort of seriousness and worry that he had detected in her voice the previous evening when they had walked on the lawn. But as soon as her eyes met his, the look disappeared, and she offered him a pleasant smile. Seeing her response, Linda turned and blinked unsurely at Athreya before giving a quick smile and turning away again.

The three guests were nervous. His imagination suggested that they were waiting for something to happen. Something was planned. Abruptly, the lounge floor became a chessboard in his mind's eye. The five guests became chess pieces. Ipshita was the queen, Purbhi a bishop, Dhavak a rook, Sarosh a knight and Linda a pawn.

Athreya shook himself out of his vision and glanced at Dhavak going up the front stairway to the terrace with a cigarette packet in one hand and a lighter in the other. With smoking in the lounge prohibited, the ones who wanted a dose of nicotine would need to go to the terrace. Athreya suspected that Dhavak, a heavy smoker, would make several trips before the evening was out.

Javed and Sarosh were sitting on a set of sofas around a low glass table near the centre of the lounge, between the two stairways. Seeing his host wave to him, Athreya joined them and took a single-seater sofa beside Javed. As before, Sarosh, whose distinctive moustache looked freshly gelled, was trying to talk Javed into upgrading Peter Dann to a luxury destination. A minute after Athreya sat down, he ended his spiel and went to join the others, where he began monopolizing Ipshita.

'Good timing,' Javed smiled. 'I was getting tired of Sarosh's endless sales-talk. Did you notice an edginess in him yesterday?'

Athreya nodded. 'Purbhi is anxious too, Ipshita is pensive, and Dhavak seems angry. Only Linda—'

'Linda is normally quiet,' Javed interrupted in an undertone. 'She is talking a lot more than usual. Typically, Asma talks and Linda listens. This time around, it is the opposite. There is a nervousness in her that is making her talk.'

'She seems afraid tonight. She spoke a lot to me at dinner last night. About her Gurgaon days with Asma, about crime and grief and about her late brother.'

Javed's eyebrows crept up. 'That's unusual for her. She is generally a private person; opens up only to Asma. She's a lovely girl too—very caring and gentle. And devout. She was a great help to Asma after Naira passed away. I was terribly worried about how Asma would cope with her mother's death. I was so relieved that she had found a close friend in Linda.'

'United in grief,' Athreya mused. 'That's how Linda put it.'

Javed nodded as he contemplated her from a distance.

'They are all tense,' he rumbled softly. 'All five of them. They've come here to Peter Dann for a reason. I wonder what they are up to.'

'Something is coming to head,' Athreya added in an undertone.

'Mrinal and Kinshuk will be joining us shortly. They checked in a little while ago. How old do you think Mrinal is?'

'A couple of years older than Asma, perhaps. Twenty-five?'

'Looks like that, doesn't she,' Javed chuckled. 'But she is thirty-two.'

'Thirty-two?' Athreya's eyebrows shot up. 'You're sure? How could I have misjudged so badly?'

'You are not the only one who did. I saw her ID when she checked in. She is thirty-two and certainly doesn't look her age. Incidentally, she and her fiancé *have* had a quarrel. She was not speaking to him when they checked in, and she looked as if she had been crying.'

Javed broke off as Dhavak came down the stairs after his smoke and passed close to where the two sat. He went to the far end of the room and took a chair near the window furthest from where Athreya and Javed sat. He was keeping his promise of staying out of Athreya's way. He probably expected Athreya to do likewise.

'There is something I need to tell you,' Athreya said in a low voice. 'I don't know if it has anything to do with the riddle of the five guests, or if it's more mundane, but someone has pinched my power bank from my room.'

He quickly narrated what had happened, and said that he would speak to Maazin about it.

'Do that,' Javed said. 'I'll check too, but I don't think any of the staff would have done that. They are very reliable.'

Just then, the door of Room 3 opened and out came

Kinshuk, wearing a tight pair of trousers and a sleeveless T-shirt that was a size or two too small for him and show-cased his muscled torso. Maazin, who had been ensuring that the arrangements were in place, came up and wel-comed him. He introduced Kinshuk to the others.

Athreya watched as he met his fellow guests. There was no overt sign of prior familiarity as they shook hands. The celebrity trainer, Athreya noticed, held Asma's and Ipshi-ta's hands a little longer than was normal. The handshake with Sarosh was formal, as was the gesturing when the two men approached the bar. Unsurprisingly, the latest arrival promptly took a couple of selfies with the group. To all appearances, Kinshuk was meeting them for the first time.

Soon, the party warmed up. Everyone, including Maaz-in, had a glass in hand. Dhavak had a bottle of whisky for himself on the coffee table in front of him. Chatter and laughter produced a continuous hum that was punctuated by different notes—Linda's silvery laughter, Sarosh's loud-ness, Ipshita's clear, musical voice and Maazin's guffaws. Purbhi too seemed to have relaxed and was smiling and talking.

After a fruitless attempt to monopolize Ipshita, Sarosh had joined Dhavak at the far end of the room, where he held a desultory conversation with him. Meanwhile, Kin-shuk had managed to corner Ipshita's attention, much to Sarosh's evident annoyance. Athreya and Javed fell into reminiscing about the days they had been together, drawing an indulgent smile from Asma as she passed them. Playing the hostess, she divided her attention between the three groups, offering a snippet here and a smile there. Her sling had become a mere inconvenience.

The party was purring along and everyone seemed to be having a good time. Even the taciturn Dhavak seemed to have opened up, and was chatting with two young men, showing his yellowed teeth from time to time as he grinned at a tipsy Kinshuk's jokes or needled Sarosh. Dhavak and

Javed went up to the terrace. The party hum had become continuous and steady. Athreya was finishing his second drink when the noise abruptly ceased. Silence fell. It was as if someone had turned off a tap. Athreya turned to see what had caused it. Everyone was looking south towards the guest rooms, so he too glanced in that direction.

There stood Mrinal, looking resplendent in a deep-blue silk kurti and light-blue leggings. A matching metallic hairclip held her hair together in a ponytail, and she had her mobile phone loosely in her left hand. She was the only woman in the room wearing traditional Indian attire. She stood there a few feet away from Athreya, midway between the two stairways, smiling hesitantly. Under her minimal make-up, her face looked haggard, and her tentative smile seemed to conceal sorrow.

For some reason, Mrinal's arrival had overshadowed everything else. It was almost as if the others had been waiting for her. And when she arrived, the lounge was plunged into silence.

8

Mrinal hadn't uttered a word, but every pair of eyes was turned on her as she stood there unsure and uncomfortable. Her large, clear eyes seemed to be searching for something familiar, someone she knew. Athreya was the closest to her, and when her gaze fell on him, her smile widened a trifle and something akin to relief passed over her face. She took half a step towards him.

As on the earlier occasion, Athreya felt sorry for her. It was a small, involuntary pang that was not the result of any conscious thought process. As before, the dominant perception on seeing her was that she looked alone and vulnerable. That evoked an avuncular, protective feeling towards her. But before he could greet her, another voice spoke.

'Welcome, Mrinal. Good evening.'

Asma's measured but warm voice cut through the silence. She strode forward towards Mrinal with a beaming smile and stretched out a hand.

'Oh, hello, Asma,' Mrinal replied in her soft and low voice. 'I hope I'm not late? I had some work to finish and that took more time than I had expected.'

'Not at all,' Asma assured her. 'We are not prisoners of time in this part of the world. Let me get you a drink. What will you have?'

'I brought a bottle of gin. It should be somewhere around. May I have that please? With tonic, ice and lemon? Thanks.'

'I'll get it, Asma,' Maazin called from the bar. 'I have

your bottle here, ma'am.'

He reached under the counter and pulled out an un-opened bottle of Gordon's Gin. Meanwhile, Mrinal stepped forward to Athreya and shook his hand.

'Good evening, Mr Athreya,' she said with a pleasing smile. 'How was your horseback ride?'

'We had a wonderful time,' Athreya replied. 'I'm a bit sore here and there, but nothing that won't go away in a day or two.' He gestured to the sofa next to him. 'Come, sit.'

Mrinal flashed Asma a smile and both of them sat down. Talk in the lounge resumed. Kinshuk, however, remained silent, watching Mrinal from a far corner with a worried expression on his face. He didn't get up and come to her. On her part, she ignored him. Javed was right—they had had a quarrel.

Mrinal's drink arrived just as Javed returned from the terrace. He boomed a greeting to Mrinal and sat down beside Asma, as Dhavak went to join Kinshuk and Sarosh. Athreya and the others began with small talk, and soon they were discussing Peter Dann, when Mrinal reminded Javed about his promise to expound on the castle. He repeated the story of the bishop and the monk who had taken refuge in the castle, but he added many embellishments and a sense of drama. It, however, was essentially the same as Dave Clarkson had briefly narrated two nights before. Javed's tale, told in a storyteller fashion, was a lot more entertaining and funnier, and brought laughter to his audience of three.

'Any dungeons, secret passages or hidden treasures?' Mrinal asked amusedly, as she went on to her second gin and tonic. 'No castle is complete without them.'

'We have a basement,' Javed rumbled, scratching his beard. 'We can pretend that it is a dungeon.'

'There are tales about a secret passage too!' Asma piped up. 'How else do you think word reached the British soldiers that the bishop was under attack? The castle was surrounded, but one of the bishop's boys escaped through the secret passage at night and reached the British camp on foot.'

'Why didn't that bishop escape through the secret passage?' Mrinal asked.

'For one, he was probably too portly to negotiate it and the forest on foot. But more importantly, the forest was considered dangerous at night. That's why they took refuge in the castle in the first place.'

'Where is the secret passage?'

'No clue.' Asma laughed and continued dramatically, 'Lost in the mists of time, I presume.'

'And what about buried treasure?'

'One of the many fabrications—' Javed began when Asma cut him off.

'Dad! Don't be so unromantic!' she admonished him and turned to Mrinal. 'Do you know that the walls of this building are over five feet thick in many places? Maybe even more.'

'Wow!' Mrinal's eyes widened. 'Five feet! That is as thick as I am tall.'

'Remember, this castle is made of stone,' Javed said. 'The whole two storeys of it along with the roofs and all. The walls on the ground floor have to support an immense weight. They *have* to be thick and solid.'

'Thick enough to hide treasure!' Asma chirped. 'Come, Mrinal, let me introduce you to the others.'

The two women rose and went towards the cluster of chairs where Sarosh, Purbhi, Linda and Ipshita were chatting. Kinshuk and Dhavak were at the far side of the lounge. As they walked over, Athreya observed that from behind, they might have been sisters. The only difference was that one was wearing a skirt and shirt while the other was clad in traditional Indian attire.

* * *

Athreya didn't know what happened in the intervening time, but when Mrinal returned twenty minutes later, she was rattled. Gone were the smile and gaiety that Javed's storytelling had stoked in her. The haunted look had returned to her face and her fingers were trembling slightly. Asma had introduced her to Sarosh and the three women, after which Asma had gone on to chat with Kinshuk and Dhavak. Now, seeing a visibly unnerved Mrinal return to Javed and Athreya, Asma came and sat down beside her. Concern was etched on her face as she enquired if anything was amiss.

Mrinal shook her head but said nothing. She emptied her glass and looked pitiably at Asma, who took her glass to the bar and brought her a refill. A few sips seemed to steady Mrinal, and soon, she offered a watery smile.

'It's nothing to worry about,' she said. 'It's just that I have received a bit of a shock. A personal matter. Oh, please don't blame Sarosh or the others… it's just that our conversation reminded me of something very distressing. I'll be fine soon, don't worry.'

'What did you talk about—' Asma began, but Mrinal cut her off.

'Let's not discuss it please. I'm sorry to interrupt you, but I want to get it out of my mind. Let's talk about something else. Please?'

'Certainly.'

Asma began talking about the trek the next day, and asked if Mrinal had packed. She answered distractedly, but Asma continued chatting as if nothing was amiss. Athreya watched the twenty-three-year-old handling the situation with uncommon maturity. Soon, Mrinal was looking better and began munching on the snacks Maazin had brought for her.

Athreya continued to watch, contributing minimally to the conversation, but observing Mrinal as well as the others. Ipshita, Purbhi and Linda had resumed their conversation, but they seemed a little subdued. Sarosh had joined Kinshuk and Dhavak in a far corner and was pensively fingering his moustache. Over the next fifteen minutes or so, Dhavak went up to the terrace twice to smoke.

On his second return, he picked up his guitar and strummed it. Mrinal, who had her back to him, didn't turn to look, but Asma did.

'Oh, good!' she exulted. 'Another drink for you, Mrinal?'

Mrinal nodded for her fifth drink. That surprised Athreya. Even after consuming over a third of the bottle of gin, she didn't seem tipsy. Clearly, she was accustomed to drinking.

She had taken a couple of sips when Dhavak began his first song. By the guitar notes that preceded the lyrics, Athreya recognized Simon and Garfunkel's 'The Sound of Silence'.

At the first few notes from the guitar, Mrinal, who was bringing her glass to her lips, froze for a moment. The next instant, the glass resumed its journey, but her fingers seemed to have lost some of their steadiness.

Dhavak began singing.

Mrinal froze again. The glass stopped at her lips. As Athreya watched, she paled. Colour drained from her face to the extent that even her pink lips become bloodless. Inch by inch, as if in a trance, she lowered her drink and put it on the table. She clutched her hands together and stared down into her glass. And that's how she remained—silent and motionless—until Dhavak completed the song. Everyone in the lounge applauded. Except Mrinal.

'Where is the nearest place I can get fresh air?' she asked Asma softly in a quavering voice. 'You said something about a rooftop terrace. How do I get there?'

'Sure,' Asma replied, puzzled. 'If you want to. Are you sure you're okay?'

Mrinal nodded. 'I just want to be by myself. Can you

show me the way please?'

Together the two women went up the front stairway. Dhavak continued singing, but Athreya's mind wasn't on it. He was staring unseeingly at the sofa that Mrinal had just vacated, and his right index finger was furiously tracing invisible words on the armrest. Javed watched silently, alternating his gaze between the finger and Athreya's face. He knew from their old days that the surest sign that Athreya's mind was churning was his finger acquiring a mind of its own.

Asma came down a few minutes later. She and Maazin took up Mrinal's bottle of gin along with a glass, ice and some tonic. Once they had come down, Kinshuk went up to the terrace and returned after five minutes. Periodically, Maazin, Asma or one of the staff took something for her. On being asked, both Asma and Maazin discouraged Javed from going to the terrace to enquire after Mrinal.

Returning from one of his trips to the terrace, Maazin came to Javed and spoke softly, 'Mrinal has dropped out of tomorrow's trek.'

* * *

By the time the dinner buffet opened at 10:15 p.m., Athreya was hungry. A tiring day on horseback and multiple rounds of drinks had stimulated his appetite considerably. He and Javed went immediately to the food counter and picked up plates. When none of the younger ones showed interest in food, Maazin reminded them that they had an early start the next morning. Thanks to additional encouragement from Asma, they began picking up their dinners at 10:30 p.m., while Athreya and Javed had finished theirs, and were enjoying some of Margot's liqueurs.

Suppressing incessant yawns, Kinshuk took a plateful of food to the rooftop terrace and returned empty-handed a few minutes later. Athreya wondered if he and Mrinal had patched up their quarrel. And with Mrinal having dropped out of the trek, was he going or not? A sleepy Kinshuk was the last person to eat dinner, after which the food counter closed, and the staff began removing the food and taking it downstairs.

By then, the time was 11 p.m., and a drowsy Athreya was ready to go to bed. Even as he contemplated calling it a night, he saw Kinshuk pick up a large brandy and take it into his room.

Ten minutes later, with his eyelids growing heavier by the minute, Athreya wished Javed and the others goodnight and retired. Javed too called it a night, and the party wound up as the others emptied their glasses and rose.

Once inside his room, Athreya found that a part of him was fighting sleep. Even in the face of mounting drowsiness, he was agitated somewhere deep down. For what reason, he didn't know. His right index finger made spasmodic attempts to trace invisible words but gave up. He glanced at his watch. It was 11:15 p.m., and the sounds outside his door had ceased.

Refusing to give in to sleep, he sat on his bed without changing into his nightclothes, for once he did, he knew that he would succumb. Before that he wanted to determine the cause of his agitation. Without realizing it, he lay back on the pillows. Even as he churned his sluggish mind to identify the reason for his tension, his eyelids closed and he drifted off.

He dreamt that he was sinking into a welcoming and comforting darkness, and tried to struggle out of it. He rose a little from the dark embrace only to fall back again. How long this struggle went on, he had no way of knowing. But sometime during it, he thought he heard voices… and the sobs of a woman. And a thump.

Then, sleep took him.

9

Athreya was awakened by persistent knocking on his door. He surfaced reluctantly from sleep and opened his eyes. For a moment or two, he was disoriented, not recognizing where he was. When he regained his bearings, he snapped awake and sat up. Sunlight was streaming in through the large east-facing windows that offered a spectacular view of the Himalayas.

The next set of knocks had him hurrying out of bed to unbolt his door. Outside stood Javed and a middle-aged man whom Javed had earlier introduced as the staff manager, Mr Baranwal.

'You okay?' Javed demanded as soon as he saw Athreya. 'We've been knocking for a couple of minutes.'

Athreya nodded groggily. 'What's the time?' he asked.

'Past eight-forty-five. Almost nine.'

'Nine! I've slept for almost ten hours! Must have been all that alcohol.' He let out a yawn.

'Want to sleep a little more?' Javed's voice was concerned.

'No, no! Time to get up.'

'You sure you're okay? You fell asleep in your day clothes.'

Athreya looked down and realized with a mild shock that he was still wearing his party clothes. He hadn't changed for the night.

'Give me fifteen minutes,' he mumbled. 'I'll come down for breakfast.'

A quarter of an hour later, he entered the dining room and apologized to Javed, who had waited for him to have breakfast. None of the other guests was in the room, and Athreya realized that they must have left on their trek. Maazin had planned an eight o'clock start.

'Eight of them have gone on the trek,' Javed said as they began eating. 'Mrinal and Kinshuk dropped out. They are still asleep.'

'Kinshuk was pretty drunk last night,' Athreya said and gave a wry grin. 'Looks like I was drunk too—slept like a log!'

As they ate, Athreya considered what he had just said. For some reason, that didn't seem right. The woozy feeling he was having was not similar to his usual hangovers. This was different. Was it the peach and almond liqueurs? He had enjoyed more than a couple of shots of them. At that thought, something stirred in his mind. He went to the sideboard, pulled out the bottle of peach liqueur and examined it against the light streaming in through the large windows. Yes, there was some cloudiness but...

He picked up a liqueur glass and poured a small amount into it after shaking the bottle. He brought the glass to the dining table and let it stand for a few minutes. He then sipped the liqueur and peered into the remnants in the glass.

'What is it?' Javed asked.

Athreya didn't answer. Instead, he turned to Baranwal.

'Have you collected all the glasses from the party last night?' he asked.

'Yes, sir.' Baranwal nodded.

'Have they been washed?'

'Not yet, sir.'

Athreya leapt up from his chair. 'Show me the glasses!'

A minute later, they were standing over an assortment of unwashed glasses of different shapes and sizes as the kitchen staff looked on with puzzlement. Only one of them was a liqueur glass—Athreya's.

He picked it up and examined it against the sunlight. A moment later, he called Javed over and pointed to the dregs.

'See?' he said in an undertone. 'There is a sediment... a white powder.'

'Good lord!' Javed exclaimed.

'That was no hangover, Javed,' Athreya said, as he carried the liqueur glass to the dining room, 'I was drugged.'

* * *

A short while later, they were outside Kinshuk's room. Baranwal was knocking furiously on the door. After several minutes, it opened and a groggy, disoriented Kinshuk stood there in the clothes he had been wearing last night.

'Wha-... ' he asked hoarsely. 'What happened?'

'How are you feeling?' Athreya asked.

'Rotten.' Kinshuk's voice slurred a little. 'My mouth feels like a sewage pipe. What's up? Why all the ruckus?'

'It's past ten. We were concerned about you.'

'Ten! Bloody hell! He swayed and clutched the door jamb for support. 'What did you guys serve last night? It knocked me out like—'

'Can I come in?' Athreya asked. 'I saw you take a glass of brandy into your room when you retired. I need to look at it.'

'Whatever for?' Kinshuk demanded. 'There's nothing left in it. I had all of it before I went to bed.'

When Athreya remained resolute, he shrugged. 'Oh, well. If you want to.'

Athreya and Javed entered the room. Athreya went straight to the low table beside the bed and picked up the empty glass. A few millimetres of dark-brown brandy remained in the glass. In the slight depression at the centre of the bottom was a powdery sediment. Athreya wordlessly held it up for Javed to see.

'We should have this analysed,' he said. 'And my glass

too.'

Just then, there was a loud knock at Kinshuk's open door. A middle-aged maid, whom Baranwal had sent to check on Mrinal, had returned. Athreya held up a hand to prevent her from speaking. He stepped out of the room and went to a corner of the lounge, where he asked her to speak softly.

'Madam is not in her room, sir,' she said. 'The bed hasn't been slept in. The security guards at the door and the gate haven't seen her.'

'Lock her door,' Athreya instructed at once, 'and don't let anyone enter the room. *Anyone*. Understood?'

'Yes, sir.'

As the maid hurried away to do his bidding, he turned to Baranwal.

'Mrinal didn't go on the trek, right?' he asked.

'No, sir. She and Kinshuk dropped out. That's what Maazin told me last night.'

'Send all the staff you can spare to search every corner of the castle and the grounds. Search the stables, generator building, staff quarters, everywhere.'

'Yes, sir!'

As Baranwal turned to set things into motion, Athreya gave him the last instruction. 'Send me the keys to the roof-top terrace. Immediately. I'll be waiting here.'

Once the manager hurried away, Athreya turned to Javed, whose face was set in grim lines.

'Your premonition,' he said. 'It might have been well-founded after all.'

* * *

Javed opened the door at the top of the front stairway and stepped out onto the rooftop terrace. Athreya came up behind him and both men stood there for a moment, surveying the terrace. A few yards in front of them was a large circular lily pond that was three feet high and a couple of dozen feet across. The water, which stood an inch below the edge, was fully covered by broad lily leaves. A few water lilies of different hues pushed up here and there.

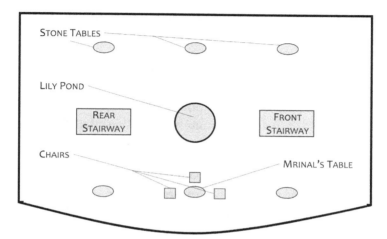

ROOFTOP TERRACE

Beyond the pond, Athreya could see the closed door of the rear stairway. He knew that it was locked from the inside. Six stone tables stood at regular intervals in the northern and southern halves of the terrace. Several wrought-iron chairs, painted white, stood near them.

On an oval stone table to his left, the middle of the three tables on the southern side, stood a near-full bottle of gin. Beside it was a glass with an inch of juice, an empty can of tonic water, a hair clip and a closed ice bucket, with an empty dinner plate and a fork at the far end. Four paper napkins fluttered on the floor underneath. Draped on the back of a chair was a grey shawl. This was the table Mrinal had used the previous night.

Athreya approached it with Javed behind him, and stood

looking at it for a long moment before pulling out his mobile phone and clicking several pictures of the table and the chairs.

He then walked around the terrace, checking all the tables and chairs for anything that might be on or under them. He also scrutinized the floor and the crenellated parapet wall. They only found two ashtrays—one on the parapet wall on the northern side and another at the eastern side, close to where Athreya had watched the play of light on the Nanda Devi three evenings ago.

Finally, he went to the lily pond and moved around the large circular lily leaves until he was satisfied that they didn't hide anything.

'Something is wrong,' Javed growled, as they returned to the table Mrinal had used. 'She isn't in her room, she hasn't left the castle, and she isn't on the terrace.'

'Let's wait for Baranwal to finish searching,' Athreya muttered. 'Something may turn up.'

He looked up and gazed southwards at a peculiarity that had intrigued him on his first evening at Peter Dann. He had wanted to ask Javed about it as soon as he had seen it, but as the sun had been close to setting when they had arrived on the terrace, he had hurried to set up his camera and tripod, lest he miss the opportunity to photograph the famed sight on a clear evening.

'Javed,' he asked, pointing to the large outcrop of bare rock half a mile away to the south. 'What's that?'

It was a single, monolithic protrusion of stone that rose at least two hundred feet from the ground. The column of rock had weathered and cracked over time, littering the flat top with car-sized boulders and smaller chunks. Its sheer walls rose vertically from the greenery below. As far as Athreya could see, there was no way up. Yet, a rough stone structure stood on top.

'A temple of sorts,' Javed explained as he led Athreya to the southern periphery of the terrace.

'Not a functioning temple, I suppose?' Athreya laid his palms on the parapet wall and leaned forward.

'It is a live temple. Pujas take place every full moon. There's a deity in there that the Cochha tribe worships.'

'Fascinating! Are there steps on the other side of the outcrop then?'

'No steps. The men of the tribe scale the rock face.'

'Two hundred feet?' Athreya asked in surprise. 'Every month?'

'They are extraordinary climbers. They scale the steepest rocks and walls like monkeys. Talking about that, do you know which God is the deity of that temple?'

'Hanuman?'

Javed shook his head.

'Good guess, but no. It's one of the lesser *vanara* deities; a relative of Hanuman, I believe. Did you know that it is forbidden to say Hanuman's name in Nanda Devi's shadow?'

'Really? Why?'

'Remember Ramayana? Hanuman was sent to fetch the Sanjeevani herb when Lakshman was lying at death's door?'

'Yes, I remember.'

'When Hanuman couldn't identify the herb, he ripped off a piece of the Dronagiri Mountain and flew off with it to Lanka. Legend has it that he did that without getting Nanda Devi's permission. That made the goddess furious, and she decreed that Hanuman would not be worshipped in her domain. That's why you don't find Hanuman temples around here.'

'I see,' Athreya mused. '*Vanara* devotees who are excellent climbers... they build a shrine atop an outcrop that nobody else can scale... interesting. Did they build the temple in such an inaccessible place so that others can't reach it?'

'I guess so. The Cochhas are pretty possessive about the temple and its deity.'

Athreya dropped his gaze and looked down from where he was standing. Peter Dann Castle had been built on the very edge of the gigantic rock to which it was anchored. While the other three sides of the castle overlooked the flat top of the hillock, the southern face stood right at the edge of the rock precipice. The green floor of the woods was at least two hundred and fifty feet below him. It was a sheer drop, with only a crenellated parapet wall between him and a perilous fall. Feeling giddy, Athreya involuntarily took a step back.

'Yes,' Javed said, addressing Athreya's unspoken question. 'The Cochhas can scale this too. That's why the doors to the rooftop terrace are heavy and placed behind iron grills. You sometimes hear noises from this terrace when it's supposed to be empty.'

'Could the bloody handprints have been made by them?' Athreya asked.

Javed nodded. 'I fear so.'

* * *

An hour later, there was still no news of Mrinal. Most of the castle and the grounds had been searched. Javed made a quick call to Dave Clarkson to check if she had somehow gone there. She had not. As time progressed and no sign of Mrinal emerged, Javed grew increasingly contemplative and grave. Something was running in his mind, of which he had said nothing to Athreya. Athreya was glad that the five guests and Asma were away. Finally, Javed drew him aside.

'There is one place we haven't looked,' he whispered. 'Come.'

He summoned the man in charge of the stable and a stable boy. Together, the four of them set out through the gate. They went down the length of the private road to the southern side of the hillock where it met the public road. There, Athreya halted and looked up. Perched majestically atop its gigantic rock, soaring above him, Peter Dann Castle looked impregnable and out of reach. No wonder they had called it a castle.

The precipitous, featureless rock face merged with the castle's wall to give the impression of a cliff. The two rows of windows in the stone wall were heavily barred. There was no way in unless you scaled vertical stone and leapt over the parapet wall onto the rooftop terrace.

Athreya recalled how giddy he had felt when he had looked down from there an hour and a half earlier. The memory brought beads of sweat to his forehead—a fall from there would be fatal for sure. Bringing his gaze back to the ground at the foot of the rock face, he saw several large boulders with lush green foliage growing and filling the gaps between them.

Athreya's sluggish brain, still recovering from the drugging, was slow to catch on. When it did, his eyes widened as he realized why Javed had brought them there. A vision of a blue-clad figure plummeting in darkness assaulted his mind. He felt physical pain when it ended with the figure hitting a rock.

The two men from the stable were already making their way to the foot of the precipice. Athreya hurried after them, looking up and gauging where Mrinal had been sitting last night. Then, drawing an imaginary vertical line from that spot to the foot of the precipice, he saw a large boulder surrounded by thick shrubs.

He hurried to it. When he was fifteen feet from it, he saw a splash of deep blue through the greenery. With a sinking heart, he ran forward, recalling that Mrinal had worn a deep-blue silk kurti last night.

He clambered over the boulder, parted the foliage and peered down. There was Mrinal, lying face up with her eyes half-open, arms out flung and her neck twisted at an impossible angle.

There was no doubt that she was dead.

10

The discovery blew away the cobwebs from Athreya's mind. The first instruction he issued to the men from the stable was that news of Mrinal's death should stay within Peter Dann. He further insisted that nobody should inform Maazin or Asma of the tragedy, even if they were to phone. He wanted the trekkers to be kept ignorant. After a brief discussion, he and Javed decided to leave the body where it was until the police arrived. They posted two men at the spot and returned to the castle.

Javed was in shock. Not a sound passed his lips as they went up the road to Peter Dann. His eyes, looking haunted, had gone wide. Though Athreya and he had worked together on several murder cases in the past, Athreya had not known him to be so affected by the sight of a corpse. Was it because this had happened at Peter Dann? Was it because he had taken a liking to Mrinal? Or was it something else? When they reached the castle, Javed went to his room, leaving Athreya in charge.

Athreya found Kinshuk on a sofa in the ground-floor hall. He had fallen asleep sitting with his head thrown back on the headrest and tilted to one side. A tiny rivulet of spittle had drooled down from the corner of his half-open mouth to his chin. One of the staff told Athreya that a disoriented Kinshuk had been struggling to stay awake while waiting for word about Mrinal. Unable to do so, he had succumbed about half an hour ago.

Athreya picked up a couple of tissues and shook the

sleeping man's shoulder, but to no avail. Then, by calling his name a few times, as well as shaking him, Athreya managed to rouse him.

'Here, wipe your mouth,' he said as Kinshuk awoke and looked at Athreya in confusion.

Clearly, he was still disoriented. Athreya opened Kinshuk's eyelids with his fingers and peered into his eyes. The pupils were dilated. Twelve hours had elapsed but the drug had not yet worn off. That could be dangerous. A doctor had to examine Kinshuk as soon as possible.

'A general practitioner is on her way, sir,' Baranwal whispered in his ear. 'A car has gone for her. She should be here any time now.'

'Don't worry,' Kinshuk slurred, struggling to an upright position. 'I'll be fine. Maybe, I drank too much last night.' He looked up at Baranwal. 'Can I have some coffee? Black, no sugar.'

Baranwal nodded and strode away.

'How much did you drink last night?' Athreya asked.

'Oh, I lost count after the fifth.' Kinshuk said. 'Once we had dropped out of the trek, there was no need to hold back. But I shouldn't have mixed drinks. I had both whisky and vodka, and finished off with a large brandy.' His voice dropped. 'Dhavak and I also shared a couple of joints.' He looked at Athreya quizzically. 'Say, did you find anything in my brandy glass? I know that you looked at it, but I can't remember what you said after that. My recollection is all too fuzzy.'

'There was some sediment, but I don't know what it is. Don't worry about it. I wanted to talk to you about something.'

'Sure. Hey! Any word of Mrinal?'

'Not yet,' Athreya lied. He felt rotten, but consoled himself by acknowledging that it was necessary—there was something he *had* to find out from Kinshuk first. 'Talking about Mrinal, she seemed very distressed last night.'

'Yeah… yeah.' Kinshuk looked dejected.

'What happened? Why was she upset?'

'I don't know.' Kinshuk spread out his hands. 'I asked her several times, but she didn't tell me.'

'Why did she go up to the terrace?'

'That's what I asked her. She wouldn't say.'

'You went up a couple of times to see her. How did she seem to you?'

'Very upset. Very, *very* upset. She was miserable.'

'Why didn't she tell you what was upsetting her?'

'Well—' Kinshuk looked sheepish and dropped his eyes. 'Well, we had a fight yesterday.'

'Before you came to Peter Dann?'

Kinshuk nodded.

'Actually, we had the fight the night before last. Both of us said things we didn't mean.'

'She was not talking to you when you checked in here, right?'

'Yes. I apologized, but she gets hurt easily. But she usually recovers in a day or two. She'll be fine today. We'll make up, don't worry.'

'You tried to make up yesterday?'

'Yes. I must have apologized a dozen times.'

'Tell me what happened when you went up to the terrace.'

'The first time she told me to go away. She didn't want to talk to anyone. Said she wanted to be alone for a while. But when I took up dinner for her, she spoke a little bit. She had begun to thaw.'

'What did she say?'

Kinshuk frowned as he tried to remember.

'She first mumbled "thanks", which is a sign that she was thawing. She said that she had dropped out of the trek… she didn't want to go with "those people". She then began crying bitterly. When I tried to comfort her, she said that life had been very unkind to her. She seemed devastated, but she asked me to leave her. Said she'll be okay in the morning.'

'Did you believe her?'

'That she would be okay in the morning? I don't know. I've never seen her so upset. She was quite broken, actually. Something happened in the lounge that caused this. Whatever it was, was so overwhelming that it overshadowed her anger with me.'

He stopped as Baranwal came with a cup of hot black coffee. Athreya waited for him to take a couple of sips before continuing his questioning.

'Did Mrinal know Dhavak from before?' he asked.

Kinshuk shook his head. 'I don't think so. Why?'

'And the three women—Ipshita, Purbhi and Linda—did she know them from before?'

'Not as far as I know. But she knew Sarosh, though. I know him too from Mumbai.'

'How come?' Athreya asked.

'He and I had some discussions about setting up a chain of high-end fitness studios that combined multiple disciplines—gym, yoga, massage, Kerala oil treatment, sauna, et cetera. He was considering investing in it.'

'Where did those discussions go?'

'Not yet concluded. Both of us are thinking about it. Why are you asking all this?'

'In a minute. Were you in Nainital about six weeks ago?'

'No,' Kinshuk slurred. 'I haven't been there in ages. What dates?'

Athreya gave him the dates and Kinshuk consulted the calendar on his mobile phone.

'No,' he said shortly. 'I was in Bangalore that weekend. We had a three-day workshop at a five-star hotel.'

'Was Mrinal with you too?'

'No. She was in Delhi or Dehradun or some such place. Now will you tell me what is this all about?'

There was no way to break it gently, but Athreya tried

his best. He let Kinshuk finish his coffee and gave him the news. Kinshuk went into denial at once and grew aggressive.

'Don't be stupid!' he yelled. 'Don't play games with me. Dhavak told me how you cops lie through your teeth. Is this your idea of a bloody joke?'

'I'm sorry, Kinshuk,' Athreya replied mildly. 'I am not lying. We just found her.'

'Where?' Kinshuk demanded.

He was becoming increasingly aggressive. Baranwal and another staffer came closer, just in case the agitated celebrity trainer assaulted Athreya. His raised voice also brought Javed from his room.

'Where?' Kinshuk demanded again, standing up unsteadily and glowering at Athreya. His fists were clenched and his muscles bulged. He looked weird with a flushed face, flaring nostrils and dilated eyes. His speech was still slurring. 'You're lying!'

'No.' Javed's deep voice intervened. 'I'm really sorry, Kinshuk. Mrinal is dead. She seems to have fallen from the terrace.'

Kinshuk's head snapped towards Javed. He stared at his host for a long moment.

'No!' he breathed. His voice was hushed.

He swayed dangerously. Baranwal came up and supported him.

'No... she didn't... she didn't actually do it!' His voice was no more than a whisper.

Athreya's interest was aroused. What was Kinshuk implying? That Mrinal had considered leaping off the terrace? If so, why? An image came to his mind. It was dark but he could see a blue-clad woman in his vision. She was standing in the gap between two crenellations and looking down. She was leaning forward dangerously...

'Do what?' Athreya demanded.

But Kinshuk wasn't listening. He swayed again and

collapsed on the sofa. Just then, the general practitioner walked in.

* * *

Athreya, Javed, Baranwal and a staffer were on the rooftop terrace. Once the doctor took charge of Kinshuk, Baranwal had taken Athreya there where the young man awaited them.

'This is Ravi,' Baranwal said. 'He was serving the guests last night at the party. He has some information for you.'

He turned to Ravi and nodded.

'I was at the food counter last evening, sir,' he began in Hindi. 'After dinner, we took all the food and plates and everything downstairs.'

'Do you remember what time that was?' Athreya asked.

'Yes, sir. One or two minutes before 11:20 p.m. I looked at the clock when I reached the kitchen. It was 11:20 p.m.'

'Okay. Go on.'

'We then had our dinner, washed the vessels and plates and put everything away. I was about to go to bed when Maazin Sir told me to go up to the terrace and ask Mrinal Madam if she needed anything. I came up here and asked her. She said that she didn't want anything, and that she would be going to her room shortly. I went down and told Maazin Sir. After that, I went to bed.'

'What time was it when you came up to the terrace?' Athreya asked.

'One or two minutes after 12:20 a.m. Both Maazin Sir and I looked at the time before he sent me up.'

'Where was Mrinal Madam when you spoke to her?'

'On this chair.' Ravi pointed to the middle chair near the table Mrinal had used last night. 'She was sitting and look-ing that way.' He pointed southwards over the parapet wall.

'What was she wearing?'

'I think it was this shawl, sir.' Ravi pointed to the grey shawl draped over the back of the chair.

'How could you see? It was dark.'

'The moon was out, sir. I could see a little.'

'The shawl was over her shoulders?'

'Yes, sir. It was wrapped around her shoulders and arms. Her hair was hanging in a ponytail outside the shawl.'

'How did she sound when she spoke to you?'

'I can't say, sir. I think she sounded normal.'

'Did you go down after that?'

'Yes, sir. And I told Maazin Sir that she didn't want anything and that she would be returning to her room shortly. He said that he would go up soon.'

'Did he go?'

'Don't know, sir. I went to the staff quarters. Almost all the staff had gone there. It was well past midnight.'

'Who was in the lounge when you came up?'

'Nobody. It was empty. Only the night light was on.'

'What else did you see when you were here on the terrace?' Javed asked.

'I saw the bottle of gin, the ice bucket and a can.'

'Plate, phone, et cetera?'

'Not sure, sir. They might have been hidden behind her as she sat in the chair.'

'Was there anyone else here?'

Ravi hesitated. He frowned as he tried to remember. At length, he shook his head.

'I don't think so, sir. But I can't be sure.'

'Why not? You said the moon was out.'

'Yes, sir. Half-moon, sir. I saw Mrinal Madam clearly because she was moving slightly, and I was looking directly at her. If there was someone else a little to either side, or if he had stayed still or crouched, I might have not seen him.'

* * *

The general practitioner had finished with Kinshuk when Athreya and Javed went down to the hall. She had sent him up to his room and had asked one of the boys to stay with him.

'He's been heavily drugged,' the GP said. 'And heavy drinking last night has compounded the problem. He needs to sleep, but I dare not give him anything for that. I don't know what drugs are present in his blood. He needs to consume lots of fluids so that the stuff in his blood is flushed out.

'He blacked out when he got angry with you, Mr Athreya. That happens when the level of the drug in the blood is high. I've taken a blood sample, but it'll take a while to analyse it. Can you tell me what happened?'

Athreya summarized the party and what Kinshuk had told him.

'Nasty combination!' the doctor exclaimed. 'Alcohol, marijuana and a sleeping drug.' She cocked her head and looked at Javed. 'I hear that a young lady is dead? Kinshuk's fiancée, I believe?'

'Yes.' Javed's voice was heavy. 'There's been an accident. She fell from the rooftop terrace.'

'Oh God!' the GP's eyes widened. 'Not again? Javed, I'm *so* sorry.' She reached out and took his hand. 'Are you okay? Can I check you?'

Javed let out a long sigh. 'I'm okay. But no harm in that, now that you are here.'

Over the next few minutes, she took Javed's pulse, blood pressure, breathing and other vital parameters. Athreya watched silently, wondering why the GP had said 'Not again?' What did that imply? Had someone fallen from the roof in the past? Was that why Javed was taking it so hard?

'You seem okay, Javed,' the GP said, straightening up. 'Take it easy if you can. Who is this lady who died? Someone you knew well?'

Javed shook his head.

'A guest who checked in yesterday. This isn't going to be pleasant, you know. Once the police get here. There will be questions.'

'I know. Shall I stay? Where is Asma? Maazin?'

'Gone on a trek.'

'Then,' she said with finality, 'I'll stay till the police are done troubling you.'

* * *

The Clarksons had almost finished their lunch when Athreya reached their place. Margot welcomed him effusively and offered lunch, which he politely declined. Not wanting to ruin their meal, he indulged in small talk for a couple of minutes. Once they finished eating, he broke the news to them.

The immediate reaction was that of shock and grief. Tears welled up in Margot's eyes and Dave looked as if he had been punched in the stomach. Like Javed, the Clarksons too seemed to have taken a liking to Mrinal, although she had stayed with them only for a couple of days. Both Margot's and Dave's reactions made that much clear.

'An accident?' Dave asked when he recovered his breath. 'How did it happen?'

'She seems to have fallen from the rooftop terrace,' Athreya replied, watching the middle-aged, mismatched couple.

Dave's mouth fell open and Margot blanched. She clutched her husband's arm with an unsteady hand.

'Fell from the terrace?' Dave repeated. 'Where? On the southern side?'

Athreya nodded. 'At the furthermost point of the curved southern side.'

'Oh Lord!' Margot gasped, visibly shaken. 'Not again!'

Athreya's eyes snapped to her face. It was pale and stricken. Tears welled anew and cascaded down her face.

She seemed oblivious to them. She had unknowingly uttered the same words the lady doctor had used at Peter Dann—'not again'.

'Why do you say that, Margot?' Athreya asked softly. '"Not again"? Has this happened before?'

'Don't you know?' she asked.

Her husband had still not recovered enough to converse.

'Know what?' Athreya asked.

'About Naira?'

'Javed's wife?' It was Athreya's turn to be shocked. 'No.'

'That's exactly how she died,' she said brokenly. 'She fell from the same spot… fell two-hundred-and-fifty-feet… and died.'

'Accident?' Athreya asked.

'Yes.' Margot nodded firmly. 'It was an accident.'

Dave turned to her as if to say something but she didn't give him a chance.

'It was an accident, Mr Athreya,' she repeated. 'No doubt about it.'

'How did it happen?' Athreya asked.

'You need to understand Naira's medical history first,' Margot replied and rose unsteadily. 'Dave will tell you. I must go and pray for the poor girl's soul. Excuse me.'

Dave took a long breath and blew out through puffed cheeks.

'I need a drink,' he muttered. 'This has been a shock. Poor Mrinal.' He lumbered to his feet. 'Can I get you a drink?'

Athreya shook his head. A couple of minutes later, Dave was back in the chair in front of him with a large shot of apple brandy.

'Naira was a lovely woman,' he began. 'Truly a wonderful person. Warm and accommodating. Everyone here loved her, and she was so generous in return.

'But she had a problem; a big one. She suffered from

a combination of mental illnesses, including depression. When it hit her, it was debilitating… like a ton of bricks. It was not as frequent in her younger days, but towards the last few years of her life, it became more and more frequent. In her last year or two, she was constantly depressed.

'Doctors treated her and did whatever they could, but they couldn't cure her of the affliction. When they increased the drug dosage, she would become terribly drowsy and unsteady, and would spend all the time in a stupor. That would make her feel worthless and a burden on everyone else. And that aggravated the problem further. She was stuck in a vicious cycle—her waking hours would be miserable for her because of her depression, while the rest of the time was spent in drugged stupor.

'Along with her, Javed also suffered. It must be terrible to watch your wife suffer so much with no hope of recovery. The once breezy and cheerful Naira became a grey shadow of herself. It tore Javed's heart apart, and Naira's illness also affected the business. Unable to devote enough time and energy to it, Peter Dann also began suffering. Being a sharp woman, Naira realized that, and it further worsened her mental condition. She felt that she was the root cause for every little thing that afflicted Peter Dann and her family. She felt that she was caught in a trap with no exit. And that she was dragging her family down with her.

'She took to walking on the terrace for hours, saying that sunlight, the openness of the mountains and the magnificent sight of the Nanda Devi were the only things that lifted her spirits. Except her daughter, of course. On the one hand, she was depressed. On the other hand, the medicines she was taking made her drowsy and unsteady.

'This was the situation when she fell from the terrace all of a sudden. Of course, there was a rumour that she might have deliberately jumped off. That was idle speculation of a mischievous mind. Her doctors believed that it was an accident, and reiterated that several times.'

Silence reigned when Dave finished his narrative. For a long moment, Athreya sat in contemplative silence. He then looked up and nodded at Dave.

'Thank you,' he said softly. 'This is what Margot meant when she said "not again".'

'Yes,' Dave agreed. 'Javed must be shattered. We must go to him.'

'Certainly. As soon as Margot finishes praying. Before that, I have a question to ask.'

Dave nodded.

'You told me the other day that whatever happens at Peter Dann, happens for the good. What you told me about Naira was certainly not a good thing.'

'Depends on your perspective,' Dave mumbled. 'Look at it this way… nothing they tried seemed to work. It was devastating both the family and the business. Peter Dann takes a fair bit of money to run. With fewer and fewer guests coming, it was bleeding them dry.'

'In addition,' said a new voice, 'we don't know how it was affecting young, impressionable Asma.' Margot came and stood by their table with a hand on Dave's shoulder. 'Naira was *very* worried about that. She told me so herself. Many times.

'So you see, Mr Athreya, why Naira's passing was a good thing? For her, it was an escape from a living hell. And for the family, it was a release from a prison. They could now return to living their lives unencumbered; something that was their right.'

Athreya stared at her. He didn't agree with her. However grave Naira's illness might have been, he was certain Javed and Asma would have preferred that she lived. He decided not to contest the matter.

'In many ways,' Margot concluded, 'Naira's death was the best thing that could have happened for everyone concerned. What happened that day at Peter Dann, happened for the good.'

11

The first thing Athreya did on returning to Peter Dann was to gather all the information available about the seven guests—the five who had checked in earlier, and Mrinal and Kinshuk. Armed with a carte blanche from Javed, he hustled the reception staff to collect every scrap they could lay their hands on and collate it into one document.

Full names, addresses, father's names, phone numbers and email ids were picked up from the reservation paperwork. Copies were made of the ID documents the guests had shown while checking in. Some of them had offered different IDs the two times they had checked in. Ipshita, for instance, had given her driving license the first time and her Aadhaar card the second. Those offered two potential avenues for gathering her background information.

Athreya then went through Peter Dann's emails and picked out messages exchanged with the seven guests. From these, he obtained bank accounts and some credit card details in addition to miscellaneous information from the questions raised and answers provided.

Then, with Javed's help, he reached out to contacts in Kolkata and Mumbai police departments and sent them what he had collected. He requested them to gather as much background information about the seven guests and their histories as possible. He and Javed then placed calls to senior police officers to ensure that the juniors they had spoken to went about their tasks with speed and without hindrance. As an unnatural death had occurred in an ex-police-officer's home, Athreya and Javed were assured that their requests would be taken up as a priority, and that they could expect to receive information from the next day onwards.

Athreya made a special request regarding Dhavak to the Kolkata police. He suspected that the singer had changed his last name to Strummer, but he didn't know when or where he had done that. Further, it was possible that he might have changed his first name too. And as Dhavak's driving license had been issued in Dehradun three years ago, he sent the information and his request to the Dehradun police as well.

And finally, Athreya sent a request to the Nainital hotel, asking for the list of people who had been staying there on the day Javed had seen the five guests and their two friends. To ensure that he received a reply, he roped in the local police.

By the time he did all this, the time was past 3 p.m. Leaving Javed in the Clarksons' care, he went to the kitchen and spoke to several staff members. Nothing new emerged, but Ravi's testimony about the previous evening was confirmed by a couple of them.

All this while, something about the rooftop terrace was gnawing at the back of his mind. He didn't know what it was, and wondered if it would help if he went there again.

And so, he returned to the rooftop, stood by the table that Mrinal had used the previous evening and let his imagination wander. Several fragmented possibilities crossed his mind as he stood there thinking of Mrinal and Naira. Both women had met very similar deaths. In Naira's case, the speculation seemed to have been limited to accident or suicide. The Clarksons had not alluded, even in passing, to the third possibility.

In Mrinal's case, however, all three options were open. Now that Javed's riddle of the five guests had turned dark, murder was a very real possibility. The five guests and two more had plotted something in Nainital and carried it out at Peter Dann. The obvious question was whether it involved Mrinal's death. And the accompanying question was whether Mrinal and Kinshuk had been the sixth and the seventh of the group in Nainital. Curiously, all seven had denied being in Nainital on that day six weeks ago.

Athreya sat down on one of the wrought-iron chairs with his sketchbook and pencils. As his mind wandered, he began sketching the protrusion of rock to the south. He absent-mindedly drew the column and the dilapidated temple on top of it. Without consciously meaning to do so, he added a couple of men scaling the vertical rock face.

Without deliberate thought, he turned the page and began sketching again as his mind grew busy trying to fit the few facts at his disposal into a pattern. But he failed—it was just too early in the case. What he knew was far too little, but a stray subliminal thought was still gnawing at the back of his mind. That was why he had sat down to this activity—he wanted see if sketching would give expression to his subliminal thought. Even as his conscious mind was trying to parse the scant information he had gathered, his long fingers acquired a mind of their own. They began sketching furiously.

Fifteen minutes later, he snapped back to reality and stared at what he had done. The first drawing was a good representation of the column of rock and the temple. The men scaling the rock face—presumably the Cochhas who worshipped the *vanara* deity in the temple—were his imagination's addition.

The second sketch showed two glasses that he recognized right away—his own liqueur glass and Kinshuk's brandy glass. That was how the two men had been drugged. With them out of the way, the five guests would have had a free run of the first floor and the terrace to do as they pleased. It was during this ten-hour period, when Athreya was in a drugged stupor, that Mrinal had fallen off the terrace although the doors to it must have been locked a short while after he had fallen asleep.

The third sketch surprised him. It was a drawing of the bottle of gin that had stood on Mrinal's table. He stared at it for a long moment, thoughts rushing through his head.

Of course!

* * *

When Athreya went down to the first floor, he found Kinshuk sitting in the lounge with a pot of green tea. Freshly bathed and shaved, he looked up as Athreya approached. He had regained his composure and was looking much calmer, even if grief-stricken.

'I believe I shouted at you and said some uncharitable things,' Kinshuk said as Athreya sat down opposite him. 'I don't remember what I said, but I apologize. I'm really sorry. I can't think what made me be nasty to you.'

'Don't give it a second thought,' Athreya assured him. 'People often are not themselves just in the aftermath of a nasty shock. What do you remember about today?'

'It's all very hazy... like some dream. Or a nightmare. I believe Mrinal fell off the terrace and died.'

His voice shook even as he tried to say it evenly.

'Unfortunately, that's true,' Athreya replied. 'Do you remember what you said just before you passed out?'

'No... what did I say?'

'Just after I told you that she had fallen off the terrace, you said: "*No... she didn't... she didn't actually do it!*" You seemed to be speaking to yourself. What did you mean?'

'*I* said that?' Kinshuk stared at Athreya in amazement. '*I?*'

Athreya nodded, watching him. 'Those were your exact words.'

'Really? I have no idea what I might have meant.'

'Okay. Try and think what you *could have* meant by

those words.'

Kinshuk spread out his hands and his mouth turned downwards as he shook his head. He seemed to be puzzled.

'Come on, try,' Athreya persisted. 'There is something you know that fits with what you said. Even if it is a tenuous connection. Try and find it.'

Kinshuk stared unseeingly as he tried to recall. His eyebrows came together in an apparent effort to remember. At length, he shook his head.

'Could you have wondered if Mrinal had deliberately jumped off the terrace?' Athreya asked.

'Oh God! No!' Kinshuk's eyes flew open wide. 'That couldn't be true!'

'Did it occur to you that she might have taken her own life?'

'Oh God!' Kinshuk, suddenly unnerved, buried his face in his hands. His shoulders shook as if he were sobbing. His voice cracked, 'Oh, God!'

Athreya waited. A minute later, Kinshuk raised his head. His face was wet with tears. He bit his lip as he tried to control himself. Athreya was not sure if he saw a shadow of guilt on his face.

'I don't know,' he whispered at length, staring across the lounge as if he were in a trance. 'I don't know. I remember something Mrinal told me. Apparently, someone told her that a woman had done just that at Peter Dann a few years ago—jumped off the terrace. By jumping, the woman had ended her misery.'

'Who told her that?'

'Don't know… she didn't tell me. It could have been someone at Clarkson's… or at the village we had stopped at before coming to Clarkson's. Mrinal talked about it afterwards… said she could understand why sometimes life could be overwhelming.'

Suddenly, he snapped out of the trance. His eyes regained focus and he clenched his jaw. He squared his shoulders and looked Athreya directly in the eye.

'But that is bunkum,' he said crisply. 'Mrinal was *not* the kind of person to commit suicide. She loved life too much.' He thought for a moment and continued, 'It may sound inappropriate to say this about a dead person, but Mrinal loved herself too. She was not necessarily a self-sacrificing person. She was generous and did a lot for others, but in doing so, she loved herself for what she was doing. She had a good, positive self-image. Such a person does not kill herself.'

Athreya remained silent, giving Kinshuk the freedom to say whatever he chose.

'Do you know that her start-up teaches kids in five different countries plus India?' the younger man went on. 'It's an internet-driven venture that teaches English, music and life skills to kids. She has done a lot for kids in and outside India. She did it because she wanted to help. And having succeeded at just thirty-two, she thought well of herself too. Why would such a person kill herself?'

Athreya nodded and changed the topic.

'We need to inform the next of kin,' he said. 'You would know—'

'She had no kin,' Kinshuk cut in.

'No kin?' Athreya's eyebrows shot up.

'She lost her parents in the 2010 riots near Kolkata. Rioters burned her house down in North 24 Parganas district and killed her parents in the process. She has a brother somewhere, but he is a weirdo. As long as I've known Mrinal, she hasn't spoken to him. Her phone might have his number, though. His name is Pralay.'

'How long have you known Mrinal?'

Kinshuk's voice trembled with emotion as he replied. 'I've known her well for the past two years. Before that, I met her a few months after she came to Mumbai from Kolkata.'

'She hasn't spoken or corresponded with her brother for

the past two years?'

'Not as far as I know. She has no relatives in Mumbai for sure.'

'We need to find some kin. I take it that her family name is Shome. Can you provide some details of her family in Kolkata? Where she lived, her parents' first names, address or locality, and such? Any information that can help us trace her brother, uncle or any relative?'

'She had lived in North 24 Parganas district near Kolkata when her parents died. I can give you their names. I'll see what else I have.'

'Anything you can give us will be helpful. The police will also search her flat in Mumbai. Now, there is something more I want to know. How was Mrinal in the recent past? Did she have any problems? Anything unusual?'

Kinshuk leaned forward and held his head in his hands. He remained silent for a long moment except for his laboured breathing. At length, he looked up and tried to talk, but choked as he did so. No words came. Embarrassed, he poured himself some more green tea and began sipping it. Athreya waited.

'Well… ' Kinshuk began and stopped to clear his throat. 'Well, she was troubled for the past two months or so. Something was bothering her, but she didn't confide in me. I now wish that she had. I remember that it started gradually. Initially, she was a little pensive occasionally and showed some nervousness once in a while. But bit by bit, her anxiety grew and it began affecting her sleep. She also began drinking heavily.

'In the last few weeks, it became worse. That is when she decided to take a holiday. She wanted to get away from Mumbai to a place where nobody could bother her. A trek in the foothills of the Himalayas sounded ideal. We were to come here a couple of weeks ago, but cancelled it at the last moment. Work at Mrinal's office prevented us from coming. Fortunately, the trekking season hadn't yet started, and we were able to change the booking to shift it to this week. Everything was fine until the party in the lounge yesterday evening. Suddenly, things went haywire.'

'Yes,' Athreya agreed. 'Something happened at the party that upset Mrinal badly. What was it?'

Kinshuk shook his head and dropped his gaze. Guilt returned to his face.

'I wish she had told me,' he moaned. 'What a rotten time to have a fight! Like I told you earlier, we had a fight the night before we came here. Because of that, she didn't talk to me yesterday evening. I asked her what was wrong, but she wouldn't tell me. I asked her many times. I wish we hadn't fought.'

He placed a hand over his forehead and eyes. He sighed deeply as he shook his head in anguish.

'She was very upset last night, wasn't she?' Athreya asked.

'Honestly, I haven't ever seen her so distressed. She was really, *really* distraught.'

'Why did Dhavak's song upset her so much?'

'You saw it too?' Kinshuk asked. 'Yes, that's what sent her to the terrace. I have no idea why.'

'Are you sure she didn't know Dhavak from before?'

'She didn't, as far as I know.'

'She was very upset last night,' Athreya said. 'Yet, you rule out the possibility of her taking her own life.'

Kinshuk let out a long sigh,

'You are a man of the world, Mr Athreya,' he said. 'You've been a police officer. Poor Mrinal is dead. What purpose will it serve if her name is tarnished by speculation of suicide? It won't bring her back.'

'Do you know if she wrote a will?'

'No idea. How many thirty-two-year-olds write wills?'

'All the more reason to locate her brother.'

'Yes… I suppose so.'

'One last question, Kinshuk. Is there nothing you can

tell me about what was troubling Mrinal for the past two months? Even if it is speculation?'

'Nothing… nothing … except one suspicion.'

'What?'

'Remember it is only a suspicion. I don't know for sure. Nor do I have any evidence.'

'That's okay. Tell me.'

'I think Mrinal was receiving some letters. They are connected in some way to her anguish.'

'Why do you say that?'

'She wouldn't let me see them. That was not the case earlier—all letters used to be kept openly on the table in the hall. But during the past two months, she used to put away her letters in her steel cupboard.'

'Then, we should be able to find them in her flat. All we need to do is to open the cupboard.'

'Unfortunately not,' Kinshuk replied. 'On three different occasions, I saw her burn or shred letters. The last time was on the day before we left Mumbai to come here.'

* * *

Athreya returned to his room and sat still, reviewing all that he had learnt since they had discovered Mrinal's body. Unsurprisingly, his right index finger began tracing invisible words on the sofa's upholstery. His erstwhile colleagues used to say that if they could find a way to decipher what that finger wrote, they would crack their cases in half the time.

Now, as Athreya sat in his room, his mind went back to the previous day when he and Javed had ridden out on horseback. With a jolt, he sat upright. Mrinal had burnt something at Pottersfield! Just as Kinshuk had said she had done in Mumbai. Was that why she had stamped on the ashes? If she had burnt a letter, she would want the ashes reduced to powder so that no information could be retrieved from it.

Which meant that, for what it was worth, he had to examine the ashes. With luck, he might still be able to decipher something from the remains. He would do that tomorrow with Javed. He wondered if his friend was still in his room, where he had gone to snatch some rest.

Right now, Athreya had another task to do—he would enter Mrinal's room and see what it offered as evidence or pointers.

12

Athreya opened his door to step out into the lounge and found his way blocked by Javed and a woman in uniform. Javed's arm was raised to knock on the door, but Athreya had opened it before he could complete the action.

'Ah!' Javed grunted. 'The police are here. This is Assistant Commissioner of Police Shivali Suyal.'

'Good afternoon, sir.' Shivali stepped forward and shook Athreya's hand with a firm grip. She was a tall, lean but muscular woman in her early thirties with short, straight hair. 'Pleased to meet you. I've heard of you, of course. It would be my pleasure to work with you.'

'Good evening, Ms Suyal,' Athreya replied, noting her purposeful, no-nonsense air. 'We are fortunate to have an ACP personally looking into this affair.'

'Not at all, sir,' she replied briskly. 'Mr Javed being a respected ex-officer, this is the least we can do. I had no idea you were here too until Mr Javed told me. I presume you just happened to be visiting Peter Dann?'

'Well, it's a little more than that, Ms Suyal—'

'Please call me Shivali, sir,' she interposed.

Athreya nodded. 'It's a little more than that, Shivali,' he repeated. 'I'll tell you all about it. You drove down, I guess?'

'Yes. I was just a couple of hours away when we received the news. I decided to come down right away with a doctor. A couple of constables are bringing the body up.'

'Excellent! We will need the doctor's opinion on a few

matters. We also have a few things that need to be analysed.'

'Such as?'

'The dregs in two glasses and a blood sample from the deceased's fiancé, Kinshuk. Two people were drugged last night—Kinshuk and me.'

'You?' Shivali exclaimed in surprise.

'Yes. There are a number of things I need to update you on. There is also a bottle of gin that needs to be analysed.'

'No problem,' she replied assuredly. She threw a quick glance at Javed. 'I will have the samples sent to the lab as soon as I get them.'

'I've asked Baranwal, the staff manager, not to empty the wastepaper baskets in guest rooms or the common areas. The rubbish will be retained if you wish to examine it.'

'Thank you. That would be helpful—with luck, we may just find an empty drug strip with fingerprints on it. Anything else, sir?'

'The biggest task is this: we need to gather as much information and history about seven guests. Javed and I have started the process by sending out requests to Mumbai, Kolkata and Nainital. It would be a great help if you could put your weight behind it.'

'Mr Javed told me about it. I'll push it from my side too. While the constables are bringing the body up, I wanted to look at the deceased's room. I believe you have the key, sir?'

'I do. We had it locked as soon as we discovered that Mrinal was missing, and I refrained from entering the room until you arrived. Shall we go now?'

'Yes, sir. I'll call the photographer and the fingerprint man.'

'Excuse me,' Javed said. 'I have some work to do.' He turned and went down the stairs. He hadn't spoken a word after introducing Shivali. Athreya had an inkling of what was bothering him.

Minutes later, Athreya and Shivali were standing inside Mrinal's room as the forensic men began photographing it and dusting it for prints. It was large but not as big as Athreya's. A king-size bed stood at the centre, with luxurious furniture arranged around the room. It was tastefully decorated in a classic mould, with heavy curtains, framed paintings and three carpets. The south-facing window was wide open and the bed had not been slept in.

A suitcase lay flat on an iron-and-wood table while another stood vertically beside it. When one of the forensic men opened the cupboard, Athreya saw clothes neatly folded on the shelves, and toiletries were stowed away at the rear of one. A few garments were up hung on hangers. First impressions suggested that Mrinal had been an orderly and tidy person.

Athreya's gaze went to the writing table near the window. Except for what the hotel had provided, there was nothing on it. Not even a pen or book that might have belonged to Mrinal.

He dropped his eyes and peered under the table. Initially he saw nothing. Then, he noticed a tiny splash of red on the floor behind one of the table legs. He went closer and knelt down. The red seemed to be a torn scrap of paper. Behind it lay another tiny piece that was white. The scraps looked glossy.

Athreya silently pointed them out to Shivali, who directed the forensic men's attention to them. Athreya walked around the room very slowly, studying every piece of furniture and peering under them. After he completed one round, he went again, looking at the walls and ceiling this time. He found nothing of interest.

He went to the bathroom next. Within a minute, he found another scrap of paper, this time inside the toilet bowl. The rest of the yielded no evidence.

It appeared that Mrinal had torn up some paper and flushed the pieces down the toilet. She had probably been sitting at the writing table when she tore it up. A breeze coming through the window must have blown some pieces to the floor. Two that had fluttered to a corner had lain unnoticed by her. And finally, a scrap of wet paper, being light and sticky, had clung to the toilet bowl.

Was this a sample of the letters Mrinal had been receiving and subsequently been destroying?

Leaving the forensic men to complete their work, Athreya and Shivali went up to the rooftop terrace. There, Athreya briefed her on all that he knew—from the riddle of the five guests that had brought him to Peter Dann to the bloody handprints, to him and Kinshuk being drugged, to what Kinshuk had just said about Mrinal receiving letters and destroying them.

However, he did not speak about Javed's premonitions, the conversation he had overheard, and some other fragmented notions that were floating in his mind. When he spoke about the column of rock on which the temple stood, Shivali's response was quick and simple—she would have someone inspect the temple. Either she would find a man who could scale the rock face, or she would use the police helicopter that monitored the area to drop a man onto the top.

Athreya found himself warming up to Shivali—she was an efficient police officer who didn't lose a minute. She seemed to command her men with ease too, and they, in turn, responded with alacrity.

Once Athreya had said all he had to say, Shivali began quizzing him. First, she asked him about the guests—what did he think of each of them? Did he have any specific suspicions? What had Asma said about Linda? Why had Dhavak been rude to him? Then, she went to where it all started.

'You came to Peter Dann because of the riddle of the five guests?' she asked.

'Well… ' Athreya hesitated. 'I had promised to come

here anyway and found myself just two hours away. Javed is an old friend, as you know. He insisted that I come, and so did Asma.' Athreya's justifications didn't seem very convincing to himself. He wondered how Shivali was receiving it. Would she be suspicious? 'I had no reason to decline the invitation, especially when my wife was going overseas in a couple of days. I accepted and came here.'

'That's fine, sir.' Shivali smiled pleasantly. 'There's absolutely no reason not to visit an old friend, especially in a place like this. Coming back to the five, was he absolutely positive about his identification when he saw them again at Peter Dann?'

'Yes. I quizzed him about it. He told me about the physical peculiarities of each one and why he remembered them clearly.'

'But did Asma see them at Nainital?'

'No. She was not in the restaurant then,' Athreya replied. 'She had gone out to the market.'

'I see... then, there is no corroboration.' She turned to look him in the eye. 'Is there, sir?'

'No.' The word was dragged out of Athreya. 'I had no reason to doubt Javed once he had explained to me why he remembered each of the five.'

'Ah!'

Shivali was expressive in her brevity. She was neither accepting Athreya's assessment, nor was she suggesting anything about Javed. Athreya began to get a sense of where she was heading. Clearly, she had her own ideas about the investigation, and was not going to be led by him. Nor would she accept his views just because of his age and experience. Her next question reinforced that feeling.

'Are you aware, sir,' she asked, 'that a *very* similar death took place here a few years ago? A lady fell off the rooftop terrace almost exactly where Mrinal fell?'

'Yes.' Athreya nodded. 'Javed's wife, Naira.'

'What can you tell me about her, sir?'

'Very little. I hardly knew her.'

'Okay... what about the way she died?'

'Nothing. I haven't spoken about it with Javed or Asma. I wasn't here when she died, and it was only four hours ago that I learnt about the manner in which she died.'

'Before today, you didn't know how she died?' Shivali was studying his face.

Athreya shook his head. 'No.'

'Are you aware that there was speculation about her death?'

'Yes. I believe she was depressed. Some may have wondered if Naira had committed suicide.'

'Yes... that was one speculation—accident or suicide. Many people wondered about it.' Shivali paused for a long moment. 'There was another speculation too... about a third possibility.'

Athreya didn't respond. There was nothing he could say. The penny had just dropped in his mind—so, that was why an ACP had come to investigate! Instead of sending an inspector as usual, the ACP had decided to come herself. The two deaths were remarkably similar and they had happened at the home of a retired police officer. That required an experienced and more senior officer.

Athreya decided that the best way forward was to speak about it openly.

'I understand the implications, Shivali,' he said. 'I will be honest in saying that I have not considered the possibility you allude to. As far as you are concerned, I would understand if you felt that I may not be entirely objective when it comes to a friend being a suspect. It's therefore best that you pursue that line of investigation without involving me. Meanwhile, you have my assurance that I will not speak to Javed about it. What you choose to tell me will stay with me.

'However, I would be happy if we could collaborate on the other lines of inquiry. Without a dossier on each of the seven guests and without forensic analysis, this case can't be cracked. I need you and your resources for that. And if I may be open enough to say so, I would welcome the opportunity to work with a sharp young officer.'

'Thank you, sir,' Shivali replied immediately with a hint of relief on her face. 'It would be my pleasure to collaborate. It is not often that we get the chance to work with really senior people. Is there anything specific you want the lab or the doctor to look at?'

'No specific instructions for the lab—we just need them to identify the drug in the remnants in the two glasses and in the blood sample the GP took. We also need to determine if the gin in the bottle is contaminated in any way.

'As far as the police doctor is concerned, I'd like him to examine Mrinal's fatal injuries in minute detail. A two-hundred-and-fifty-foot fall could obscure or even erase the signs of injuries she might have sustained beforehand, unless the earlier injury was a bullet or a knife wound.'

'Understood, sir. I'll ask him to examine all major injuries very closely. Anything specific you are looking for?'

Athreya nodded.

* * *

Back in his room, Athreya sat down with a pot of tea to take stock after his conversation with Shivali. She had brought into sharp focus some things that had been lurking at the back of his mind, something that he had been uneasy contemplating.

The foundation of his suspicions so far was built on one assumption: that Javed had spoken the truth about seeing the seven young people together in Nainital. But there was no corroboration at all. When five of them had pretended to be mutual strangers when they came to Peter Dann, the puzzle was born. The whole puzzle had only one source—Javed. What if it was a lie? What if the five had not met in Nainital as they have always maintained? What if they *really* had been strangers when they came to Peter Dann the first time? Except Ipshita and Purbhi, who were friends from school.

If Athreya were to view it clinically, he would have to acknowledge that his view of the five had already been coloured before he came to Peter Dann, before he met them.

Moving on to the other uncomfortable issue: what if there had been foul play in Naira's death? Had Athreya not been Javed's close friend, wouldn't he have considered the similarity between the two deaths as being relevant? Just as Shivali had? Had his friendship got in the way?

There was no denying Javed's potential motives in Naira's death. Not only did the valuable Peter Dann property come to him, but also it broke the shackles that bound him for years in so many different ways. Naira's passing also brought financial prosperity to Peter Dann. And it had unfettered Asma as well.

So, to take a page from the Clarksons' book, what had happened at Peter Dann that day had happened for the best, at least as far as Javed was concerned.

The logical thing to do now was to delve into the circumstances of Naira's death. But Athreya didn't want to do that. The reason or excuse—he didn't know which—was that Shivali was doing that, and she seemed to be very competent. There was no need for him to investigate his friend and host.

Athreya paused for a long moment as he considered his own feelings. He was distinctly uneasy, but he would stick with that decision for now. His right index finger was scribbling furiously on the sofa upholstery, but he gave it no attention. Instead, he picked up his phone and called his wife—something he often did when he felt unsettled. A chat with Veni always brought back the right perspective and balance.

'Oh, Hari!' she said when he told her about Mrinal and

her death. 'Why does murder follow you around so? I hope you are okay? You sound as if something is troubling you.'

Trust Veni to catch on! He had not yet talked about his unease.

Over the next ten minutes, he briefed her about the case and spoke of Naira. He also told her what the Clarksons had said. Finally, he rounded it off by talking about his own predicament.

'Hari,' she told him, 'You are no longer in the police force. Nothing *requires* you to investigate Naira's death. It is not your duty, and nobody has hired you to do it. And as far as Javed is concerned, you two are close friends who trust each other. Don't start doubting him without a strong reason. Let me tell you this, Hari: he would *not* have brought you into this if he was guilty. He has too much respect for your abilities.'

Listening to her, he felt the confusion in his mind diminish. Veni always gave good counsel.

'I agree with Margot,' Veni went on. 'I'd suggest that you too see the wisdom in her insistence that Naira's death was an accident. Nothing is to be achieved by raking it up now. It's over! It's the past. All's well that ends well.'

By the time he hung up five minutes later, he had decided to follow Veni's advice. At least for the time being. He would focus on Mrinal's death and determine which of the three possibilities it was—accident, suicide or murder.

* * *

Pangs of hunger reminded Athreya that he had missed lunch. He had lost all appetite on discovering the body. Before that, his breakfast had been an incomplete and meagre one that had been cut short by his discovery that he had been drugged the previous night. As dinner was a couple of hours away, he went down to the kitchen and asked for a sandwich.

He wondered where Javed was. He hadn't seen his host after he had brought Shivali up to meet Athreya.

Javed was an uncommonly sharp man who picked up many non-verbal cues from the way people spoke and behaved. Had he figured out that Shivali suspected him? He would surely have grasped the significance of an ACP coming to investigate instead of the usual inspector rank. If so, he would not want to put his friend, Athreya, in a difficult spot. One way of ensuring that was to avoid Athreya.

Athreya was eating his sandwich and sipping his tea when Javed and Shivali entered the dining room.

'Missed lunch?' Javed asked. 'So did I. Wolfed down a sandwich half an hour ago. Have you recovered from the sleeping drug?'

'Oh, yes! Entirely. I guess the shock of finding Mrinal drove it from my system.'

'This is bad business, Athreya,' Javed rumbled, as he took a chair opposite him. Shivali sat beside him. 'Asma is going to be shattered when she learns about it.'

'Why?' Shivali asked. 'Was she fond of Mrinal?'

Javed shook his huge head like a disgruntled bear.

'No,' he said. 'She hardly knew Mrinal. They had met just a few hours earlier.'

Javed paused and let out a long breath as a waiter brought tea for himself and Shivali. He waited till the man had gone and the door had closed behind him. He turned in his chair and faced the ACP.

'There is no point in playing hide-and-seek, Shivali,' he said in a voice that was gruffer than usual. 'You know it and I know it. Everyone else is probably talking about it. That's probably what brought you here to Peter Dann in the first place.

'So, let me confirm this for you—Mrinal fell from exactly the same spot from which Naira did. From the furthest point of the curve of the southern parapet wall. She fell on the same rock too. You would be remiss in your duty if you did not consider this obvious similarity. I'm sure you have a copy of the testimony I gave after Naira's death. You probably read it in the car on the way here. I have nothing to add, and nothing to change. But if you have any questions, I'll answer them.'

'Thank you, sir,' Shivali responded. She didn't seem embarrassed or fazed in any way. 'I don't have any questions about your wife's death. You have answered every possible question many times over. But I do have questions about Mrinal—did you know her before she came here to Peter Dann?'

'I met her for the first time on the day before she came here.' Javed spoke in a measured and deliberate manner. 'She was staying at Clarkson's. Athreya and I had gone there to sample Dave Clarkson's apple brandy. That's when I met her, saw her and spoke to her for the very first time. That's when I knew of her existence on God's Earth. The same goes for her fiancé, Kinshuk.'

'As far as you could tell, did she know you or know of you?'

'I don't think so. Athreya can corroborate this… when I was introduced to her by the Clarksons, it looked as if I was as much a stranger to her as she was to me. She was surprised to learn that I was the owner of Peter Dann, the hotel she would be moving to two days later.'

'Thank you, sir. The other issue is about the five—or seven—young people you saw in Nainital six weeks ago. Five of them came to Peter Dann two weeks ago. Are you *absolutely* sure that they were the same five people you saw in Nainital?'

'Yes, I am sure. There is no doubt in my mind.'

Shivali nodded her head pensively. She stopped talking and began sipping her tea. As the silence dragged, Javed gave a soft grunt and stood up.

'I don't expect you to trust what I've said,' he said. 'I'm sure you'll form your own opinions. All I'll say in my defence is this: if I was planning to kill Mrinal, I wouldn't have brought the country's best investigator to the crime scene. I wouldn't have invited Athreya to Peter Dann.'

With that, Javed excused himself and left the room. For a moment, Athreya sat stunned. Javed had said *exactly* what Veni had told him a short while ago. Why hadn't it occurred to Athreya himself? Did he have too much humility? Was he overly modest? A good investigator needed to know his shortcomings.

He mentally brushed away the thought and turned to Shivali.

'So, you heard it from the horse's mouth,' he said. 'Are you convinced that it was the same five people Javed saw in Nainital?'

Shivali took her time to put her cup on the table.

'I have just heard from the Nainital police, sir,' she said in a measured fashion. 'They scrutinized the guest ledgers, the computer system and the financial transactions for those dates six weeks ago. Mr Javed's and Asma's names are in the guest list. They were there as he claimed.'

'And the other five—Ipshita Lahiri, Purbhi Chakradhar, Linda Mathew, Sarosh Gulati and Dhavak Strummer?'

'No, sir.' Shivali shook her head. 'None of them was there. We examined all guest data for a week prior to that day and a week after. None of those five names figures in the guest list or credit card transactions.'

Interlude

Asma was growing increasingly puzzled. This trek was turning out to be very different from earlier ones. This group was far too quiet—none of the five guests had said much from the time they had left Peter Dann.

Chetan, the thirty-five-year-old local guide, who was acting as Maazin's assistant, had arrived at Peter Dann early in the morning. Coming from a local mountain tribe, he was short, wiry and strong, and could climb mountain slopes almost effortlessly. His straight black hair had the habit of falling over his eyes, making his attempts to push it back an exercise in futility. He had the endearing habit of breaking out into a crooked grin at the slightest opportunity, displaying his yellowed teeth to anyone who cared to look.

That morning, he had checked their supplies and had inspected each person's shoes and attire as and when they had appeared. He had then hustled the groggy guests in his broken English, and had ensured that they departed a little after eight o'clock.

Two vehicles had driven them down to Pottersfield, from where they had proceeded on foot. In all the years Asma had been walking this trail, this picturesque plain, framed against the lofty Himalayas and crowned by the majestic Nanda Devi, had seldom failed to draw gasps and evoke awe in hikers. The first sight of the vista, as they came upon it suddenly, was the surprise that often ushered in a buoyant mood.

But not this time. The five guests, silent and inexplicably glum, just gazed at the magnificent sight and said nothing. When prompted by Maazin, they mouthed half-hearted admiration rather unconvincingly. In all the hikes Asma had been on, a group was at its chattiest from Pottersfield for about two hours, when tiredness would begin taking its toll. But this group might well have been a funeral procession from the start.

After they crossed the stream at the end of Pottersfield, Maazin had paused and spoken to the guests. This was one of the most beautiful sights in the country, he said. By this time, most people would have taken a couple of dozen snaps. But this group hadn't taken one! Why, he asked. Chetan chipped in with Urdu and Hindi poetry, and sang a local song about the foothills. That seemed to shake the guests out of their lassitude. Smiles appeared, voices rose, and cameras clicked. Dhavak hummed an English song about the Rocky Mountains, and Ipshita chipped in with a Hindi song, which Chetan heartily joined in. At last, the mood lifted and they resumed their journey in higher spirits.

But that didn't last for long. Within half an hour, they seemed jaded as if the temporary sprightliness had required conscious effort. Silence returned, save for the chatter between Maazin, Asma and Chetan. Sarosh, who had talked incessantly at Peter Dann, had gone pensive and mute. Asma was chatting and laughing and turned to Linda with more than a trace of concern.

'What's the matter?' she asked in a low tone. 'Not feeling well?'

'No, no,' Linda replied, 'I'm okay. I guess I have a bit of a hangover from the party. Should be okay soon. I'm already feeling better.'

Linda offered a wide smile. But Asma knew her friend well. She could make out that the smile was put on. But after that, Linda made a conscious effort to keep up a desultory chatter, except when going uphill gave her a pretext for keeping talk at a minimum.

The other two women were a dozen yards behind Asma while Dhavak and Sarosh led the group with Chetan and Maazin. Despite being a heavy smoker, Dhavak strode effortlessly up the incline with long strides even as Sarosh struggled to keep up.

Glancing back at Purbhi, Asma felt that something was amiss. Clad for the first time in something other than jeans, the gawky, ferret-faced young woman was visibly anxious. It showed clearly on her face and in her manner. Ipshita, looking elegant as always and particularly attractive in her tracks and tee, was trying to comfort her. But Purbhi was growing increasingly agitated and snappy. Asma wondered why.

Realizing that Ipshita was trying to calm her childhood friend, Asma refrained from falling back to help. She hoped that there was no major problem. They would have no network coverage for several hours until they reached the midway camp; getting help was near impossible. And there was little Asma could offer with her own arm in a sling.

She alerted Maazin to Purbhi's condition. For the first time, she could see concern on Ipshita's face, as if something was getting out of hand. Maazin decided to call a halt and give the party a rest for fifteen minutes. They came together and sat down. Though it was not the normal thing to do in the middle of a trek, he and Chetan lit a solid fuel stove and brewed tea. Dhavak lit the inevitable cigarette.

Grinning and pushing his hair back from his eyes, Chetan told a couple of jokes, which for a short while distracted Purbhi from whatever was troubling her. For a minute or two, her face softened, much to Ipshita's relief. But once the jokes had been told and laughed at, anxiety returned to her face. She jumped up and began pacing rapidly and aimlessly. When Ipshita rose to go to her, Purbhi snapped at her and told her to stay away. Ipshita sat down again, taking no offence. But her worried eyes darted to Purbhi repeatedly. By now, everyone had noticed Purbhi's fretfulness.

When the fifteen minutes were up, Maazin called for the trek to resume. Ipshita went to Purbhi and tried to hold her hand. But Purbhi jerked it away and snarled at Ipshita.

'It's your fault!' The words came faintly to Asma, who was upwind from Purbhi, and she wondered what they meant. She had no idea what their disagreement was about.

Later, they stopped for lunch, which would have turned out to be a quiet affair but for Dhavak and Sarosh. They made small talk and pulled the others into their chatter. Linda responded with banter and Ipshita chipped in here and there. But Purbhi was beyond help. She was visibly angry now, scowling and snapping at her best friend, who still took no offence.

By afternoon, Purbhi had gone to pieces. There was no restraint any longer and no pretence. Her anger had gone beyond Ipshita. But at the same time, she looked like a trapped animal—frightened and restless. Her legs, despite the tiredness she must be feeling, wouldn't stop. Her face was haggard, and her efforts to listen to music on her mobile phone didn't seem to soothe her at all. Repeatedly, her eyes brimmed from whatever was tearing at her heart.

It was early evening when they reached Mid Camp. It was a permanent campsite with wood-and-canvas structures serving as a kitchen and two bathrooms. Tents were the sleeping quarters. This was where they would spend the night. Supplies had already arrived by vehicle from Peter Dann, along with a cook and a helper. At one spot above the camp, a weak mobile phone signal was available, but it worked only for BSNL phones.

Maazin promptly called Baranwal at Peter Dann to report their arrival and to ask if there was anything at the castle that he needed to be aware of. On being told that there was none, he rang off. Purbhi and Ipshita tried in vain to catch a signal for their mobiles.

As darkness descended and the group settled around a campfire, Dhavak produced a bottle of whisky from somewhere. The full bottle looked small in his large hand as he hefted it effortlessly.

Half an hour later, he was singing. Not having his guitar with him, he borrowed a couple of tins from the kitchen, which he used as makeshift drums. Purbhi, who was nowhere to be seen during the singing, materialized at dinnertime, looking more haggard. But the edge of anxiety seemed to have disappeared. After dinner, she flopped into her sleeping bag and fell asleep.

The night turned out to be a strange one for Asma. The four women shared a tent while the four men shared the other. Her injured arm troubled her in the cramped tent, interrupting her sleep several times during the night. On one such occasion, she saw that Purbhi's sleeping bag was empty. Too tired to think about it, she went back to sleep.

Later, when she awakened once again, she saw that Purbhi had returned but Ipshita and Linda were missing. Asma thought she faintly heard Ipshita's clear voice, but she couldn't be sure. It was cold and the wind was howling outside. Asma snuggled into her sleeping bag and went back to sleep, not noticing that the zip of her backpack was open.

13

Athreya and Javed set out on horseback the next morning after breakfast. Athreya wanted to speak to the trekkers before they became aware of Mrinal's death. With no motor track that could take him to their walking route, he and Javed had decided to use horses. By riding fast, they would overtake them in three hours or so. That would give Athreya a few hours to talk to them before they reached their destination, from which they would return to Peter Dann the next morning by vehicle.

But along the way, Athreya had two things to do first. As soon as he and Javed set out of Peter Dann's gate, he turned to Javed to ask about the first one.

'Can we ride to that rock outcrop?' he asked. 'I'm curious to see the rock face the Cochhas scale so easily.'

'Sure,' Javed replied. 'There is no road to it, but it is accessible through the trees.'

They went along the road to where they had found Mrinal's body the previous day. On the other side of the road, the ground sloped downward into a shallow valley, beyond which rose another hillock. On the top of it stood the monolithic column of stone with the *vanara* temple. Javed turned his horse into the woods towards the outcrop.

A short while later, they were at the edge of a wide ring of boulders that surrounded the outcrop. There was no way to reach it without clambering over a forbidding tangle of rock and bramble.

'The ring goes all the way around,' Javed said. 'Geologists say that the outcrop was once a much larger rock. Some centuries ago, it split vertically in several places, and the outer parts toppled away outwards, leaving the inner column standing alone. Time and the elements turned the fallen parts into this ring of boulders that you see.'

'That's remarkable,' Athreya replied. 'I wonder why it split vertically at every crack.'

'It's got something to do with the internal structure, I'm told. Rocks split along the weakest facet of their lattice structure, which runs through them as flat, two-dimensional planes. This rock happened to be oriented at an angle that made these planes perfectly vertical. So, when it began cracking, it splintered vertically. It is unusual, no doubt, but by no means unique. There are similar cases, both in India and overseas.'

As they rode around the ring of rock, Athreya saw that all the sides of the outcrop seemed equally unclimbable. That the Cochhas scaled it every full moon seemed incredible. If they could scale this, they could scale the Peter Dann's rock face with ease.

They returned to the road where Athreya paused and looked up at the castle. At first, the southern wall of the castle seemed plain and featureless, save the barred windows. On a closer look, he saw some vertical projections on the wall, about a foot high, and horizontal ones a few feet below the windows of both floors. At the middle, they joined a vertical projection that ran down to the bottom of the castle, where it stopped abruptly.

'Drainage pipes,' Javed explained. 'Originally, the rooms did not have bathrooms. When we added them, we had to make provision for water and drainage. So that the pipes don't stand out uglily, we attached stone-like cladding on them.'

'Makes it easier for someone to scale the castle wall, doesn't it?' Athreya asked.

'I guess so. But the person would have to be light. The

cladding won't take the weight of someone like me.'

They then started the horses trotting swiftly eastward. Once in the open, they sent them galloping across Pottersfield and reached the stream in a couple of minutes. There, they dismounted to do the second thing Athreya had in mind.

He knelt down beside the ashes of the fire Mrinal had lit about forty-eight hours ago. It had been a small fire that had been kindled using twigs and paper. The wind had scattered the ashes, and small bits of grey lay around the centre. With a stick, Athreya raked the charred remains at the centre to see if anything lay under the surface. Small flat grey pieces suggested that paper had been burnt there. Mrinal had stamped the fire after extinguishing it, to grind down the ashes to powder. But she had not had the time to do a thorough job of it. There was no hiding the fact that she had burnt paper here.

'She came all the way here to burn something?' Javed remarked. 'Wonder if it was one of those letters Kinshuk was talking about.'

'Likely,' Athreya replied. 'Maybe, she wanted to ensure that nobody saw her burning it. That's why she walked all the way here. The alternative was to enter the woods to burn it, which she might not have wanted to do.'

'Can you make out what kind of paper was burnt here?'

'No, I can't. It's all charred beyond recognition... Ah! What's this? We may be in luck!'

Athreya bent forward and peered into the ashes he had just raked. With his forefinger and thumb, he held something and lifted it out of the ashes. It turned out to be a small piece of stiff paper that had not fully burned. Holding it carefully, he blew on it till it was free of the dirt and ash. He rose and held it out for Javed to see. It was the corner of a thick, smooth paper that was mostly white. Near the charred edge away from the corner, there was a few millimetres of red. And the paper itself was glossy.

'Similar to what we found in her room,' Athreya said softly. 'Glossy white paper with some red. Know what it is, Javed?'

He shook his head.

'Mrinal has been destroying photographs,' Athreya continued. 'She burnt one here two mornings ago and tore one up the same evening at Peter Dann.'

'Photos?' Javed echoed, his brow furrowed. 'Someone has been sending her photos? Was she being blackmailed?'

'Don't know.' Athreya dropped the scrap of paper into a small ziplock bag, which he carefully placed into his wallet. 'Whatever it was, I suspect that there is a hidden past here that needs discovering.'

* * *

It was early afternoon when the riders reached the trekkers. In three hours, the horses had covered the distance that had taken the walkers a day and a half. The riders had just crested a low, verdant hill when they spotted the party beyond a lush, shallow valley a mile away. They were in three groups on the undulating carpet of green with no discernible track. Three men were leading it—Chetan, Dhavak and Sarosh. A hundred feet behind them were Asma and Linda, with Maazin walking a few yards to their left. Ipshita and Purbhi brought up the rear another hundred feet behind.

Maazin was the first to notice the riders. He turned and stopped, gazing at the approaching horses. Seeing him, Asma also turned. They recognized the horses simultaneously and waved.

'What's brought Dad and Uncle here?' Asma asked softly. 'I hope everything is okay.'

'I hope so too,' Maazin agreed in a worried tone. 'This is unusual.'

The rest of the party came to a halt, remaining where

they were. Chetan ran down past Maazin and Asma, and took the reins of Javed's black horse as the riders dismounted. Maazin took charge of Athreya's dun and rubbed its neck as the horse nuzzled him affectionately.

Athreya stretched after dismounting to ease his aching muscles. Three hours of hard riding had made him rediscover muscles whose existence he had forgotten since his ride a few days ago. He walked for a few minutes on the welcoming grass until the bunched muscles loosened and he was ready to begin his interviews.

Meanwhile, Maazin, Asma and Javed exchanged a few quiet words, after which, Maazin waved to the others to resume walking. Dhavak and Sarosh at the head of the party turned and started uphill as Asma and Linda fell into step with Javed. Chetan followed with the horses.

At Athreya's request, Maazin joined him, and they drifted away from the group till they were out of earshot. Ipshita and Purbhi had resumed their pace, ensuring that they maintained their distance from the others.

'Before you begin, sir,' Maazin said as they strolled uphill from the charming valley, 'I wanted to apologize, but I didn't get a chance. I am very sorry for what happened at Land's End the other evening.'

'Are you talking about Dhavak?' Athreya asked in surprise.

'Yes, sir.'

'Why should *you* apologize for *his* rudeness? You were as surprised as I was.'

'It happened at Peter Dann—'

'Come on, Maazin. You can't be held responsible for what your guests say to each other. Anyway, why did Dhavak behave the way he did?'

'No idea, sir. As you said, I was shocked too. Dhavak is actually a nice person, even if he does seem a little… er… odd at times. He accommodates our requests and sings for us. Many celebrities wouldn't. He is nice to talk to as well, although he doesn't say very much. And finally, he comes from a reputable family.'

'No idea why he hates cops?'

Maazin shook his head again. 'No, sir.'

'Is Strummer his real name or a professional pseud-onym?'

'It's his real name. His ID says "Dhavak Strummer". I saw it when he checked in.'

'I wonder what made him hate the police so. Or was it something to do with me? Did anyone say anything to him about me to cause such a reaction? *Somebody* must have told him that I was once a police investigator.'

'He overheard the ladies discussing what you had said at dinner that evening. He then asked Purbhi if you had been a police officer. That's all.'

'Fair enough. Do you know him from before?'

'No, sir. He's just another guest. He's come here for the trek, and has come alone. He strikes me as a loner—wanders on his bike, keeps his own timings, does what he wants when he wants and isn't particularly fond of company. But that's fine. We get all sorts of people on treks. Compared to some of the groups we've had in the past, this is a quiet group.'

'Do groups form by themselves, or does someone as-semble them?'

'We put our trek schedule on our website. It gives the details and shows how many slots are available. Whoever wants to go registers online and pays an advance. Some-times, if a group becomes too large, we split it into two and stagger them. We also organize hikes for groups who want to go unaided by themselves, as long as they stay at Peter Dann. It's one way to drive occupancy.'

'Makes sense.' Athreya paused for a moment. 'Let's leave that aside for now. What I wanted to talk about is something else.'

'Yes, sir?'

Athreya knew that Maazin would be curious about his sudden arrival, but whatever Javed had told him was probably preventing Maazin from asking outright.

'There has been an incident,' Athreya said. 'I need to talk to you and the others. I am not in a position to share any details now. I'll do so once I've spoken to everyone.'

'Sure. What do you want to know?'

'I want to talk about the evening of the party. I need you to recall people's movements during and after the party as accurately as you can.'

'Okay. Where do you want me to start? When the party began?'

'Why don't you start when Mrinal came to the party? Remember that?'

'Of course. She came in a little late. It was getting towards 8:30 p.m.'

'That's right. You remember everyone fell silent?'

'Yes, I do.'

'Why did everyone fall silent?'

'I don't know,' Maazin replied, drawing out each word. 'It was one of those sudden silences that interrupt parties, I suppose.'

'Every eye turned to her. Everyone stopped talking.'

'Well, sir,' Maazin offered a half-smile. 'Mrinal does catch the eye. She's not a glamorous lady or a head-turner, but there is something about her that catches people's eye. In addition, she was wearing a bright dress that evening.'

'Is that all? Was there nothing else?'

'Not as far as I could see.'

'Do you think that people were waiting for her to arrive, and automatically turned to see her when she did?'

'That's possible.'

'Where were you when she arrived?'

'Behind the bar.'

'Do you know Mrinal from before, Maazin?'

He shook his head. 'No, sir. This is the first time she has

144

come to Peter Dann.'

'What do you think of how she behaved during the party?'

'Well… that's not for me to say, sir. She seemed okay in the beginning. But later on, something upset her badly.'

'Any idea what might have upset her?'

'I don't know, sir. Asma and I were talking about it yesterday. We were both surprised too.'

'Do you remember when she got upset?'

'I noticed it was just before she went to the terrace. I was busy serving drinks and managing the snacks. I didn't speak to Mrinal at all before that.'

'How was she when you went up to the terrace?'

'As you just said, sir—*very* upset. Upset enough to leave the party and sit by herself.'

'Was she crying?'

'She seemed stunned… like in a trance. She was staring wide-eyed and seemed to be trembling. She didn't say a word to me even when I asked her if she was okay and if she needed anything. It was almost as if she wasn't aware of my presence. The first time I went up, I left the bottle of gin on the table along with some tonic and ice. I then sent up a plate of assorted snacks.'

'You went up a few times, didn't you?'

'Yes, sir. She had recovered a little when I went the second time. But she spoke very little. As it was getting cold up there, Asma had brought her a shawl.'

'Grey shawl?'

'Yes.'

'Was it Asma's or Mrinal's shawl?'

'Asma's, sir. She sent one of the staff girls to fetch it from her room. She then went up and gave it to Mrinal.'

'What else did you send or take up to her? More tonic, I presume?'

'No, sir.' Maazin cast an enquiring glance at Athreya. 'She stopped taking alcohol once she went to the terrace.

She only drank orange juice.'

'Are you sure, Maazin?' Athreya asked.

'Yes, sir. You can check with Asma too. Mrinal had her last alcoholic drink in the lounge.'

'And dinner?'

'Kinshuk took it up to her. I am not sure if she ate it or not.'

'When did she tell you that she was dropping out of the trek?'

'When I went up the second time.'

'Do you remember the time?'

'Yes, sir. It was 10:10 p.m. My recollection is that she went to the terrace at around 9:45 p.m. I went up the first time a few minutes after that. I went up again at 10:10 p.m. to ask if she needed anything. That's when she told me that she was dropping out.'

'Did she say why?'

'No.' Maazin shook his head. 'I asked her, but she didn't reply.'

'What do you think? What could have been the reason?'

'Maybe… I'm just guessing here, sir. Maybe she decided that she didn't want to go with this group.' He jerked his head towards Dhavak and Sarosh a hundred feet in front. 'Remember, it was Dhavak's song that sent her to the terrace.'

'What about Kinshuk? When did he tell you that he was dropping out?'

'As soon as he learnt that Mrinal had dropped out. I don't remember the exact time, but it must have been about half an hour after dinner began. Kinshuk was yawning uncontrollably. He must have been very sleepy—he could hardly keep his eyes open. He told me that he too was dropping out, and then went to pick up dinner.'

'What time did dinner end?'

'At 11 p.m. I remember that clearly. Five minutes later, Kinshuk took a large brandy and retired to his room. You

and Mr Rais followed him after another five minutes.'
Maazin threw him a quick glance. 'You too were very
sleepy, sir. I guess you must have been tired after all that
riding.'

Athreya didn't respond. 'Who poured the large brandy
for Kinshuk?' he asked instead.

'I am not sure, sir. I was at the food counter then. Kinshuk, Dhavak and Sarosh went to the bar counter together.
One of them poured it, or the boy behind the bar would
have.'

'When did the party wind up?'

'Just after you and Mr Rais left. That must have been
ten minutes past eleven. The staff cleared the lounge, and
we were all down in the kitchen at 11:18 p.m. I remember
seeing the kitchen clock. Asma told me that she checked on
Mrinal at 11:20 before retiring to her room.'

'You didn't go up after that, I suppose?'

'I did, sir. I went up to lock the terrace doors.'

Athreya's eyes snapped to Maazin. 'You went there?'

Maazin nodded. 'Of course, that was much later.'

'What time?'

'It was 12:30 a.m.'

'Did you go out onto the terrace before you locked up?'

'Yes, sir. I always do that to ensure that nobody is locked
out on the terrace.'

'Was anyone there? Mrinal?'

'No, sir. It was empty.'

'Are you sure, Maazin? This is important.'

'Very sure, sir. I made a quick round of the terrace to see
if any guest was sitting on any of the chairs up there. The
terrace was empty.'

14

Asma was waiting to grill Athreya when he finished with Maazin. She had sensed that something was wrong but her father had refused to tell her anything. On her part, Asma had refrained from demanding answers in Linda's presence.

'What's wrong?' she asked as soon as she and Athreya were out of earshot of the others. 'You wouldn't have ridden out so far unless something was amiss. Dad no longer undertakes such long rides.'

'There has been an incident,' Athreya told her. 'I am not going to tell you about it yet. I need to speak to everyone before doing that.'

'You can tell *me*!' she protested. 'I won't tell the others. Peter Dann is my home!'

'I'm sure you wouldn't tell anyone, Asma, but you have a very expressive face. You have to trust me on this.'

The spirited girl stared at him for a long moment, trying to decide whether to give in to his assumed authority or to continue fighting.

'Your father trusts me,' Athreya added softly. 'So should you. It's for a good reason. You'll know in a couple of hours.'

'Okay,' she conceded reluctantly. 'This… incident… made you come all this way to talk to us? It must be a big incident.'

Athreya shrugged.

'What do you want to talk about?' she asked. 'I'm sure the others already suspect something.'

'That can't be helped. Before I start, how has the trek been so far?'

'It's interesting that you ask that, Uncle. This is a funny group. They have been very silent and have shown very little enthusiasm. I've never been on such a quiet trip. Their reaction to these spectacular mountains is less than luke-warm.'

'Feels as if they are just going through the motions? Their hearts not in it?'

'Exactly!' Asma flashed him a curious glance. 'You don't seem surprised.'

He shrugged. 'What about Linda? Has she been subdued too?'

'Yes. I wonder if she is thinking of Aaron.'

'Aaron?'

'Her brother. They were very close, you know. He died a few years ago. Whenever she thinks of him, she goes silent.'

'How did he die?'

Asma's voice dropped a notch. 'He committed suicide. She hasn't reconciled herself to it.'

'Sometimes, people never reconcile themselves to some events.'

'That's exactly what she says. It's near impossible, she says.'

Abruptly, a question that Linda had asked during the first dinner flashed through his mind: '*Solving the crime helps with reconciliation, doesn't it?*' He wondered if that had any bearing on the present.

'Why did Aaron commit suicide?' he asked.

'Is it necessary to talk about that, Uncle? Can we let the past be the past?'

Athreya thought for a brief instant and decided not to pursue the matter. He nodded and changed the topic.

'Let's talk about the party the evening before last, he said. 'What did you think about the way Mrinal behaved?'

'I was surprised, and frankly, quite concerned. She seemed very distraught, but didn't confide in anyone.'

'You tried asking her when she was in the lounge but she didn't confide. Didn't she say anything on the rooftop terrace either?'

Asma shook her head. 'No. Initially, she was stunned almost speechless. When she did begin speaking, she said very little. She didn't want anyone near her—neither Maazin nor me, nor her fiancé.'

'What did she do on the terrace? She was there for a long while.'

'Nothing. It's really puzzling. She just sat there staring out into the night or at her fingers. I got the impression that she was thinking hard.'

'Did she drink much on the terrace?'

'No. I mean, she didn't drink alcohol. She had some orange juice.'

'You tried to talk to her, I suppose?'

'Yes, but not with much success. Beyond a point, it seemed intrusive to keep asking her. Only when I went up for the last time did she say anything.'

'What did she say?'

'She thanked me for the concern I had shown and told me not to worry about her. She was going through a difficult patch, she said, and she would be okay soon. She said something about life being tough and about her having to make some difficult choices in the past. She asked me if the party was nearly over. To which I said that it might be another fifteen minutes or so.'

'Did she seem depressed?'

Asma's eyes snapped to Athreya. They bored into his for a moment before she responded.

'Why? Why do you ask that?'

'I want to understand her state of mind,' Athreya replied, choosing his words with care. They were treading very close to Naira's death.

'Has something happened to Mrinal?' Her eyes were searching his face.

'Just answer the question, Asma. Please.'

'Was she sad? Dejected?' she thought aloud and frowned as she tried to recall. 'Hmm… she was agitated, she was worried… but she was not dejected. I got the feeling that she was trying to decide what to do next. There is no question that something significant had happened during the party. She was trying to devise a response.'

'What do you think upset her?' Athreya asked.

'I remember what she said to you, Dad and me: "*I have received a bit of a shock A personal matter… please don't blame Sarosh or the others… it's just that our conversation reminded me of something very distressing.*" So, something in the conversation with Sarosh and the girls upset her. Then came Dhavak's song. She went white when he sang "Sound of Silence".'

'I remember. I am trying to find out why the conversation upset her and why the song unnerved her.'

'Why don't you just ask her?' Asma asked.

An instant later, she froze in her tracks. Her eyes grew wide and her head swivelled to face Athreya. Her face had blanched.

'Something *has* happened to her!' she whispered. 'Uncle? Isn't that so? You can't ask her… that's why you are asking me. *Oh God!*'

'Get a hold on yourself, Asma,' Athreya cautioned. 'You'll know everything very soon. Meanwhile, your face must not tip off the others. Now, I believe you saw her last at 11:20 p.m. After that, you went down to your room. Is that right?'

Asma nodded wordlessly. Her face was drawn and white.

'Is the time right? 11:20 p.m.?'

She nodded.

'She was not disconsolate then, correct?'

She nodded again.

'Was she crying?'

Asma shook her head.

'I don't think so,' she rasped. Her voice softened as she went on. 'But it was difficult to make out as I couldn't see her face very well. She buried her face in her hands a couple of times, making her hair fall over her face and obscure it. I am therefore not sure if she was crying. I got the feeling that she was trying to get a hold on herself.'

'Was she wearing the shawl you lent her?'

'No.' Asma cleared her throat and resumed walking. 'But I told her to keep it as it was getting colder on the terrace. I said I'd collect it later, or she could just leave it in the lounge.'

'What was on the table when you left her?' he asked. 'Do you remember?'

'Her mobile, an empty dinner plate, half a glass of orange juice, a half-full bottle of gin, an empty can of tonic, an ice bucket and some napkins. I also saw something small colourful and metallic behind the bottle, but I am not sure what it was.'

'That's very precise! Did you see anyone else on the terrace?'

'No. All the other guests were in the lounge. You and Dad had retired. Kinshuk had already gone to his room. All the staff had gone down. Everyone was accounted for.'

'Could anyone come from the outside?' Athreya asked.

'Outside?' Asma echoed. 'Nobody can enter the castle without the security guard seeing them. How else?'

'Could someone have scaled up the rock face and the southern wall of the castle?'

Asma's eyes widened.

'I hope not,' she whispered. 'But it's happened before.'

* * *

Linda was frightened when Athreya began talking to her. The fingers of her right hand were caressing her engraved silver cross. The guarded expression on her open face and the wide-open eyes seemed to suggest that she had her back against the wall. She merely nodded when Athreya said that he wanted to talk to her, and offered no comment or question when he told her that there had been an incident at Peter Dann.

When he asked her about her movements on the night of the party, she said that she had been in the lounge all evening before retiring to her room with Purbhi and Ipshita at 11:15 p.m. or so. She added that she had not gone up to the terrace at all.

Yes, she had noticed Mrinal's strange behaviour; no, she had no idea why Mrinal went up to the terrace. She had also noticed that Kinshuk and Athreya had been very drowsy towards the end of the party.

'Upset after talking to us?' Linda asked, when Athreya told her that Mrinal had been troubled after speaking with Sarosh and the three women. 'Why?'

'What did you talk about?' Athreya asked, not answering her question.

'I don't remember. Some small talk, I guess. I said very little because I hardly know her. She is also much older than I am, and a successful entrepreneur. I have very little in common with her.'

'Do you remember what the others said?'

Linda shook her head. 'Nothing very important, I think.'

'Did someone say anything that could have reminded her of some past event?' Athreya asked.

Linda thought for a moment and shrugged, turning her palms upwards to signify ignorance.

'Were you in Nainital six weeks ago, Linda?' Athreya asked, abruptly changing the topic.

'Nainital?' she asked after a momentary pause. 'No. Why?'

'Just wondered,' Athreya answered. 'Why did you come to Peter Dann?'

'To visit Asma and to go on the trek.'

Athreya wondered whether it was significant that the usually spirited girl took no umbrage at his blunt, rude questions. She seemed to be subjecting herself to the interrogation rather meekly. It seemed out of character after his dinner conversation with her three days ago.

'You don't seem to be enjoying the trek very much,' he said.

'I think I overdid it on the night of the party and was too tired yesterday. I'm quite enjoying it today. Look at these lovely mountains, Mr Athreya—how can one not enjoy them? Having said that, the climb is steeper today. I'm often out of breath.'

'When did you decide to come to Peter Dann?'

'About a month ago. I spoke to Asma and she was delighted.'

'Why did you select Peter Dann?'

'Why? Because of Asma, of course. She has been suggesting it for a while.'

'Is there another reason as well, Linda?' His voice was soft, encouraging.

'Another reason?' she echoed without looking at him. 'No. What other reason could there be?'

That, Athreya told himself, was something he would discover.

* * *

Athreya's chat with Ipshita went along very similar lines with Linda. Leaving Purbhi in Asma's care, Ipshita came to talk with him without any protest or query. Nor did she display any curiosity about the 'incident' Athreya mentioned.

Her account of the evening was clear and succinct. She had been in the lounge during the entire duration of the party, and had gone to the room she shared with Linda and Purbhi at about 11:15 p.m. The three were sharing the dormitory-style room due to cost considerations, but it was sufficiently large. They had not left the room till the morning. No, she had no insight to offer regarding Mrinal's 'funny' behaviour.

No, she had not gone up to the terrace—why should she? Particularly when the party was happening in the lounge? If Mrinal wanted to go up, it was her choice. Oh, she was thoroughly enjoying the trek, except that having to take care of Purbhi was cramping her style.

'Purbhi is having a bit of a problem,' she explained when Athreya probed. 'It's a personal matter that I don't want to discuss.'

Unlike Linda, who had appeared frightened and unsure, Ipshita was in complete control. Yes, she was chaperoning Purbhi, she seemed to be saying, but that was none of Athreya's business.

'Mrinal was upset after she talked to you, Sarosh and the other two women,' he said. 'Any idea why?'

'No.' Her answer was straight and blunt. It left no room for discussion.

'What did you talk about?' Athreya persisted.

'Mr Athreya,' she replied, as if she were explaining to a child, 'how do you expect me to remember? We were talking non-stop for hours! We'd had several drinks too. How can I recollect some inconsequential chit-chat with someone who was at the party for a short time?'

'Are you saying that you didn't know Mrinal from before?'

'Did I give you the impression that I did?' she countered.

'Why did you come to Peter Dann, Ipshita?' he asked.

'Why not? Is there a problem with my being there?'

'No,' Athreya answered patiently, 'I was wondering what prompted you to choose Peter Dann.'

'That's an entirely different question,' she replied, seeming to grow in confidence. 'Purbhi and I looked up several websites offering treks, and came upon Peter Dann. It seemed to be just what we wanted, and we signed up.'

'Was it before or after you went to Nainital?' he asked.

'Nainital?' she answered at once, without missing a step. 'You must be mistaken. I've not been there recently.'

'Have you been there before?'

'Yes. Some years ago. Why?'

Athreya smiled inwardly. He had enjoyed this conversation with this sharp, confident woman. It was time to wrap it up.

'Perhaps,' he acceded, 'I am mistaken.'

* * *

If Linda had been frightened and Ipshita assured, Purbhi was openly combative when she met Athreya. Her narrow face was contorted into a scowl and she was given to making quick, restless movements. She continuously fidgeted with her phone and gripped it as if she was afraid she'd lose it. Her eyes were open wider than usual and darted nervously all over. The strange mixture of anger and anxiety lent her an air of a cornered feline. Had she possessed claws, Athreya thought, she would have bared them.

'What gives you the right to go around interrogating people?' she demanded belligerently, not bothering to keep her voice down.

'Nothing,' Athreya replied calmly. 'You are free to walk away if you wish to. There is nothing I can do if you choose not to talk.'

'I have nothing to tell you,' she almost snarled. 'I didn't want to come on this lousy trek in the first place. I've had nothing but grief since yesterday morning.'

Despite her words, she didn't walk away as he had suggested.

'Not enjoying the scenery?' Athreya gestured towards the rising mountains around them. 'It is a beautiful sight, and the day is perfect.'

'You didn't come here to talk about the mountains and the weather,' she sneered.

'Well… I did come to talk about the trek, you know,' he said conversationally, in complete contrast to her belligerence. 'Why did you come to Peter Dann, Purbhi?'

'It was Ipshita's idea. A foolish idea. She made me come.' She then fell to imitating and mocking her friend: '"Come, you'll love it, Purbhi. It'll do you a world of good!" Bullshit! I would have been happy at Peter Dann.'

'So, you like Peter Dann but dislike the trek? Why?'

'None of your bloody business! I don't need your approval to like or dislike anything.'

She glanced at her mobile phone in her hand and her scowl deepened. Her free hand adjusted her spectacles.

'Don't like the walking?' Athreya asked. 'Not enjoying being away from civilization? What—'

'It's for four bloody days! Four lousy days doing nothing but walk and be cut off from the world. Today is only the second day. We are not even halfway done!'

'Would you like to cut it short by two days?'

Her face jerked around to him. For a moment, the scowl vanished. Hope was writ large on her face.'

'You serious?' she demanded.

Athreya nodded.

'How?' she challenged.

'The trek is two days up to Top Camp and two days down. You reach your destination tonight and turn back tomorrow morning.'

'Yes, but it'll still take two days' walk back to the castle. Unless you teach me to ride a horse overnight and give me yours.'

'That won't be necessary. Javed has arranged for vehicles to take you back from Top Camp to Peter Dann.'

'Really?' It was a squeal of delight. Her manner changed abruptly. 'Really, Mr Athreya?'

'Upon my word.'

Her ferret face lit up with delight and she hugged him impulsively.

'This is the best news I've heard for ages! Thank you, Mr Athreya.' She broke into an embarrassed smile and her face softened. 'I'm sorry that I was rude to you. I shouldn't have been.'

'No need to apologize, Purbhi,' he smiled. 'Now, look around… aren't the mountains beautiful?'

'They are!' She took a deep breath and swept the vista with shining eyes. 'They are truly beautiful.'

'See? It is just a matter of your state of mind.'

She let out a self-conscious laugh.

'Now, tell me Purbhi. What has been bothering you? What has been making you so unhappy?'

She exhaled a long breath before replying.

'It doesn't matter, Mr Athreya. It's over and done with. I'm happy now and the mountains look lovely.'

'They look lovely from Nainital too, don't they?'

'Oh, yes! They do.' She caught herself on the verge of saying something and bit back her words. To her credit, she recovered in an instant and went on smoothly. 'You meant Peter Dann, didn't you? Not Nainital.'

'No, I meant Nainital. Didn't you notice that the mountains look charming from there too?'

'I don't know.' The answer was curt. 'I've never been there.'

He changed the topic to Mrinal's behaviour and asked her the same questions he had asked the others. He got nothing new from her. All she did was to confirm what Linda and Ipshita had said.

As she answered his questions, she was more interested in peering into her mobile phone than in talking to him. Speaking in monosyllables and short phrases, she offered minimal information.

By the end of the interview, he realized that what the three women had told him was remarkably similar. Not just in content, but also in the words they used. And all three had been clear that they had gone to their room at 11:15 p.m. and had not budged out after that.

The sameness in the three testimonies was probably because they were speaking the truth. It was equally possible that their testimonies had been rehearsed.

15

Sarosh was looking distinctly uncomfortable. Deprivation of his grooming paraphernalia and the comforts of his bedroom had left his usually polished appearance a little tarnished. His proud moustache drooped, its ends pointing to the green turf under his feet rather than to the azure sky above. The luxurious thatch of hair on the top and back of his head was in disarray and even the two mismatched earrings looked dull. Athreya wondered idly if the angel investor was vain enough to polish them every day.

Also gone were his self-assurance and loquacity that had characterized him in Athreya's mind. There was no doubt that he had watched, perhaps with nervousness, Athreya interviewing the others one by one. Speculation about the reason behind it must have occupied his thoughts for the past two hours. And so, when his turn came, Sarosh chose to listen than to speak first.

'Enjoying the trek?' Athreya asked as he and Sarosh strolled away from the others.

'Yes,' Sarosh replied unconvincingly. 'It is very pictur-esque. This is probably the most stunning scenery I've seen on hikes.'

'Been on many?'

'A few, but mostly in the Ghats. The Himalayas are something else.'

'How long have you known Mrinal?' Athreya asked out of the blue.

Sarosh blinked rapidly. A couple of seconds later, he

spoke.

'Why do you ask?' he queried.

'I'll tell you in a little while. I'm trying to understand something.'

'Well… maybe for a couple of years.'

'And Kinshuk?'

'About the same time, I guess. I met them separately. It was only later that I came to know that they were engaged.'

'How do you know them? Socially or professionally?'

'Professionally. Kinshuk is a very sharp guy—the kind of person I'd like to invest in. He and I are considering starting a chain of wellness centres.'

'Wellness centres?' Athreya asked. 'What are they?'

'Oh, an interesting concept where we combine multiple disciplines into an integrated wellness regime. In addition to the usual gym stuff, we'll offer yoga, meditation, Kerala oil massages and some other traditional approaches. We think there is a market for it, especially among the well-heeled. You could call them fitness studios.'

'You would provide the funding, I suppose, and Kinshuk would run the chain?'

'Yup. Same formula. He knows the fitness business inside out.'

'Is Mrinal involved in it too?'

Sarosh shook his head. 'No.'

'Then, what's your connection with Mrinal?'

'Nothing.' Sarosh's answer was immediate.

'Sure?'

'Sure.'

His tone was flat and brooked no challenge. There was no resentment or indignation at Athreya doubting his answer. It was as if he had expected the question, and was delivering his pre-prepared answer. Athreya let it pass.

'What brought you to Peter Dann?' he asked instead.

'I told you earlier—I came to scout for properties to invest in. I'm also considering an adventure-sports start-up.

Mountains and rivers are ideal for it.'

'And what about this trek?'

'That too. Three-in-one.'

'How did you discover Peter Dann?'

'Discover?' Sarosh turned an enquiring glance at Athreya.

'How did you come to know of Peter Dann?' Athreya explained. 'Did someone tell you about it? Did Kinshuk or Mrinal suggest it?'

'Oh, I see what you mean. No, nobody told me about it. I think I got an email or something. I had just started looking for hotels on the web when I got a message. You know how it works—companies spy on your surfing history and send you messages and emails about the topics you've googled.

'I checked out Peter Dann on the web, and it seemed a good place. The location was perfect and the photos looked nice. The website also mentioned treks, and I signed up for this one.'

'Did you know who the others would be when you signed up?'

'Nope. All I could see was how many slots were available.'

'So, when you got here, the others were strangers to you, right?'

Sarosh nodded.

'Were you in Nainital six weeks ago?' Athreya asked.

'Nope.'

Again, it was an immediate, incurious answer that felt pre-prepared. Sarosh did not want to know how Nainital entered the picture or why Athreya was asking the question out of nowhere.

'What did you think of Mrinal's behaviour during the party,' Athreya asked, changing track.

'What behaviour?' Sarosh asked. 'What do you mean?'

'Didn't you feel her behaviour was strange during the

party?'

Sarosh shrugged and shook his head.

'Didn't you think that it was strange that she went away to the terrace? In the middle of the party?'

'That's her choice. She wanted to go up, so she went up. What's the big deal?'

'Okay... what time did you turn in after the party?'

'Let's see... ' Sarosh frowned as he tried to recall. 'It was pretty late. Dhavak and I spent some time strolling on the lawn. I'd say, about 12:40 a.m. or so.'

'So 12:40 a.m.?' Athreya asked. 'That's a good hour and a half after the party wound up. What were you doing?'

'Oh, this and that.' Sarosh seemed to brush it off as unimportant. 'He and I hung around in the lounge for a while and checked our trekking gear and rucksacks in Room 2. We were shuttling between our rooms, the lounge and Room 2 while doing that. I then went to my room, but didn't feel sleepy. I heard Dhavak's door open and close, and realized that he too was still awake. We decided to go down for a stroll.'

'What time was that?'

'About 12:15 a.m. We walked around for about twenty-five minutes until we felt sleepy. We came up and I crashed.'

'Did you meet anyone?'

Sarosh nodded.

'We saw one of the staff boys on the ground floor before we went outside. I think there was also the security guard at the front door. There must have been a guard or two on the castle grounds as well.'

Athreya made a mental note to obtain corroboration. The staff boy was likely to be Ravi. He might have seen Sarosh and Dhavak just before going up to the rooftop terrace to ask Mrinal if she needed anything.

'The party wound down at about 11:10 p.m.,' Athreya went on. 'If you went out at 12:15 a.m., you were in the

lounge or your room for a little over an hour before you
went for your walk. Is that correct?'

'I guess so,' Sarosh replied nonchalantly.

'Did you go up to the terrace?'

'No. Whatever for?'

'Not even once?'

'Nope.'

'Did you see any of the women in the lounge?'

'After the party wound up? No. They went to their room
at 11:15 p.m. or so. The next I saw them was in the morning.'

Athreya terminated the discussion. His suspicion that
the four testimonies were rehearsed was turning into conviction. Each person's testimony was neatly confirming the
others'. Too neatly.

* * *

Athreya had left the thorniest interview to the end. Considering how the singer had rebuffed him at Land's End,
he was not sure if a discussion would even take place. But
now with his growing conviction that the five guests were
somehow hand in glove with each other, he suspected that
Dhavak would not pass up an opportunity to reinforce the
testimonies the other four had given. Nevertheless, he took
Javed with him.

'I thought I had said that we would keep out of each
other's way,' Dhavak began, in as hostile a tone as the one
three days ago. 'I have honoured my end of the bargain. I
expect you to do likewise.'

'It is not out of affection or a desire to befriend you
that I approach you,' Athreya replied without any trace of
rancour or resentment. 'I do it because I must. You probably know what it is about. I noticed that two of the women
have already talked to you after my chats with them. You
are not obliged to speak to me and are free to walk away.

I can't and won't stop you. However, know this: you have the choice of talking to me or to the ACP who awaits your return at Peter Dann. Javed will tell you that you are perhaps better off choosing me over her.'

'Indeed!' Dhavak mocked. 'You would say that.'

'Dhavak,' Javed rumbled before Athreya could respond. 'You don't know Athreya from Adam. That is perfectly understandable as you have never met him. But, if you ever wanted a fair-minded investigator to talk to when your back is against the wall, you would find no one better than him.

'I have worked with him for donkey's years. Let me assure you—bluntly—that he does not frame people. He would rather let the guilty go free than pin a crime on an innocent man. You cannot find a person with a stronger sense of fairness and justice than him. If you must place your faith in anyone, I suggest that you place it in him.'

Dhavak remained silent, thinking and staring unseeingly at a distant mountain ridge. He seemed to be taking Javed's counsel seriously.

'I don't as yet know why you resent the police,' Athreya added after a couple of silent moments. 'But be assured that I will find out in the next twenty-four hours. And once I do, the ACP will come to know of it as well.'

Dhavak grunted and turned his weary gaze to Athreya, studying him for a second or two before nodding.

'What do you want to know?' he asked gruffly.

'A number of things,' Athreya replied. 'But before I start, let me thank you for talking to me. It is so much easier this way.'

Dhavak nodded silently.

'The first thing I want to ask is about your name,' Athreya went on. 'When did you change it to Dhavak Strummer, and what was it before that.'

Anger flashed in the singer's eyes briefly before he brought it under control.

'Why?' he demanded.

'Because it is relevant to the matter at hand.'

'And what,' he challenged, 'is the matter at hand?'

'Your relationship with Mrinal,' Athreya answered evenly, his eyes not missing anything as they took in Dhavak's face and body language.

An angry flush rose to his heavily bearded face, and his eyes hardened as they stared at Athreya. The investigator returned the gaze unflinchingly. Half a minute passed in silence as Javed looked on. Abruptly, Dhavak turned and began walking uphill.

'We may as well walk while you interrogate me,' he growled.

Athreya and Javed hurried to catch up with him.

'What if I don't tell you?' Dhavak asked when the older men were abreast with him.

'It wouldn't go in your favour as far as the police are concerned. Chances are that we will have this information tomorrow morning anyway.'

'Okay.' Dhavak seemed to come to a decision. 'I changed it about three years ago.'

'In Dehradun?' Athreya asked.

Dhavak threw him an unfathomable glance. 'Yes.'

'What was your name before that?'

Dhavak inhaled deeply and let out his breath as he looked skywards. He brought his gaze down and kicked a small rock that happened to lie in his path. He cursed under his breath.

'I will tell you,' he conceded. 'But if it is not relevant to whatever you are investigating, you must keep it to yourself.'

'Why?'

'Because that was a different life!' Dhavak snapped. 'I am over and done with it. I never want to go back to it, and I am trying my best to forget it. Going back will serve no useful purpose to anyone. Least of all to me! That's why!'

'It's outside your and my control, Dhavak,' Athreya said

in a low voice. 'It's going to come out anyway. You may as well prepare for it.'

Dhavak cut loose a string of expletives as his eyes sought another rock to kick. Not finding any, he threw his trekking pole violently to the ground and then picked it up with a large hand. Athreya waited for him to regain control of himself.

'Okay,' Dhavak said at length. 'My name was Kumud… Kumud Malakar.' He gave it reluctantly, as if it was drawn painfully from him.

Something stirred at the back of Athreya's mind. The name was vaguely familiar. He had come across it a few years ago, but he couldn't remember the context. There seemed to be some association in his mind with Kolkata. He made a mental note to send out an enquiry as soon as he returned to Peter Dann.

'Thank you,' he said aloud. 'Why did you change it?'

'No.' Dhavak shook his head firmly. 'No. I am not going into that. You can find out what my earlier name was, but there is no document anywhere that tells you why I changed it.'

'Whatever caused you to change your name… was it the same thing that made you dislike the police too?'

'I am not going to talk about it,' Dhavak repeated.

'Okay.' Athreya nodded and let it go. 'Let me ask you another question: how long have you known Mrinal?'

Dhavak stopped in midstride and glared at Athreya.

'I never said I know her,' he hissed. His big hands were clenching and unclenching repeatedly. The trekking pole looked like a long pencil in his hand. 'Don't try to pin things on me.'

'No, you didn't say so,' Athreya agreed. 'But it's apparent that you and Mrinal know each other from before. Your song made her flee to the rooftop terrace.'

'You call that evidence?' Dhavak challenged. 'You jump to conclusions on something as flimsy as that and go about calling yourself an investigator?'

'I won't insult your intelligence by answering that. You know exactly what I mean.'

'Is there anything else you want to ask me?' Dhavak asked. It was apparent that he was not going to answer Athreya's latest question.

'Yes.'

He asked about Dhavak's movements on the evening of the party. Being a heavy smoker, the singer had gone to the terrace several times, but did not remember how many how often or at what time. However, he corroborated what Sarosh had said about packing and going for a walk, and confirmed the time at which they had gone down and when they had returned. Yes, a staff member and the security guard had seen them.

'I had no idea who the other trekkers would be,' he said when Athreya queried him on why and how he had chosen Peter Dann. 'I just picked it from the internet—it looked like a nice place. I spend a lot of my time in Dehradun and know Uttarakhand pretty well. I wander about quite a lot on my bike. I like the solitude of the mountains.'

'Have you been to Nainital?' Athreya asked.

'Several times.'

'Were you there six weeks ago?'

'Maybe,' Dhavak replied without hesitation. 'I don't have my diary here with me. So I can't say for sure. What's all this about?'

'I'll tell you shortly.'

* * *

Top Camp was situated on the eastern side of a hill, near the top. A huge outcrop of rock sheltered it from the winds that whipped over the top. The camp itself—a collection of tents and semi-permanent wooden structures—sat on a flat natural terrace protected under the outcrop. The ground sloped sharply away to the east to a long, lush valley that had a stream flowing at the bottom.

Beyond was a huge mountain that dwarfed their hill and the valley. It rose abruptly, often precipitously, for a couple of thousand feet before culminating in a craggy ridge that loomed over Top Camp. It was comprised of vast faces of flat rock at different angles, which were entirely devoid of vegetation. Even the toughest of grasses could not withstand the gales and the whirling snow that whipped the ridge day and night. Large parts were covered in ice.

This was the highlight of the trek; another spectacular show was in the offing at dusk.

As sunset approached, the group gathered at the centre of the terrace, facing eastwards. The crest of their hill had already cut off the sunlight, plunging the valley below into gloom. The rays from the gradually reddening sun lit the massive mountain ridge. In contrast, the valley below seemed almost as dark as night.

Athreya had witnessed the sunset over the Nanda Devi peak four evenings ago. He had watched the distant peak from far away. Now, he was about to witness a similar spectacle, but from very close up. The ridge that loomed over him filled his entire range of vision as he and Javed stood a dozen yards behind the others and watched the play of light on the mountain.

As the sunrays turned yellow, the ridge lit up as if it were made of gold, vast slabs of gold. Some gigantic faces of rock at right angles, reflected the sun onto the terrace like a mirror. Such was the brilliance of the reflected light that it cast shadows of the people on the terrace. Cameras and phones clicked away rapidly. Few words were spoken; only gasps of wonder and delight.

Gold turned to orange and then to red as darkness crept steadily upwards from the valley towards the ridge. The shadow line quickened as it climbed, and scaled the last few hundred yards so swiftly that it was almost as if the plug had been pulled on the show.

Abruptly, they found themselves in darkness, except for the fire and the reflected light from high clouds. After a brief period of stunned silence, excited talk erupted.

Athreya watched the others in the light of the campfire. Sarosh was attired in high-end gear, with exclusive shoes, pole, rucksack, jacket and tracks. Even to Athreya's lay eyes, his outfit seemed more expensive that the others'.

Ipshita, on the other hand, although wearing mid-range stuff, looked as graceful as at Peter Dann. Somehow, her jacket and tracks, like everything else she wore, seemed to suit her. She looked attractive even from the distance and in the gloom. Her school friend, however, was scruffier than ever.

Asma and Linda, with the similar stature and body structure, looked like sisters. Except for the colours, their tracks and jackets were very similar. Dhavak was no different from before, except he had traded his dark, rumpled jeans for dark, rumpled tracks, but the rest of him looked the same.

Ten minutes after the show on the ridge ended, dinner was brought out and placed on an iron contraption over the campfire to keep the food hot. The hungry group wasted no time in digging into it. Even as they ate, the food on their plates cooled rapidly as the cold air stole the warmth within minutes.

Fifteen minutes later, expectant gazes began turning towards Athreya. It was time for the promised explanation of his interrogation. He gestured towards chairs arranged around the campfire, inviting everyone to sit.

Athreya chose to stand behind his chair with his hands resting lightly on its back. Stooping with weariness at the end of a hard day, and with his fine hair thrown into disarray by the incessant wind, he looked like a slender weeping willow tree. No amount of running his long fingers through the mane restored order. The cold, dry wind had robbed it of all moisture.

The five guests were in chairs on the other side of the campfire from Athreya, while Asma joined her father to Athreya's left. To his right were Maazin and Chetan. The reason Athreya was standing despite his tiredness was to have a clear view of the five faces. He wanted to see their reactions when he told them about Mrinal's death.

'I told you that there had been an incident at Peter Dann,' he began, speaking slowly and clearly so that there was no misunderstanding. 'But I did not tell you what the incident was. I will say it now.'

He paused for a moment to ensure that he had the undivided attention of all of them. When he was sure, he delivered it bluntly and without preamble.

'Mrinal,' he said,' is dead.'

As soon as he said it, he scanned their faces, as he knew Javed too would be doing. He focused on the five guests, throwing only quick glances at Asma and Maazin. He was not sure what he had expected, but what he saw left him stunned.

He was stunned because he saw no expression on any of the five faces. They returned his stare, showing no surprise or trepidation at the announcement, or at what it could potentially mean to them. They had absorbed the news without any semblance of shock or surprise.

To his right, he saw Maazin's mouth fall open. The young man stared at Athreya in horror before exclaiming, 'I'm sorry,' he said. 'I don't think I heard you right.'

'You heard me right, Maazin,' Athreya replied, as he threw a quick glance at his shocked face. 'Mrinal is dead.'

'When?' Maazin asked.

'On the night of the party.'

Athreya's eyes were still scanning the five faces before him as he spoke. Still no expression had yet registered on them.

'Then, I guessed right,' Asma said from his left. There

was unmistakable sorrow in her voice. 'How did she die?'

'She fell from the rooftop terrace.' Athreya's diction was clear and precise.

A gasp and a groan sounded simultaneously. Maazin's face contorted with a tortured moan. There was no doubt in Athreya's mind that it was genuine. There was palpable pain in it.

The gasp had come from Asma. Through the corner of his eye, he saw her clutch Javed's muscular arm and lean on him.

'Same place?' he heard her ask her father in an agonized whisper.

Javed nodded. He wrapped an arm around her shoulders and drew her to him. With a sob, Asma buried her face in her father's chest. Athreya resolutely kept his gaze away from them. This was a time of private grief. The inescapable similarity between Naira's and Mrinal's deaths must be heart-wrenching for Asma.

But what made Athreya's heart sink was not her anguish. Rather, it was the complete lack of reaction from the five guests. That could mean only one thing—that they already knew of Mrinal's death. Not only that, but they also knew of the manner in which she died. Athreya felt a cold hand touch his spine.

Ipshita was the first of the five to realize that some sort of a response was called for.

'I'm really sorry to hear that,' she said. 'I guess it must have been an accident.' She threw a quick glance at Asma and lowered her voice. 'I believe it has happened before.'

'We don't know yet,' Athreya replied. 'It's too early to draw any conclusions. There is nothing to tell us if it was an accident, suicide… or murder.'

The last word finally elicited responses from the five. Shock and dismay sprang to four faces. A mouth fell open and three hands flew to three mouths. Four pairs of eyes flew wide open and stared at him in horror as the implication sank in. For the moment, they had been rendered speechless.

But not the fifth guest. His jaw was clenched and his eyes were ablaze with fury.

'So, that's why you came here,' Dhavak snarled, rising from his chair and glowering at Athreya in unbridled anger. His large hands were clenched into fists and his head was thrust forward pugnaciously. 'That's why you interrogated us.'

He rose to his full height and laid a protective hand on the shoulder of the woman sitting beside him.

'Don't let his honeyed words fool you, Ipshita,' he growled. 'He wants to pin it on one of us.'

16

Athreya sat on the chilly hillside early the next morning, warming himself with a hot mug of tea and soaking up the slanting sunrays. The sun had cleared the high mountain ridge to the east and was bathing Top Camp and the valley below with wholesome warmth.

A short distance away, Maazin and Chetan were preparing to ride the two horses back to Peter Dann. Two 4x4 vehicles had just arrived to ferry the rest of them over a combination of dirt tracks and potholed roads.

As Athreya watched Maazin and Chetan making their final preparations, Asma emerged from her tent, wrapped in a thick, hooded jacket. She came to Athreya and pulled up a plastic chair to sit beside him.

'How was the night?' he asked her, as he gazed at the two horses that seemed impatient to start.

'Not good, I'm afraid,' she replied. 'I took a long time to get sleep. But once it came, it thankfully knocked me out for four hours.'

'How did the others in your tent sleep?'

'Fitfully, I think. Linda was crying. One or two of them muttered in their sleep. They were uneasy after your news last evening.'

'Guilty conscience?' Athreya suggested.

'Why do you say that?' Asma turned to study his face, as he continued looking at the impatient horses. 'You don't think that one of them had anything to do with Mrinal's death, do you?'

'It's too early to say anything definitive, Asma.'

'Yes, but… surely, none of them could have… would have… ' She left the sentence unfinished.

A dozen yards away, Maazin mounted the black horse and waved to Asma before riding away. Chetan followed him on the dun. Asma and Athreya watched them in silence as they rode up the hill and disappeared over the crest. Once they were out of sight, Athreya turned to Asma.

'I'm sure you noticed it last night,' he said.

'Noticed what, Uncle?'

Her question was unconvincing; a feeble attempt to delay acknowledging a grave matter.

'The reaction of the five guests to the news of Mrinal's death.'

'But there was no reaction.' Her tone was diffident.

'Exactly.' Athreya paused, as he turned his gaze away from her face to the mountain ridge. 'What does that tell you?'

She remained silent, staring down at the valley.

'The only possible explanation,' Athreya went on, 'is that they already knew of Mrinal's death. Agree?'

Asma thought for a long moment and nodded wordlessly.

'How could they have known when your father and I discovered the death only at noon? You all had already departed for the trek; you were long gone. Nobody called you or Maazin. Everyone at Peter Dann was instructed not to spread the news. Besides, the only people who were surprised were you and Maazin.—And Chetan, of course, but he is an outsider. How is it that your five guests knew of Mrinal's death but you and Maazin didn't?'

Asma shook her head, still not trusting herself to speak.

'Nor were the five surprised at *how* Mrinal had died. It was no run-of-the-mill accident. They couldn't have guessed it.'

Asma finally found her voice.

175

'Maybe they had no interest in Mrinal?' she suggested. 'That's why they didn't react.'

'No, Asma. They were interested enough to stop talking abruptly when Mrinal came to the lounge. They stared at her for a long moment with considerable attention.'

'Where does this lead, Uncle?' Asma whispered. 'One of the five is my close friend. Linda wouldn't harm a fly. All this seems to implicate her too.'

'It does,' he agreed. 'That's all the more reason for us to clear up this affair.'

'Us?' Her eyes searched his face.

'I need your help, Asma. You are one of the very few who is in the clear.'

'Why?

'Because I believe that you didn't know Mrinal before she checked in at Peter Dann.' His thoughts went to the burnt fragment of the photo burnt at Pottersfield. 'Because death was probably stalking her before she came there.'

'What about Dad?'

'The similarity between Mrinal's death and your mother's imposes some... er... concerns about him.'

Her eyes grew wide as the import sank in.

'Uncle!' she gasped. 'You can't suspect Dad!'

'Not me, Asma. The police are at Peter Dann. An ACP has come for the precise reason that the two deaths are very similar.'

Asma's hand shot out and grabbed Athreya's arm.

'Uncle!' she pleaded. 'You *must* clear his name. He is innocent! What would he have to do with Mrinal? He had only just met her—the same reason you cleared me.'

Athreya nodded. 'I know.'

'Mum's death was an accident,' Asma went on. Her fingernails dug into his arm, but she didn't seem to realize it. He bore it silently. 'I *know* that it was an accident. She was depressed but she would *never* have jumped from the roof. The family name was too dear to her. She knew that sui-

cide would make things difficult for Dad and me. She bore
her burden with great fortitude, Uncle. She was a *strong*
woman, very strong. And she knew that she was setting me
an example of never giving up. She assured me—several
times—that she wouldn't do anything rash. It came from
her heart.

'She fell because of the drugs she was taking. It made
her drowsy and unsteady. She had grown frightfully thin in
the last couple of years—almost emaciated. She must have
stumbled and fallen through the crenellations. That's how
thin she had become.'

Silently the tears streamed down her face. She let go of
Athreya's arm and wiped her face, leaving three red marks
on his arm.

'So you see, Asma,' he asked in a voice that didn't carry
beyond her, 'why you must help me? There is so much I
don't know and I can't ask. And there is your close friend
over whom a cloud hangs. Remember what I said at dinner
the other night? If a crime remains unsolved, it can have
very nasty side effects. You don't want that to happen to a
friend.'

'Then, you have decided that a crime has been committed?'

'I don't know yet, but I'll find out. Now, will you help
me?'

Asma nodded. 'Yes, I will. But you'll have to tell me
what to do.'

'I will. Meanwhile, get Linda to talk to you. Don't press
her too much. Assume that she is innocent. It will be easier
for you that way.'

'I'll see what I can do.' She thrust her hand into her
jacket pocket. 'But first, I have something for you—there
has been a development in one of your little mysteries.'

'My mystery?' Athreya asked.

In response, she pulled out something from her pocket.
It was flat, rectangular and dark blue in colour. She held it

out for him.

'My power bank!' Athreya exclaimed as he took it. 'Where did you find it?'

'In my backpack. Someone put it there.'

'When?'

'Last night. It wasn't there yesterday.'

Athreya frowned as his mind began racing. New possibilities flashed past his mind's eye even as his right index finger began tracing indecipherable words on his knee. Asma sat still, watching him. A full minute passed.

Abruptly, Athreya looked up.

'Do you have your phone with you?' he asked.

'Yes.'

'Show me.'

Asma pulled out it from the other pocket. Athreya's eyes went to the one thing he wanted to see.

'The battery is low,' he pointed out.

'Again?' Asma exclaimed and turned the phone to see the screen. 'It's almost gone! I charged it last evening and didn't use it at all. It was switched off all night.'

'How was it yesterday morning?' Athreya asked. 'Before you recharged it?'

'It had less than ten per cent charge. That's why I plugged it into my power bank.'

'How much charge did it have the evening before that?'

'About eighty per cent full. I had switched it off before sleeping, but it was almost fully discharged in the morning. I guess I need to change the battery.'

'Let me guess,' Athreya said in a low voice. 'You are one of the few here who has a BSNL connection.'

BSNL was a government-run mobile operator that had a developmental objective. They were the only company that served the remote, sparsely populated areas of the vast country that were intrinsically unprofitable.

Asma nodded. 'Apart from Maazin and Chetan. You get only BSNL's signal in the hills. None of the others has a

BSNL connection.'

'Check your call history.'

A minute later, Asma shook her head as she scrolled through her calls.

'It's fine,' she said. 'The last calls it shows are the ones I made yesterday.'

'Your browser history?'

She tapped the phone a couple of times and her brow gathered into a frown.

'Blank,' she said. 'No browsing history.'

'Did you clear it recently?'

'No. I can't remember the last time I cleared the history on *this* phone. I use the other phone at home.'

'Ah!' A faint smile brightened his face as his finger traced a name on his knee. 'Your battery is fine, Asma. You don't need to change it.'

'No?'

Athreya's smile broadened.

'You have cleared up one riddle,' he said. 'Elimination is a wonderful thing. Eliminating one riddle makes the remaining ones a little clearer.'

* * *

On his return, Athreya found much information waiting for him at Peter Dann. His mobile had started beeping half an hour before reaching the castle, as soon as his mobile began receiving the network signal. He had several WhatsApp and email messages, some of which had attachments. But he refrained from opening them as a quiet and pensive Linda was sitting next to him.

He found Shivali waiting for him as soon as he got to the castle. She had been busy in his absence and had news for him. She was also impatient to know what he had discovered. She buttonholed him and took him to the study on the ground floor, where the police doctor was awaiting them. He turned out to be an elderly, stooping man with round glasses. He had performed the autopsy and had come to share his findings with Shivali.

'The deceased had multiple fractures, including in her skull, neck and spine,' he summarized. 'Any one of them would have been fatal. The injuries are consistent with a fall from a great height. Bruising and flesh wounds are present in the area of impact where she hit the rock. There are no knife wounds and there is no evidence of strangulation.'

'Drugs, sedatives or poison?' Shivali asked.

The doctor shook his head. 'None,' he said. 'There was alcohol in the blood, though. The level was not high enough for her to be inebriated.'

'Did you examine the head wounds in detail, as Mr Athreya had requested?'

'Yes, I did,' the doctor said, adjusting his glasses. 'It's interesting because there are two severe wounds—one on the back of the head and the other to the front and left. The skull is fractured in both places.'

'Why is it interesting?' Shivali asked.

'I am not sure how the deceased acquired *two* skull fractures on *opposite* sides of the head when her fall would have caused a single impact. The injury to the front left of the skull has a large impact area—about the size of my palm. The bone underneath has been crushed, and the scalp there torn and partially sheared off. That is what we expect in cases of a fall from a great height. But the impact area of the other injury—the one at the back of the head—is small and focused. Also, the tear in the scalp is narrower than expected. Such an injury is not consistent with a two-hundred-plus-foot fall.'

'Excellent!' Athreya breathed. 'Did you examine the second injury in detail?'

'Yes, sir,' the doctor went on, adjusting his glasses reflectively and speaking slowly. 'When I examined it under a lens, I found two small fragments embedded in it. One was a tiny sliver of glass that had partially embedded itself into the scalp. The other was a small piece of paper caught between the glass and the scalp. Was that what you had expected, Mr Athreya?'

'That's what I had *feared*,' he mumbled.

His brows were drawn down in intense concentration. Several bits of facts were swirling in his mind, trying to fit themselves into a pattern. Was the injury at the back of Mrinal's head inflicted *before* she fell? If so, by what? And by whom?

His right index finger had once again acquired a mind of its own. It was scribbling away on the desk before him, writing invisible words. Shivali and the doctor watched him silently.

All of a sudden, the penny dropped in Athreya's mind. His head jerked up and his eyes locked onto the doctor's face.

'Was the paper yellow in colour?' he asked.

'Yes!' The doctor blinked at him in surprise. 'How did you know?'

'A hunch.' Athreya leaned back in his chair. His face had cleared. 'And my second request?'

'The lab is looking into it, sir. I haven't heard back from them yet.'

'Have you been able to narrow the window for the time of the death?'

The doctor shook his head.

'Unfortunately not. At least eighteen hours had elapsed by the time I examined the body. My best estimate is that death took place between 11 p.m. and 3 a.m. I don't think that helps you very much.'

'Thank you, doctor.'

Once he had left the study, Shivali turned to Athreya.

'So,' she said, 'Mrinal was hit on the head before she fell.'

'Possibly. The only other possibility is that she hit her head twice during the fall.'

'Which is unlikely. How did you know that the paper was yellow?'

'Like I said, it was a guess. Let me sort out my thoughts before I speak about it.'

Shivali acquiesced and asked him about his interviews with the trekkers. He summarized his findings, and once he finished, she pulled out a sheet of paper.

'This is a summary of what we have been able to gather about Mrinal so far,' she said. 'What we have is sketchy, but I think it's a decent start. We'll add more details once we meet her colleagues and bankers. We will be searching her Mumbai flat as well.

'Mrinal was thirty-two-years-old and hailed from North 24 Parganas in West Bengal, near Kolkata. Her parents were killed during riots in September 2010. You may remember the riots that swept North 24 Parganas district, in which arson was rampant. Many buildings were razed to the ground by the rioters, including Mrinal's house. Her parents were trapped inside when it burned down.

'She has a brother by the name of Pralay, whom we are trying to trace. He is her next of kin. We haven't been able to locate any other relatives so far. Her parents' assets passed on to Mrinal and Pralay. As Pralay was a minor, Mrinal managed the inheritance.

'We were told that she was prudent and conservative in investing the money. By all accounts, she looked after the inheritance well. She tried her hand at a couple of business-es and did reasonably well. She sold two businesses at a modest profit before she set up the current one—an online education business that focuses on teaching English, mu-sic and life skills. This start-up has done very well. As the business grew, she shifted the head office to Mumbai, but retained a small office in Kolkata. That's when she moved to Mumbai. I don't have the exact date, but it was three or four years ago.

'After going to Mumbai, she has managed to raise two

rounds of funding for her start-up. It has now spread to five countries outside India which have an underserved need for English and music education. I believe the start-up is valued at several million dollars.'

'Several million dollars?' Athreya echoed in surprise. 'She was a wealthy woman, then. Somebody stands to gain handsomely by her death.'

'Her brother, in all probability. Unless she has made a will to the contrary. Guess it's unlikely that such a young person would have written a will.' Shivali dropped the paper and looked up at Athreya. 'That's what we have on Mrinal so far. We'll get more soon.'

'That's a lot of information, Shivali,' Athreya remarked. 'You have done a good job. From what you said, there is one area I would like to probe in more detail.'

'What's that?' she asked.

'The rioting incident in which her parents died. Can we get the Kolkata police to obtain every little scrap of information related to the incident? Who were the neighbours? What did they see? What do they say about the tragedy? Was the fire really due to arson and rioting, or were there some other whispers? Was anyone apart from Mrinal's parents affected by the fire? How did Mrinal and Pralay cope after the tragedy? Who were the neighbours or relatives who helped them? Find out *everything* you can, and get hold of contact numbers on which we can speak to them.'

'Got it, sir. I'll do it right away. One of my ex-colleagues is with Kolkata Police. Meanwhile, I have some more news for you. We found an empty strip of Nitrosun 10 mg tablets in one of the wastepaper baskets in the lounge. Nitrosun is a brand name for nitrazepam, a drug that is used for inducing sleep. It is given for insomnia and certain mental disorders, I am told.

'As soon as we found the strip, I had the dregs of your liqueur glass tested specifically for nitrazepam. Bingo! The drug was there. You seem to have ingested a pretty strong dose of it, sir.'

'The strip was found in the lounge?' Athreya asked. 'Then, it could have been discarded by anyone.'

'Correct.' Shivali's voice dropped a notch. 'We also searched the rooms and belongings of the guests to see if any of them uses Nitrosun. We found nothing.'

'It is unlikely that the person who drugged me would have retained the drug in his or her possession. That would be a dead giveaway. Everyone had access to the lounge. It is a good place to get rid of the strip.'

'Did you notice anything about the guests that suggests that one of them has sleep problems, sir?'

'No.'

'How about Purbhi? You said that she was behaving strangely. Maybe, it was withdrawal symptoms after taking nitrazepam. What you described sounds like that.'

'Possibly, but I doubt it. Asma didn't say anything in particular about Purbhi. All of them had difficulty sleeping last night after hearing about Mrinal. Did you have Kinshuk's brandy glass tested too? And his blood sample?'

'I've asked them to do it, but there has been some delay. Apparently, additional testing is required for his glass. The blood testing might take another day.'

'Okay.'

'The next thing I wanted to tell you is that Mrinal's mobile phone is still untraceable,' Shivali went on. 'It is switched off and we have not been able to find it anywhere. We've searched the terrace, her room, the lounge and the entire castle.'

'What about the spot where she fell?'

'There too, sir. We thoroughly searched the entire area within a hundred feet from where she fell. We also used a metal detector. Of course, there is dense undergrowth, and the phone might be particularly well-hidden, but my gut feel is that it isn't there. It's a pity that we can't find it. We could have got her brother's number from it. But we found some other things that are a little puzzling.'

'Such as?'

'A hammer, a coil of strong nylon rope of the kind trekkers use, a couple of wooden pegs that would be hammered into the ground to tie down tents and a pair of gloves. All of them look as if they have recently fallen.'

'Trekking supplies?' Athreya mused. 'We should ask Chetan and Maazin if they are missing any of these.'

'One of my men is doing that as we speak. We will know shortly—'

The ringing of her phone interrupted Shivali.

'Ah!' she said, glancing at it. 'Dr Farha is calling. She was the psychiatrist who treated Mrs Rais. I asked her to call me when she had a few minutes.'

She answered the phone and put it on speaker. Dr Farha spoke slowly and in a pleasant voice. It was the kind of neutral, unthreatening tone Athreya had heard doctors adopt with patients. Once the initial pleasantries were over, Shivali took charge of the conversation.

'I've read the report you submitted after Naira Rais's death,' she said. 'But you have left one crucial question unanswered.'

'What is that?' the doctor asked.

'Whether the death was an accident or suicide.'

'As I had said to the investigating officer then,' Dr Farha replied, 'I have no basis for making that judgement.'

'Mrs Rais was acutely depressed,' Shivali protested. 'Isn't it likely that she committed suicide?'

'Ms Suyal, if you were to look at the statistics, you will find that the number of depression cases in India is *very* high. It runs into millions. Some surveys claim that as many as one in fifty adults suffer from some form of it. Yet, how many depression-induced suicides do we have in the country? Only a *very* small fraction of depressed people die by suicide.'

'Then, you believe it was an accident?'

'As I said, I have no basis for a judgement and I will not be drawn into speculation. All I can offer are the facts and my professional opinion. I've done that to the fullest extent I could in my report and in subsequent discussions. Please also note that in addition to depression, Mrs Rais suffered from other mental ailments too. It was a complex situation that the layperson simplifies by calling it "depression".'

'You would have known your patient well. You treated her for years. You must have *some* view, Doctor.'

'I used to visit Naira once every month or couple of months. The last time I had seen her was seventeen days before her death. I therefore did not know her state of mind on the day she died. Without that knowledge, it is impossible for me to form an informed view.

'Mood swings are common among the depressed. A patient may be normal one day, even mildly elated, as anti-depressants do their job. But she might become acutely depressed in a couple of days. Seventeen days is a *long* time. Besides, external stimuli have a huge impact on the patient. Good news can lift her mood and bad news could worsen it.'

'Doctor Farha,' Athreya interposed. 'If you were seeing Naira only every month or two, who was administering her medicines? Was she doing it herself or was it someone else? Did she have a nurse looking after her?'

'No. No nurse. She would self-administer under Javed's supervision. Being a psychologist, he understood the medicines and their purposes very well. He knew exactly what needed to be done. If there was any aberration in Naira's behaviour, he would call me, and I would adjust the dosage over the phone. Javed ensured that he had sufficient stock of medicines to cover all eventualities, including the medicines that were used in an ad hoc manner.'

'How did the medicines affect her physically?'

'As you may know,' Dr Farha said, 'these drugs make you lethargic and unsteady. They may cause trembling of limbs and dizziness. Occasionally, we also see uncontrolled movements.'

'In that case,' Athreya asked, 'shouldn't Naira have avoided the rooftop terrace?'

'Indeed. I repeatedly advised her not to go up there and not to go near other precipitous drops like at Land's End.'

'And what was her reaction?'

'Naira would smile and say nothing. But I knew that she was in the habit of spending time on both. She was confident that she could handle herself. Javed and I understood why she liked the terrace. When she was depressed, she felt boxed in by her mental burdens. Sunlight, the sight of the open sky and the expansive mountains had a therapeutic effect on her.'

'I can imagine,' Athreya concurred. 'Doctor, you spoke of ad hoc medicines. Can you give me an example?'

'High dosage tablets, for instance. Let's say that she was normally taking a 2.5 mg tablet of a particular drug. Javed kept a stock of 5 mg and 10 mg tablets of the same drug, which were to be used if her condition suddenly deteriorated—giving her one tablet is far easier than administering four. He also kept a stock of supplementary medicines that she did not take daily. These were taken episodically, as and when needed.'

'I see.' Athreya's face grew grim. 'Like a sedative, if Naira was unable to sleep?'

'Exactly,' Dr Farha replied. 'That's a good example.'

'What was the sedative you had prescribed, Doctor? Do you remember?'

'Yes, I do. It was Nitrosun 10 mg.'

17

Athreya found Maazin and Chetan in the hall as he came out of the study. He took them aside and asked if they had found anything missing from the supplies they had taken on the trek.

'Yes,' Maazin confirmed. 'Chetan usually carries some tools, just in case there is an emergency. A hammer, nylon cord, gloves and a couple of tent pegs are missing.'

'When did they go missing?' Athreya asked in Hindi, turning to Chetan.

'I had checked them the evening before the trip,' the short and wiry man replied, also in Hindi. For once, he wasn't smiling or grinning. 'Nothing was missing then.'

'What time was that?'

'At about 9 p.m. The party was going on then.'

'Where were these items kept?'

'In the outer pockets of my rucksack, which was with the other backpacks in Room 2.'

'Was that the last time you checked?'

Chetan nodded. 'I didn't check the next morning or during the trek. I had no reason to suspect that anything might have been removed.'

'The police showed you a hammer, rope, gloves and pegs. Were they the ones that were missing?'

He nodded again, making his hair fall over his eyes.

Leaving them, Athreya went out of the castle and onto the lawn. So, someone had taken the items after 9 p.m. There was no way to tell if they had been stolen during the party or after it. If they had anything to do with Mrinal's death, the theft might have happened after the party, when everyone had retired to their rooms.

How did that fit in with the testimonies he had heard? And what role did these items play in Mrinal's death? Somehow, he felt that it didn't fit with the fragmented patterns that had been forming in his mind. Once he was out of earshot of the castle, he parked the questions aside and pulled out his mobile phone. He had something to do right now. He plugged his earphones in and called a Kolkata number.

After interviewing the trekkers, he had borrowed Asma's BSNL phone at Top Camp the previous evening and called a man in Kolkata. He had asked him to find out as much as he could about Kumud Malakar. On Athreya's return to Peter Dann, he had found a WhatsApp message waiting for him. He called the Kolkata man.

'Your Kumud Malakar is a disgraced man,' the contact said. 'But nobody has seen or heard from him for three or four years. He seems to have disappeared from Kolkata.'

'Why was he disgraced?' Athreya asked.

'About four years ago, he was booked under sections 354A and 509—sexual harassment and acts intended to insult the modesty of a woman. While in police custody, he became violent and assaulted a couple of constables. In retaliation, a bunch of policemen beat him up badly and left him lying on his cell floor. They also drafted charges against him for physically assaulting police officers. Eventually, he was released on a personal bond paid by his father, who is a wealthy tea plantation owner.'

'The details of why he was booked in the first place?'

'He was picked up after a complaint by a female colleague whom he threatened and verbally abused. He used obscene language and also threatened her physically. Take a look at the four photos I've sent to you. They were taken by the woman as he abused her.'

As the Kolkata man spoke, Athreya scrolled through his WhatsApp messages and tapped on the photos. The first photo showed a handsome, clean-shaven man with his mouth open in a snarl. He was glaring at the camera and seemed to be shouting at the person taking the photo. Angry lines etched his face. The second photo showed his face and shoulders as if he had come closer to the photographer. More anger was evident on the face. The third and fourth photos were taken from further away, but showed the man advancing threateningly.

There was no mistaking the face despite it being clean-shaven—it was Dhavak. So, this was his run-in with the police. Was that the reason he hated them?

'There are two more photos which have been withheld at the woman's request,' the man in Kolkata went on. 'They were taken after the assault and show her shirt torn at the neck and shoulder.'

'Any idea why Kumud assaulted her?' Athreya asked.

'He had apparently taken a fancy to her. They had been working together on a project for a few months, often late into the night. He might have felt encouraged by her willingness to be alone with him in the evening. This assault took place late one Saturday evening when they were alone in the office. When he assaulted her, she ran from the office and tried to lodge a complaint at the local police station. Apparently, they wouldn't take her complaint.

'That night, the woman took to Facebook and posted these photos and gave details of what had happened. The post went viral and even the chief minister's office commented on it, praising the woman for standing up to the molester. A film actress also weighed in. Within twenty-four hours, the police acted.

'However, the woman decided not to pursue a case against Kumud. She said that he had already received his punishment, and she had no desire to punish him any further. She refused to file a written complaint and asked the police to close the investigation.

'Kumud was released from jail and went to his father's tea estate. Soon, the affair faded from public memory and Kumud also disappeared. He hasn't been seen or heard from since.'

'The woman whom Kumud assaulted… do you know her name?'

'Yes, sir. Mrinal Shome.'

* * *

While Athreya was busy with Shivali and his other discussions, Asma was dealing with her own worries, which she did not share with Athreya. They were about Linda.

When Asma had returned to her tent after talking to Athreya that morning at Top Camp, she had crossed a fuming Ipshita storming away from the tent. When she entered the tent, Purbhi was glaring at Linda. As soon as Asma stepped in, Purbhi followed Ipshita out.

Asma found that her sleeping bag had been neatly rolled up in her absence. Linda had done that when she had rolled up her own sleeping bag. When Asma had turned to thank Linda, she found her sitting on the floor in a corner and crying quietly.

'Linda,' she had exclaimed, crouching beside her distressed friend, 'what's the matter?'

Linda had shaken her head and said nothing. But she was clutching her silver cross with one hand—a sure sign of distress. There was little doubt in Asma's mind that something had happened between Linda and the two women who had just marched out. Harsh words had probably been exchanged.

'Did Ipshita or Purbhi say something to you?' she asked softly, as she laid a hand on her friend's shoulder.

'It doesn't matter,' Linda had replied. She had then risen and wiped her face with her hanky. 'Come, let's take our rucksacks to the Jeep.'

'You are riding with me!' Asma had declared.

She had bundled Linda into her father's Jeep Compass and ensured that she, Linda, Javed and Athreya went in it. She wanted to keep Linda away from Purbhi and Ipshita. They and the two male guests had no option but to ride in the other vehicle.

For much of the journey to Peter Dann, Linda had clutched Asma's hand as she sat between her and Athreya. She had been fingering her cross with the other hand. She had said very little and had stifled her sobs so that the men didn't learn of her distress.

Asma had not known why Linda was distraught, but knew her friend well enough to sense her anguish was deep. That the torment had been caused by the others, she had no doubt. She had seen Purbhi throw angry glances at Linda before the two vehicles left. Ipshita and Dhavak too had looked towards Linda several times, and Asma thought that she saw worry on Ipshita's face.

As soon as the Jeep had reached the castle, Asma had whisked Linda to her bedroom on the ground floor so that she would be away from the others. There, she sat her down and talked to her.

'You are safe now,' Asma said. 'Nobody will trouble you here. Tell me what happened.'

'It's okay, Asma,' Linda said in a small voice. 'I'll be fine.'

'You had an argument with those two, didn't you? And they were nasty to you.'

Linda bit her lip and nodded.

'Something they said hurt you,' Asma went on. 'What was it?'

'Please, Asma... don't ask... please?'

'Why not? I'll help you. You *know* that I'll help you.'

'I know... but I can't tell... I can't... *please*.'

Asma realized what her friend's dilemma was. Whatever

the disagreement was, it was of a nature that prevented Linda from confiding in Asma. At the same time, Linda didn't want to lie to her friend. That's why she was pleading with Asma not to ask her. Along with this realization came another insight.

'Fine, I won't ask,' she said. 'But it seems to me that you are thinking of Aaron.'

At the mention of her late brother's name, Linda cracked. A sob burst through her lips and tears began cascading down her face. Asma leaned forward and hugged her. Linda buried her face in Asma's shoulder and let go. For several minutes, they remained thus. Nothing needed to be said—the two friends understood each other very well. At length, Linda disengaged herself.

'Mrinal committed suicide,' she whispered. 'Just like Aaron.'

Asma remained silent, holding her friend's hand. She wondered why Linda had concluded that: was it because of the similarity of her death to Naira's? Or was it something else?

'What goes around, comes around,' Linda added so softly that Asma could hardly hear it. It was almost as if she was talking to herself.

Asma remained silent but her mind was racing. What did that mean? Was there a connection between Aaron's death and Mrinal's? When Asma had asked her earlier, Linda had said that Aaron hadn't known Mrinal. What was Linda hiding?

'Poor Aaron,' Linda went on. 'He needn't have died. None of this need have happened. We would have been so happy.' She looked up at Asma. 'I'm sorry, Asma. I shouldn't bother you with all this.'

'Don't be silly, girl. What would I have done without you in Gurgaon after Mum's death? I too went through difficult patches. Both of us understand what it means to lose someone close. Why do you think Mrinal also committed suicide?'

Linda shook her head and didn't answer. Asma let it pass. She had something else in mind, something that would help the devout Linda. At the same time, it could also help Athreya's investigation if she was lucky.

'Linda,' she asked, 'would you like to go to a church?'

Linda's head jerked up in surprise.

'Is there one close by?'

Asma nodded. 'I can take you there if you wish.'

'Would you? Oh, *thank you*, Asma. Thank you. Will it be open now?'

'I think so. Would you like to go right away?'

Linda nodded. 'Can we, please?'

A short while later, they were in the Jeep, with Asma at the wheel. They rode in silence. Asma had accompanied Linda to a church many times when they had been together in Gurgaon. A devout girl, Linda always found solace there and came away feeling stronger and happier. It was always the same routine—both of them would go into the church and Asma would sit silently a few feet away as Linda prayed. Once she finished, they would rise and leave the church. No words were exchanged.

Fifteen minutes later, they were in the tiny church a few kilometres away from Peter Dann. Linda sat in the front pew with her head bowed as Asma sat in the pew behind her. From time to time, a slight shudder seemed to pass through Linda. She prayed silently, spending more time today that she had usually done in Gurgaon. Asma waited.

After twenty minutes, Linda rose and nodded to Asma. Her face was clear, as if a burden had been lifted. They left the church without a word. Once on the road, Linda spoke.

'I'm stronger now,' she said. Her voice had lost the tremor it had acquired since her quarrel with Ipshita and Purbhi. 'I can face them. Thank you, Asma. You are like a sister to me.'

Asma reached out and squeezed Linda's hand.

'I owe you an explanation—' Linda began when Asma gently cut her off.

'No, you don't,' she said. 'Don't feel compelled to say anything.'

'Don't worry, I am not feeling compelled. I just want to tell you something that I have withheld. I told you before that Aaron was a very sensitive and caring person. He would get hurt *so* easily. He would see an injured dog on the road and be sad for days. He was also very shy, especially with girls. But out of the blue, Cupid smiled upon him and he found a girl he loved. He loved her dearly and unconditionally. He gave her everything, keeping nothing back for himself.

'But life is cruel, Asma. Within a year, the girl ditched him. Aaron was stunned. He didn't know what hit him. He couldn't understand why it had happened. A few days later, he committed suicide.'

Linda had talked about her brother many times in the past. Every time she would end up in tears. Now, for the first time, her voice hadn't quavered, and her eyes were dry.

'I didn't know that,' Asma whispered. 'Thanks for telling me.'

'There one more thing I want to tell you… the girl's name.'

Asma's eyes flew open wide. She knew instinctively what name Linda was about to say.

'Mrinal Shome.'

* * *

On their return to Peter Dann, Asma parked the Jeep and walked to the castle with Linda. Ipshita and Purbhi, who were strolling at the edge of the lawn, stopped and looked at them. Her face now clear of the worry that had bothered her all day, Linda smiled at them. The two women returned her gaze with evident curiosity.

'You girls had lunch?' Asma called to them.

'Not yet,' Ipshita replied.

'Great! I'll join you in a couple of minutes. Dining room.'

As Asma mounted the wide front steps of the castle, Linda joined the other two.

'I went to a church,' Asma heard her say. Her voice was steady and calm. 'I'm feeling much better now.'

Asma went to her room and opened her laptop. She logged into the Wi-Fi account used by guests and opened a torrent downloading application. She browsed movie torrents, picked one at random and began downloading the file. Judging by the file's size and the download speed, she estimated that it would take at least half an hour to download. Time enough to carry out the next phase of her plan as the connection speed on the guest network would be drastically reduced.

Soon, the four women sat together at lunch, eating and chatting. With the ordeal of the trek over, Purbhi seemed relaxed and happy. She seemed to have gotten over her annoyance with Linda too—perhaps, their chat while Asma was in her room had addressed the tension between them.

'Feeling better, Purbhi?' Asma asked.

'Yep!' Purbhi beamed, looking up from her mobile phone, which seemed inseparable from her. 'I was needlessly tense about the trek. It turned out okay. But I'm happy to be back here.'

For the first time since Asma had met her, she seemed at ease. She was talking a lot more and laughing without restraint, even when her fingers were flying over her phone's screen. It seemed central to her existence.

'Great!' Asma turned to Ipshita. 'I wanted to pick your brains, Ipshita. I've been wondering if Peter Dann should be done up a little bit. I have no clue how to go about even thinking about it. As you are an interior designer, could you give me some tips? Of course, I don't want you to work for free, but I thought you could guide me on how to approach this business of changing the interior design.'

'Hey, no sweat!' Ipshita responded with a smile. 'It's only when I get down to doing the design that I charge. Talking about how you should approach it is not an issue. What did you have in mind?'

'That's the problem,' Asma replied with a grimace. 'I have nothing apart from a vague question about whether we should make some changes to the castle. I don't even know what options there are, what will work for Peter Dann, or how do I even go about identifying options.' She turned up her palms in a gesture of helplessness. 'Where do I start?'

'No problem,' Ipshita said. 'The first thing you need to do is to think about what kind of themes you might like. Do you want a modern theme, or a classic one, something funky or one that is exclusive and luxurious? There are a number of possibilities.'

'But I don't want to do any structural changes to the castle.'

'You don't need to. For starters, imagine this dining room without anything—no tables or chairs, no curtains or draping, no carpet or sideboards, nothing. Just the bare walls and the floor. Then try and visualize how different themes would look and what you might like. I could show you some samples if you wish. You can choose one of them, combine different themes or come up with something completely new.'

'You have some themes?' Asma asked.

'Sure. I can show you my website and my Facebook pages. But before that, look at your walls—they are good, solid stone. Real authentic stuff, which you don't get anywhere except in genuine heritage buildings. That is a valuable uniqueness. Personally, I would be loath to supress or conceal it. I would design around it in such a way that the design brings out its grandeur.'

'Sounds great, Ipshita,' Asma enthused. 'Can we really

bring out the *true* magnificence of an old stone building? Mum used to say that it used to be *really* spectacular. Maybe, it has dulled over the years.'

'You bet, we can! Let me show you some samples.'

Ipshita pulled out her mobile phone and opened the browser. She opened her business page in the Facebook app and brought up her website in the browser. After a minute of waiting, she screwed up her face in annoyance as she watched the pages loading very slowly.

'Connection speed is low,' she complained.

'Yes!' Purbhi agreed, looking upset. 'The speed suddenly dropped a few minutes back. Websites are loading too slowly.'

'Let me try.' Asma pulled out her mobile phone and opened her Facebook app. 'What's your personal FB name?'

She typed it in and showed the result to Ipshita. 'It's loading fine on my phone.'

'Are you on the same Wi-Fi connection as me?' Ipshita asked.

'No. I'm on my personal Wi-Fi connection. You must be on the guest Wi-Fi network, I suppose. Hey, I've just sent you a friend request.'

Ipshita scowled at her screen where the pages were loading annoyingly slowly.

'Let me connect you to my personal connection,' Asma said. 'The speed in the guest network falls sometimes if too many people are on it.'

Taking Ipshita's phone, she went to the settings app and selected her personal network. When the phone asked for a password, she stopped and frowned, appearing to be stuck.

'Now, what's the password?' she mused aloud. 'I've forgotten it… No problem, I have it written down in my bedroom. Just a sec!'

She went to her room with Ipshita's phone, and keyed in the password, which she knew by heart. She then went to Ipshita's contacts list and searched for the name 'Pralay'. Earlier at Top Camp, Athreya had asked Asma if she had heard any of the guests mention the name Pralay, and she had heard Ipshita do so a couple of times. She found one contact. She took down Pralay's number on a sheet of paper, and photographed his contact picture with her own phone.

Deed done, she returned to the dining room quickly enough for Ipshita not to suspect anything. Now Asma had the phone number and photograph of the person she suspected to be Mrinal's brother.

Back in the dining room, Ipshita began showing a number of themes from her Facebook page and her website. She also accepted Asma's friend request. Over the next fifteen minutes, Ipshita gave an excellent overview of how to go about selecting an interior design theme. There was no doubt that she was very good at her work.

When they returned to their rooms after lunch, Asma opened her Facebook app and began scanning Ipshita's Facebook page. Now that Ipshita had accepted her friend request, Asma could see everything on the page. In addition to her design creations, there were a large number of personal posts and photographs, which Asma began scrolling through. In many of the photographs, the face she had seen with Pralay's name was prominent. And several of them had only Ipshita and Pralay at different locations and on different dates.

Slowly, a picture of their relationship emerged. Ipshita and Pralay were not merely friends. They were something more. While Ipshita's Facebook page said nothing about being formally engaged to him, it was clear that the two were in a very serious relationship.

And now with Mrinal dead, Pralay would inherit her assets.

18

Asma and Athreya locked the door behind them as they stepped onto the rooftop terrace. After discovering the connection between Ipshita and Pralay, Asma had knocked on his door and she said she needed to have a private chat with him in a place where they wouldn't be heard or seen. The lawn or Land's End would have been private enough, but they could be seen by all five guests. She had another reason too which she hadn't yet told Athreya. She took him to the middle of the terrace and spoke in a low voice that hardly carried.

'There is a connection between Ipshita and Mrinal's brother,' she said. 'A connection that has been hidden thus far.'

'Tell me about it,' Athreya replied equally softly.

Asma told him how she had got hold of Ipshita's mobile phone for a minute and summarized her findings from scrutinising Ipshita's Facebook page.

'From what Ipshita and Pralay have been saying to each other on Facebook,' Asma concluded, 'I suspect they are planning to get married next year. The intimacy between them, as is evident from the uploaded photos, leaves no doubt about the nature of their relationship.'

'Then, she stands to gain handsomely by Mrinal's death.'

'It appears so.'

Athreya scratched his chin thoughtfully. First Dhavak, and now Ipshita. Two people had strong motives for doing away with Mrinal.

'That's not all,' Asma went on. Her words caught in her throat as she tried to go on. After two unsuccessful attempts, she finally blurted out, 'I feel like a worm saying this, Uncle. A snake, rather. I hope I am doing the right thing.'

'About Ipshita?'

Asma shook her head. Her hair fell over her face, obscuring her troubled eyes.

'No,' she whispered. 'It's about Linda. I'm about to let down a very good friend.'

'Maybe not. Maybe you'll be helping her. Let me be the judge.'

'Okay… okay. You remember what I told you about Aaron?'

'Linda's brother?'

'Yes.'

'You said that he had committed suicide. But you didn't tell me why.'

'I can tell you now. He was deeply in love with a girl. She ditched him… he couldn't bear it… he killed himself.'

'I see… and the girl was… Mrinal?' Athreya guessed.

Asma nodded mutely, biting her lip so hard that it drew blood.

'Tell me what you know,' he said gently. 'Don't punish yourself. Once this is over, you'll be glad you told me.'

Asma looked up at him with moist eyes. 'You think so, Uncle?'

'Yes, Asma. Trust me. You are not the first person facing this dilemma.'

What he didn't tell her was that whichever way it turned out for Linda—guilty or innocent—Asma would be glad that she shared her knowledge with him. If she was guilty, Asma would have helped in bringing her to book. If she turned out to be innocent, Asma would have been instrumental in lifting the cloud of suspicion from her.

Haltingly, Asma described how she had offered to take Linda to the church, knowing full well that Linda was likely to open up to her after praying. Of course, going to the church was hugely therapeutic for Linda too—she would feel much, much better for it. Even so, there was no getting away from the fact that Asma had, to some extent, manipulated her close friend.

'We have three guests who had a prior connection with Mrinal,' Athreya whispered when Asma finished.

'Three?' Asma whispered back.

'Dhavak. I won't go into the details. Oh, I forgot! It's four—Sarosh too knew Mrinal from before. Four out of five guests! That leaves only Purbhi.'

'Purbhi and Ipshita are as close as sisters,' Asma countered. 'You can count them as one. If Ipshita knew Mrinal from before, be sure that Purbhi did too—you can take it for granted. Remember what Purbhi told you during the trek? She said: "*I didn't want to come on this lousy trek in the first place... It was Ipshita's idea. A foolish idea. She made me come.*" Purbhi is incidental to all this, Uncle. Ipshita brought her along.'

'I'm not sure about that, Asma,' Athreya said, shaking his head. 'Maybe, there is something about Purbhi we still don't know.'

'Maybe. But I think all five guests knew Mrinal, even though they pretended otherwise.'

'Your father will not be surprised.'

Asma nodded. 'His riddle of the five guests is turning out to be serious. His gut feeling was that something was amiss. His gut *never* misleads him.'

'Asma, all this is between you and me, okay? Don't breathe a word of this to *anyone*—your dad, Maazin, *nobody*. I will brief your dad. We are at a particularly dangerous juncture in the case when we have a few pointers, but we don't know who the killer is. Killers will do *anything* to prevent their identity being revealed. Those who possess *any* sensitive information become immediate targets. If you tell Maazin, you'll put him in danger. I don't want you to talk about it *at all*, lest you be overheard. Not a word. Understand?'

Asma's eyes grew wide as she nodded.

'Have you decided that it's murder?' she asked.

'More or less.' He began walking towards the southern parapet wall to the spot from which Mrinal had fallen. 'I need you to do something else for me... it's a hunch. But my gut—like your father's—has proven reliable in the past.'

'What do you need me to do? Is it on this terrace?'

They had just reached the spot. He stopped.

'Yes,' Athreya answered. 'Imagine that you are the killer. You have just killed Mrinal in the middle of the night and tipped her body over this parapet wall.' He gestured to it. 'But you still have to get rid of Mrinal's mobile phone. What would you do?'

'One option would be to fling it as far as I could into the woods below.' She pointed to the south.

'Indeed. The police are scouring the area with their eyes and metal detectors. But they haven't found it. Let's assume that the killer did not throw the phone into the woods. What else could you do? Remember, there might also be the murder weapon to dispose of.'

Without a word, Asma turned and strode to the lily pond at the centre of the terrace. She reached the three-foot-high wall and stood there, looking down into the leaf-covered water.

'My thought too!' Athreya whispered as he came and stood beside her. 'Now, do you know what I need you to do?'

She turned to him with an impish smile. 'Search the pond?'

'Can you? I didn't want to involve the police just to verify a hunch. They have their hands full with the woods and the castle grounds.'

The fact was that he had another reason too—he didn't want to let Shivali into his hunch until it was proven.

'Of course, I can!' Asma's smile widened. 'How often I entered this pond as a little girl!'

To Athreya's surprise, she peeled off her T-shirt and tracks. Underneath, she was wearing swimming trunks and a synthetic vest similar to the upper half of a swimsuit. That was when Athreya realized the significance of the towel she had brought with her.

'You came prepared!' Athreya exclaimed. 'You suspected this?'

'What do you think?' She grinned. 'I am a police officer's daughter, after all. I have heard many true crime stories too.' She unwrapped her towel. 'I also brought this.'

She held up a torchlight sealed in a transparent, water-tight ziplock bag.

'I'm impressed! Now, where in the pond do you think you have the highest likelihood of finding the phone?'

Asma frowned as she gazed at the leaves which were thick, large and circular.

'If I threw my mobile into the middle of the pond,' she said, as he contemplated the pond's surface, 'chances are that it might land on a leaf, especially in the dark. And as the leaves are strong and stiff, it might remain there and not sink into the water. If I were half-smart, I wouldn't risk that.'

'Let's assume that the killer is a more than half-smart. What would you do?'

'I'd probably reach as far as I could over the wall, put my hand under the leaves and into the water, and try and throw it underwater towards the centre of the pond.'

'Excellent! You have a very logical mind.' A faint blush rose on her face at his praise. He went on. 'Now, the pond has a long circumference. Where along it would you go?'

'The opposite end from here? The northern side? That's

furthest from Mrinal's table.'

'Possibly,' Athreya agreed. 'That would be a good place to start the search. Then work your way along the wall.'

They went around the pond and stopped at the northern side. She opened a long polythene cover and inserted her left arm into it. Athreya then tied it with a tape to her upper arm. Now, her bandages would not get wet.

With practised ease, Asma sat on the pond edge and swung her legs over into the water that had been warmed by many hours of sunlight. She switched on the torchlight inside the water-proof pouch, took a deep breath and went down on her knees so that her face was under the water.

Athreya couldn't see what she was doing underwater, especially when she disappeared below the big leaves. From time to time, she broke the surface to take a couple of deep breaths, only to disappear again.

Not finding anything in the northern side of the pond, she began going anticlockwise, searching as she went. Ten minutes passed with no discovery, but Athreya held on to his conviction. When Asma had completed a little over a quarter of a circle and she had passed the westernmost part of the pond, she jerked her torso out of the water. On her face was a triumphant grin and in her right hand was a mobile phone.

'Got it!' she enthused. 'This *is* Mrinal's phone.'

'Excellent, Asma!' Athreya almost clapped, but refrained from making noise at the last moment. 'You are a godsend. Stand where you are. I'll take a photo to record where exactly you found it.'

A minute later, he had the wet phone in his hand. He put in a plastic pouch and thrust it into his pocket.

'I need you to find one more thing,' he said. 'It is a long shot, but I am convinced that it is in the pond.'

'What?' Asma asked.

'A bottle... probably a bottle of gin.'

'Bottle of gin?' Her eyebrows shot up.

Athreya nodded. 'It may have a yellow label.'

'Wow!' Asma exclaimed. 'How do you know such things?'

Before he could answer, she went underwater again. Two minutes later, she was up again. Another wide grin split her face, and in her hand was a gin bottle.

'How ever did you know?' she hissed, but Athreya's face was grim as he snapped a couple of photographs.

He took the bottle and examined it. It was a large bottle with a big yellow label. The cap had come off and water had filled it. A corner of the label had been sheared off as if it had made violent contact with something hard. Around it was discoloration. From that spot, cracks radiated into the glass. A small place had been chipped, and missing from it was a tiny sliver of glass.

'What's this, Uncle,' Asma asked in a hushed voice as she stood drying her hair with her towel.

'My dear girl,' Athreya replied in a voice that was little more than a whisper. 'You have found the murder weapon.'

* * *

Athreya and a grim-faced Shivali sat in the study behind a locked door. The sun had already set by the time the ACP returned to the castle. As soon as she had arrived, she and Athreya had adjourned to the study, where He had briefed her about his discoveries.

'So, they lied to us,' Shivali hissed. She was visibly angry. 'Said that they didn't know Mrinal from before. Claimed that they were not linked to her in any way.'

'Of course, they lied,' Athreya responded. 'We've suspected that all along. Javed's five guests' riddle, remember?'

'That is so only if you choose to believe that Javed saw them in Nainital.'

Athreya shrugged. There was no point in contesting the

matter.

'Something happened that night after the party wound up and before Maazin locked the terrace doors,' Shivali went on. 'Something that involves these five people. All that elaborate testimony that they fed you has come to naught.'

'Perhaps. My experience suggests that criminals lie only to the extent they need to. Otherwise, they stick to the truth as far as possible. So, *not everything that they told me* may be lies. Besides, there is some corroboration from Ravi and the security guard.

'Your people must visit every hotel in Nainital, Shivali. They need to ascertain if any of the five stayed there. For all we know, they might have stayed in different hotels and they met at the Naini Retreat only to talk and plan. If your men do as I suggest, we may discover who the sixth and the seventh members were.'

'Sir, is there any doubt in your mind that one or all of these five killed Mrinal?'

'Like the Orient Express murder, Shivali?' Athreya asked with a smile. 'One of them hit her on the head and they together lifted her and threw her over the parapet wall?'

'Why not, sir?'

'Too early to say. We have a lot more to find out. For instance, what is Sarosh's motive? What do those pieces of white-and-red photographic paper have to do with Mrinal's death? What is the significance of the hammer and rope et cetera that you found? Did the five meet in Nainital? If so, who were the sixth and the seventh members of the group? Is Kinshuk entirely innocent? There are still many unanswered questions.'

'Kinshuk!' she hissed. 'I have some dope on him. And some other interesting stuff too. Let me update you on what we have found out.

'Kinshuk, not to put too fine a point, is a bloody cheat!

He has been cheating on his fiancée… very recently! While at Clarkson's, he had an amorous affair with a married woman who lives half a kilometre away. Her husband was away for a few nights, and Kinshuk visited her on two nights. He stayed there for more than an hour each time and returned to his room in the wee hours.'

Athreya's mind went back to what Dave had said: *'I fear it's only a matter of time before his attention wanders from Mrinal. I'm afraid the poor girl is in for a heartbreak.'* Had Dave seen something? Another thought struck him hard and his eyes popped open. Had Mrinal discovered Kinshuk's infidelity? That would explain the fight they had. She had refused to even look in his direction during the party.

'Kinshuk has a reputation for being a bit of a Casanova.' Shivali's wrathful voice interrupted his reverie. The ACP was voicing the anger she was feeling on behalf of the dead woman. 'Gossip from Mumbai suggests that the Mrinal–Kinshuk relationship was doomed from the beginning. The man is a narcissist who is in love with only himself.'

Those were almost the same words Dave had used to describe Kinshuk. If the engagement was falling apart, did Kinshuk have a motive to get rid of Mrinal? He asked Shivali that question.

'Possibly,' she answered. 'But if Mrinal hasn't made a will, Kinshuk is unlikely to receive anything. Yes, if she went public with her grievance, it might affect his name. But he is already known as a philanderer; he even boasts about it in private—locker room talk, as some Americans would say. Then, why resort to murder?'

'I did see him flirt with Ipshita when Mrinal was not in sight,' Athreya remarked. 'I thought it was in very bad taste.'

Shivali let out a low chuckle. 'You must hear what the castle staff have been telling my men. You will feel embarrassed just listening to it. Poor Mrinal, she must have been among the unluckiest of girls.'

'Why so?'

'Listen to what we have found out, sir. Think about it for a moment, and you'll agree with me.

'First, Mrinal loses *both* her parents to riots when she is all of twenty-one-years-old. *Twenty-one!* She was just a kid. Then, she rebuilds her life and that of her thirteen-year-old brother and works hard to conserve what her parents left them. By all accounts, she did a very good job. She not only conserved what they inherited, but also grew it.

'When her brother—Pralay—turns eighteen, she gives him his half of the inheritance. And guess what he does? He turns against her and spreads all sorts of canards. He bad-mouthed her to such an extent that they are no longer on speaking terms. Pralay was the one who severed the relationship.'

'Kinshuk said that Pralay is a bit of a weirdo,' Athreya remarked.

'Possibly, sir. Let me go on. Mrinal then gets into a relationship with a boy. A very nice boy, I believe, but hypersensitive. When the relationship breaks up, the boy goes and kills himself! I can only imagine what it would be like if such a thing happened to me.

'And then comes along one Kumud Malakar—a man Mrinal trusted, liked and even looked up to, from what we have heard. What does he do? He assaults her at night and upsets her so much that she flees Kolkata and goes to Mumbai.

'And what does this unfortunate girl find there? Kinshuk! If ever there was an unlucky woman, it was she. By the way, we are getting more dope on Sarosh, sir. Initial impression is that he too was harassing Mrinal with Kinshuk's tacit support.'

'What is Kinshuk's background?'

'A bright student at school. He did well enough to secure admission to a premier college in Delhi. Apparently, his father wanted him to enter the civil services like many of his classmates, but Kinshuk didn't have the aptitude for it. His passions were Bollywood, celebrities and fitness. After failing to get acting roles in films and TV, he found his niche in celebrity training.'

Before Athreya could ask a question, a knock sounded on the study door. Shivali opened it to find her sub-inspector standing outside.

'Found anything,?' she asked him, as she closed the door behind him.

'Yes, ma'am!' he enthused, but stopped when his eyes fell on Athreya.

'We found a mountain climber who was willing to scale the rock monolith for us,' Shivali explained to Athreya. 'He scaled the rock face and let down ropes for Negi and others to climb up. They examined the temple at the top. It looks like Negi has news.'

She turned to him and nodded.

'What a *khatarnak* place, ma'am!' Negi began. 'At least four times, I thought that I was going to fall and die. How these Cochhas climb it every full moon, I don't know. I never want to do this again.'

'How brave of you, Negi!' Shivali teased.

'You say it, ma'am!' Negi retorted with a pained expression on his face. 'It was *my* life on the line. Anyway, three of us went up to the temple at the top. The place was surprisingly clean—no garbage or rats, and most importantly, no snakes.'

'None?'

'I don't think snakes can climb up two-hundred feet of sheer rock, ma'am. Why would they climb, anyway? There is no food or rats there. Complete waste of effort for the snake. I'm sure it can do a lot better on the forest floor.'

'Never mind the snake, Negi. On with it.'

'The temple is about twelve foot square and made of blocks of stone that seem to have been hewn from the broken boulders there. The temple has no doors, and the sole entrance faces east. Inside the temple is a crude sculpture that looks like *Hanumanji*. But as we know, it is not. It is some other *vanara*. On one side is a small alcove where the puja things are stored. We searched that, and this is what we found.'

He opened the envelope he was carrying and upended it on the desk in such a way that his fingers didn't touch the contents. Out fell a ziplock bag with a postcard-sized paper in it. Athreya stared at the paper that was featureless and completely white, until he realized that it was upside-down. He flipped it over.

On the table before them lay a photograph showing a hand against a plain white background. The five fingers were spread out and curled slightly. Between the fingers, the palm was visible. It looked as if a child had dipped its hand in paint and held it out for its mother to see.

Except that the hand was that of a full-grown adult, and it had been dipped not in paint, but in blood. Three small red rivulets flowed down from the wrist to the bottom of the photograph.

It was straight out of a horror movie. There was no mis-taking the image.

It was a photo of a bloodied hand.

19

Athreya stared at the photograph in horror. If this was what Mrinal had been running from, there must be much hatred in the hearts of those who were persecuting her. For the moment, he was rendered speechless, gaping at the photo. His right index finger had gone berserk, writing invisible words on the tabletop.

A vision of a large, bloodied hand chasing a diminutive Mrinal flashed through his mind. The disembodied hand was dripping blood as she ran from fire to fire, throwing photos into the flames. As she ran from the pursuing hand, Peter Dann loomed ahead with a gigantic Dhavak strumming the guitar.

'They have been terrorising poor Mrinal!' Shivali snarled, scrambling his vision. 'For two months, they have been anonymously sending copies of this photo to her in Mumbai. She kept burning them, but they kept coming. I wonder if she came to these foothills to escape the persecution… in the hope of finding some peace and quiet. But at Clarkson's she found the bloody handprints. She also found that the same photo had followed her there too. She went to Pottersfield and burnt it. And when she came to Peter Dann, the photo appeared here as well. Probably delivered through the window by a Cochha climber.'

'Did you say that the photos were sent anonymously, ma'am?' Negi asked.

'Isn't that likely? Would Mrinal have put up with the persecution for so long had she known who was sending them? She would have gone to the police.'

'And finally at the party—' Athreya prompted.

'At the party, she must have sensed something that rattled her. She came back to you unnerved. And finally, when Dhavak sang "Sound of Silence", she realized that the heavily bearded singer was, in reality, the infamous Kumud.

'Everything suddenly fell into place in her mind, and she fled to the rooftop terrace. Just as Asma thought, Mrinal had to now figure out how to respond to what she had discovered. She planned to stay on the terrace until the party was over. Only then would she go down to her room. Dropping out of the trek was a no-brainer—there was no question of going with her persecutors.

'Also remember that she had just been shattered that morning by Kinshuk's infidelity. Her world was in a shambles. There was nothing left to do now except to return to Mumbai as soon as possible. I'm pretty sure that she planned to leave Peter Dann the very next morning while her persecutors were away.'

'But she never returned to her room,' Athreya completed the reconstruction.

Shivali spun around to Athreya. 'So, you agree with me, sir?'

He nodded. 'Something happened between Asma talking to her at 11:20 p.m. and Maazin locking the terrace at 12:30 a.m. Something that we don't yet know about. Until we discover that, we are skating on thin ice.'

'Sir!' Shivali protested. 'Look at the evidence. They had the motive, the opportunity and the means. And nobody from outside the castle could have reached the victim. Any reasonable judge would arraign the five.'

'I agree. There is sufficient prima facie evidence to arraign them, and even possibly to remand them into custody. But our objective is not that. Our goal is to obtain conviction.'

'We will, sir! We will. We have been at it for just a couple of days. With time, we'll get enough ammunition to secure a conviction.'

'Five murderers, Shivali?'

'Why not?'

'Are you convinced? *Truly* convinced? What if one or two of them are innocent?'

She squirmed. The diligent police officer in her baulked at the innocent being convicted.

'What if only one of them is a murderer and the others are protecting him or her with prepared stories?' Athreya went on.

'You are right, sir.' Shivali's chin lifted and her eyes locked with his. 'I was hasty in my enthusiasm. But I *will* get to the bottom of this. I will break them into telling the truth. Whoever is protecting the murderer will be punished for that. But the murderer *will* be named and punished.'

She turned to her assistant.

'Get everyone to assemble in the lounge at 7:30 p.m.— the five guests, Kinshuk, Asma, Maazin and Mr Javed. Instruct Ravi and the security guard to be on standby.'

Once Negi left, Athreya asked her to sit down.

'So,' he asked, 'have you decided that Javed is not involved in this?'

'I wish I could say "yes", sir,' she replied. 'But there is a thread of inquiry that casts a shadow on him.'

'What thread?'

Shivali shook her head. 'Not as yet, sir. I need to dig a little deeper.'

'Okay, but I have a request. Once you have dug deep enough and are ready to confront Javed, speak to me first. Facts, as you know, can have multiple interpretations. I don't want you to embarrass yourself by accusing a retired police officer and then having to retract. I have seen too many young officers act hastily. You have a bright career ahead of you, and I would like it to remain bright.'

She stared at him for a long moment before dropping her eyes.

'Thank you, sir,' she said. 'I'll see what I can do. But now, I need to confront Kinshuk. Shall I call him?'

Athreya nodded.

Soon, the dandyish young man was sitting across the table from Shivali. Athreya had taken a seat to the side to allow the ACP to handle the confrontation the way she wanted to. Shivali wasted no time in beating around the bush or in preparing Kinshuk for the onslaught.

'You and Mrinal stayed at Clarkson's for four nights,' she began. 'Is that correct?'

'I... guess so,' he drawled.

'Please be specific. Yes or no?'

There was no humour on her face or in her voice. Kinshuk got the message.

'Yes,' he answered.

'You and Mrinal occupied separate rooms. Correct?'

'Correct.'

'You and Mrinal were engaged to be married. Correct?'

'Yes.'

'When were you to get married?'

'Early next year.'

'Can I take it that you were committed to each other?'

'Engaged couples are generally committed to each other,' Kinshuk replied with a trace of a sneer.

Shivali ignored his sarcasm.

'Precisely,' she responded. 'So you were committed to her as she was to you. Correct?'

'Correct.'

'Then why did you visit Mrs Rathore between 1 a.m. and 3 a.m. two of the nights you spent at Clarkson's?'

'Who?' Kinshuk stammered. The abruptness of Shivali's bombshell had caught him off guard. He blanched.

'Mrs Rathore, whose husband was away on those two nights. You went to her cottage without Mrinal's knowledge and spent more than an hour in her bedroom with her. Do you deny it?'

'What the hell are you talking about?'

Kinshuk feigned indignation even as his face lost all colour.

'Don't play games, sir,' Shivali snapped back. 'You were seen.'

'Nonsense! Utter nonsense!'

Kinshuk had lost his nerve. He was groping in the dark for an escape.

'You have a choice, sir,' Shivali went on, not giving him time to recover. 'You can either accept it now, or contest it in public. But be aware that we have indisputable proof. Besides, Mrs Rathore is known for certain things in these parts. She will not back up your denials. Incidentally, a lot of blackmail stems from promiscuity.'

'Promiscuity or not,' Kinshuk thundered, 'it's none of your bloody business! You are here to investigate Mrinal's death, not harass me. What I did or did not do has no bearing on her death.'

'No?' Shivali asked with a thin smile. 'Mrinal discovered your infidelity and was livid. The two of you had a massive fight. She was so angry in the morning that she went away to Pottersfield to get away from you. From then on, she didn't speak to you. A smart prosecutor can make that sound like sufficient motive for murder.'

'Murder?' Kinshuk's hands and lips trembled. He was a far cry from the overbearing, super-confident celebrity trainer Athreya had first seen at Clarkson's. 'We are talking accident here.'

'Accident won't wash, sir. She didn't drink a drop of alcohol after going to the terrace. Suicide then? An excellent case can be made out for abetment of suicide. Ample precedents exist for infidelity and betrayal being the vehicle of abetment.'

Overwhelmed, Kinshuk fell silent. He was sweating

profusely and trembling all over. Shivali had not been kind to him. She had had no reason to be. Nor did Athreya feel any sympathy for the unfaithful man.

'Go now,' Shivali said, dismissing Kinshuk. 'Make sure that you are in the lounge at 7:30 p.m. You are not to leave Peter Dann until I say so.'

As he rose, Athreya spoke to him for the first time.

'You are in a corner, Kinshuk,' he said. 'You will remain there unless you can help prove that Mrinal was killed or pushed to suicide by someone else.'

Negi entered the room once Kinshuk left. In his hand was the envelope with the photograph of the bloodied hand, which he placed face up on the table.

'There were two more in the temple,' he said. 'I've sent them for analysis and fingerprinting.'

'Shivali,' Athreya said softly, 'do you have the piece of photographic paper we found under Mrinal's desk?'

'Yes, sir!'

A minute later, Athreya laid the scrap of paper against the photograph just where the middle of the three rivulets of blood reached the bottom of the photograph. They matched perfectly.

'So, I was right,' Shivali hissed. 'Someone put a copy of this photo in Mrinal's room. The five have indeed been terrorizing her.'

'Who would have put it in her room, ma'am?' Negi asked. 'One of the Cochhas?'

'Who else?' Shivali growled. 'He must have been paid to do it. He scaled Peter Dann's southern wall and dropped it through Mrinal's window.'

'Under whose orders?'

'That we will find out. Now, go and make sure that everyone gathers in the lounge at 7:30 p.m. And while you are at it, please send some tea for Mr Athreya and me. I need some fortification before I tighten the screws on the five.'

* * *

217

Shivali and Athreya walked into the lounge fifteen minutes late. It was by design; she had deemed it appropriate to let the suspects 'sweat it out for a while'. The five guests were seated together with Linda in the middle. On one side were the other two women and on the other side were the two men. Dhavak and Ipshita occupied the outermost seats. Kinshuk sat separately while Javed, Asma and Maazin sat together to one side.

'So,' Shivali began without the slightest trace of a smile, 'we gather here at the scene of the crime. The place where Kinshuk and Mr Athreya were drugged so that they couldn't interfere with what was to be done after the party. But let me start at the beginning.

'The five of you made fake bookings and came to Peter Dann all of you pretending to be strangers. That you had met at the Naini Retreat two months earlier was a fact that you assiduously denied. It is apparent that much thought had gone into preparing for the Nainital meeting too, as none of you stayed at the hotel where you met. You stayed at different hotels so that you left no visible link between yourselves. You paid in cash for your lunch so that you left no electronic trail there either. But unfortunately for you, you were seen. Let me assure you that I will soon have the names of the hotels where each of you stayed. Nainital is a tourist place with many hotels, but it is not very big. It's only a matter of time.

'More important than pretending to be mutual strangers is this: each of you claimed that you did not know Mrinal. Despite the fact that all of you knew her very well, and probably had reason to wish her ill. Except Sarosh, who acknowledged a passing familiarity with her. But he too didn't admit to a deeper connection.

'As you know, Mrinal was from North 24 Parganas in West Bengal. She and her brother, Pralay, lived on the same street as Ipshita and Purbhi. In fact, Ipshita, Purbhi and Pralay have been friends from childhood. Ipshita and Pralay learnt music together. Childhood friendship morphed into love. You two are planning to get married soon. So, who gains from Mrinal's death? Pralay! If he benefits, so does Ipshita. By the way, we know that Pralay is somewhere nearby. We'll get him soon.'

Ipshita had been sitting still and listening silently. Her pretty face was an inscrutable mask. Even after Shivali's declaration, she didn't respond. Purbhi, on the other hand, was restless. She fidgeted as she stole glances at her child-hood friend.

'Linda,' Shivali said softly. 'Aaron's death was no small tragedy for you. You were understandably shattered. You blamed his death on Mrinal, didn't you? There is no deny-ing that you too knew her from your Kolkata days—she was once to be your sister-in-law. Vengeance is a very strong motive for murder.'

'No!' Linda gasped, as she shook her head vigorously. 'No! I didn't kill her. She jumped to her death. It wasn't murder.'

'Wasn't it?' Shivali countered. 'We will come to that later. I have already spoken about Sarosh knowing Mrinal from before, although he claimed that he only knew her as Kinshuk's fiancée. That was just a convenient pretext. Sarosh knew Mrinal *much* better as someone with whom he had business dealings.

'The two of them had set up a venture that was to pro-vide training to schoolchildren in English communication, art appreciation and life skills. Sarosh provided the funding while Mrinal was to provide the content from her inter-net-based start-up. The same content was to be delivered through a string of physical classrooms in Mumbai. Unfor-tunately, the venture is already on the rocks with sugges-tions of financial misappropriation.

'And finally, I come to Dhavak. Even though the other four already know about your relationship with Mrinal, I will respect the request you made to Mr Athreya. It suffices to say that we know all about Kumud Malakar. Vengeance is a powerful motive.'

Shivali stopped and scanned the faces in the room. So did Athreya. Ipshita and Sarosh might have been carved in stone. Linda was in tears. Purbhi continued to fidget. Dhavak stared back at Shivali with flinty eyes that held no fear.

Javed was stoic as he sat back in his chair with his hairy, muscular arms folded. Beside him, Asma was crushing her hanky in anguish. Maazin sat stunned, with an expression of regret on his face.

'All this,' Shivali went on, 'we have managed to find out in less than forty-eight hours. There is more of which I have not spoken.' Athreya thought that he saw her eyes flicker very briefly towards Javed before she pulled them back. 'Be assured that we will find out everything there is to find out.

'In sum, the five of you have lied. Were you to repeat your lies on the witness stand, you would be committing felony. It is not as serious a charge as murder, but it could earn you a long vacation in jail. As young adults, your lives and careers would be ruined. In any case, one or more of you will face the murder charge.'

'No!' Linda whispered again. 'Mrinal jumped. Nobody killed her. Mr Athreya!' she pleaded. 'Please help! You must! I have nobody else to turn to.'

'I have a problem, Linda,' Athreya said, speaking slowly and clearly. 'Something happened that night between 11:20 p.m. and 12:30 a.m. that the five of you are hiding. Tell me about it. Only then can I help. I don't want the innocent to be accused. But I also want due punishment to be meted out in accordance with each person's crime. Believe me, ACP Suyal doesn't want to see a miscarriage of justice any more than I do. You must help me help you, Linda.'

Silence fell on the group. Nobody said a word. Linda stopped sobbing. Kinshuk was staring wide-eyed at the carpet under his feet. Asma's eyes were brimming and Maazin was looking wretched. Only Javed remained stoic.

'I would advise all of you to think about what Mr Athreya has just said,' Shivali resumed. 'For those of you who don't know, he has a reputation for fiercely defending the innocent... even when he was a police officer whose task was to bring the guilty to book. He will play fair.'

'You are trying to divide us,' Dhavak hissed. 'You are playing one against the other. I know you people—you'll try every trick in the book. Why should we even believe anything you said? It may well be empty claims to threaten us.'

Shivali returned his stare. Slowly, she pulled out something from her pocket.

'And then, there is this,' she said, showing the photograph of the bloodied hand. This is no invention of mine. It is tangible proof that Mrinal was being persecuted—'

'I've seen it before,' Kinshuk almost yelled. 'I *have* seen it. That is what Mrinal was burning. The bloody handprints were put at Clarkson's too.'

'Burning in Mumbai?' Shivali asked.

'Yes! She burned several of them.' Keen to get on the ACP's good side, he opened up and spilled the beans. 'They were sent to Mrinal anonymously and it affected her badly.'

'Did she confide in you?'

'No. She quietly shredded or burned them when she thought I was not watching.'

'Do you know what the bloodied hand signifies?'

'No.' Kinshuk shook his head vigorously. 'I wish I did.'

'When was the last time you saw a copy of this photo?'

'The day before we left Mumbai.'

'Did you know that a copy landed in her room at Clarkson's?' Shivali asked.

'Clarkson's?' the celebrity trainer exclaimed. 'In addition to the bloody handprints?'

Shivali nodded. 'Her persecutors followed her here too.'

Kinshuk's eyes snapped to the five guests. He stared accusingly with a clenched jaw. Athreya was surprised that none of the five responded with the obvious rebuttal.

'Not only that,' she went on, 'the same photograph was delivered to her room here in Peter Dann. A short while before she joined the party. She tore it up and flushed it down the toilet. That's why she was late to the party.'

She turned to the five and went on deliberately.

'So you see, the trail of evidence is clear and leads right up to Peter Dann Castle. Motive, opportunity and means... all three are clearly apparent as far as the five of you are concerned. This is ample evidence for a judge to arraign you. People have been indicted for less.'

'Circumstantial evidence,' Ipshita said in response. Her voice was calm and even. 'This is all circumstantial. You have nothing on us. Murder has not been established, nor has any intent to kill. There is nothing tangible to connect us to these photos either. What is there to say that Kinshuk is not the source of these photos? Wherever he went, the photo followed—Mumbai, Clarkson's, Peter Dann. So why try to pin it on us? This is conjecture, pure and simple. It won't stand up in court.'

Kinshuk was livid, but Shivali didn't give him a chance to respond.

'Ever been at a murder trial, Ipshita?' she asked casually. 'No? Then, you don't know what you are talking about.'

'Sarosh and I were on the lawn,' Dhavak thundered. 'We didn't return to the lounge until *after* Maazin had locked the terrace. A staff member and the security guard saw us. How do you think we reached the terrace to kill Mrinal? Fly? Let's see you come up with a theory.'

'Leaving the women to face the music, Dhavak?' Shivali asked. 'While the men give themselves an alibi?'

Dhavak reddened. For a rare moment, the implied insult rendered him speechless. In that brief instant, Athreya intervened.

'Can I take a shot at coming up with a theory, Dhavak?' he asked mildly.

All eyes turned to him.

'A long coil of nylon rope was stolen from Chetan's rucksack on the night Mrinal died. It is not long enough to scale the two-hundred-and-fifty-foot southern side. But it is enough to reach the terrace from the lawn.'

'You devil!' Dhavak exploded as gasps sounded from the others. 'How you make up stories!'

'Easy, Dhavak.' Athreya held up a hand to stop him. 'You challenged us to come up with a theory. I've done just that. I am not accusing you of scaling the northern wall and killing Mrinal. It was only an intellectual exercise intended to demonstrate what imagination can do.

'I did it to illustrate how a good prosecutor could weave theories and stories based on limited facts. Be aware that courts are sometimes swayed by credible-sounding theories.' He turned his gaze to Ipshita and went on. 'If I were you, I wouldn't place too much faith in the claim that this is all circumstantial evidence.

'With what ACP Suyal has at her disposal now, she could get the five of you arraigned. I am sure that she will gather more evidence in the coming days.

'Your salvation lies not in confronting her, but in working with us. Truth is your best defence even if it means that you have to confess to lesser crimes. Recall the conversation we had over the first dinner we had together. I will not knowingly send an undeserving person to the gallows. I've been there before, and I never want to go there again.'

'But, Mr Athreya,' Linda wailed softly, 'there has been no murder here. Only suicide.'

'Abetment of suicide is a serious crime too, Linda. The convicted spend many years in jail for it. Their lives are shattered beyond repair. Hounding a victim for two months with a horror-inducing photo and following her on a vacation to continue harrying her are very serious matters. It is enough to make the victim leap to her death. Even if your last ploy to frighten Mrinal failed.'

'What ploy?' Shivali asked puzzled.

'The man who attacked Asma made a mistake. He was to attack Mrinal and frighten her into thinking that the five were capable of killing her. Unfortunately, he mistook Asma for Mrinal when she rode out of Clarkson's that morning.'

'Yes... I had stopped at Clarkson's to say hello to Margot,' Asma whispered. 'The man attacked me soon after that.'

'Whoever hired the Cochha had described Mrinal to him. Unfortunately, you resemble her. When he saw you ride out of Clarkson's, he thought you were Mrinal.'

Athreya rose from his chair, a tired man. The day had been emotionally draining. A lot more had passed through his mind than had passed his lips.

'I urge each of you to talk to me. If you didn't kill Mrinal, you have nothing to fear. I will not frame you. If I am unable to identify the killer, I'll withdraw from the case and leave it to ACP Suyal. Goodnight.'

'I will have to return to Mumbai soon,' Kinshuk said to the ACP, as Athreya opened the door to his room. 'I can't stay here for long.'

'You will stay here for as long as it takes,' she responded. 'Till such time as the truth emerges, none of you leaves Peter Dann.'

* * *

Shivali took Athreya aside into the study after dinner.

'I will be going to Nainital tomorrow morning,' she said. 'I want to see what I can find out about the five and their two companions. I also want to recover as much information as I can from Mrinal's phone.

'I'll be away for at least a day, maybe two. Negi will be

here. He has instructions to take orders from you. He will, of course, keep me posted. He also has orders not to let any suspect leave Peter Dann. The gate is locked and two policemen will stand guard.'

'Please take the gin bottle we found in the pond,' Athreya said, 'We need to confirm that the sliver of glass and the piece of yellow paper found in Mrinal's skull are from it. Also ascertain if the discolouration on the bottle label is blood. Meanwhile, I wanted to ask if you heard back from the lab. I'm particularly interested in what they found in the gin bottle that had been left on the table on the terrace.'

'Oh, didn't I tell you?' Shivali asked. 'They found nothing.'

'Nothing?' Athreya echoed.

'The near-full bottle of gin contained only gin. No dilution, no contaminants, nothing. Pure and simple gin.'

'Is that so?' Athreya's eyes lit up. 'Now, isn't that interesting?'

'Something up your sleeve, sir?' Shivali looked at him suspiciously.

'Me?' he asked innocently. 'I only know what you know. Nothing more.'

Shivali regarded him sceptically for a moment. She shrugged and went on, 'The reason I pulled you into the study is this: fresh information has come in from Kolkata. I wanted you to hear it first-hand.'

She put her phone on speaker and called a Kolkata number.

'Mr Athreya is here with me,' she said to the man who answered. 'Can you repeat what you told me?'

'Yes, ma'am,' he said in a thick Bengali accent. 'Good evening, sir.'

'Good evening,' Athreya greeted him.

'I interviewed more than a dozen people who live on the street where Mrinal's family lived. They all remember the incident very clearly.

'To give you an idea, Mrinal's family house was on a minor street. At the end of this street is a main road. There were seven buildings between the house and the main road in 2010 and the distance to the main road is at least a hundred yards. In 2010, the police had listed the cause of the fire as "rioting and arson". But the residents of the street vehemently disagree. They say that the rioters were no-where near the house when the fire began. That the rioters were still on the main road when it was first noticed.'

'Then, how did the building catch fire?' Athreya asked.

'Not sure. But they are certain that it was not the rioters. They are also suspicious because of the speed with which the house burned down. They thought it might have been planned.'

'Someone deliberately set it on fire?'

'There are rumours, sir. The whole street was dark be-cause of a power outage. Nobody saw anything, but there are rumours about the fire. Some say that it was started deliberately.'

'To kill Mrinal's parents?' Athreya demanded. His face had grown grim.

'They can't say, sir.'

'Where were Mrinal and Pralay when the fire began?'

'In the block of flats opposite the house, sir. Mrinal had taken Pralay to his music teacher's flat for a class. Because there was talk of riots, Pralay's mother had sent Mrinal along with him, with instructions for them to run back home if she heard any commotion. Remember, Pralay was only thirteen years old. So, his mother sent his elder sister with him.'

'Did anyone else die in the fire?'

'No adult. But a baby later succumbed to the smoke.'

'Please do one thing for me,' Athreya concluded. 'Pre-pare a list of all families that lived on the street in Septem-ber 2010. Make a complete list of all names—first names and surnames.'

'Yes, sir. We have already started preparing it. You'll have the list tomorrow.'

'Thank you. You have been of great help.'

'So,' Shivali asked when she hung up. 'Do you think that Mrinal's parents were victims too? Targets of some unknown killer?'

'I fear so.'

'First, the parents are killed. A decade later, the daughter is killed. The son still lives.'

'A long shadow from the past falls on us, Shivali. I have much work to do.'

20

Athreya rose early as usual and got ready for his morning walk. The rays of the morning sun had just begun dissolving the darkness outside. This was the time of day that he enjoyed the most—a fresh new day, clean air and the inevitable dose of hope. He put on his walking shoes and a jacket to ward off the cold and stepped out of his room.

Lying sprawled on a sofa in the lounge, just outside his door, was a tall figure dressed entirely in black. It unwound itself and rose as Athreya came out.

'Dhavak!' Athreya said in surprise. 'Good morning. You are up early.'

'Good morning, Mr Athreya.' His voice was subdued. There was no sign of his usual belligerence. 'No, I didn't rise early. I just didn't go to bed.'

'Oh, I'm sorry to hear that. It has been a difficult time for you. Why don't you try and catch a few hours now? It's still pretty early.'

Dhavak shook his shaggy head. 'I wanted to talk to you. Thought I'd catch you first thing.'

'Certainly.' Athreya hid his surprise. This was a different Dhavak from the one he had seen so far. 'Where would you like to talk? I'm going out for a walk.'

'Can I join you?'

'With pleasure! I'll do a few rounds of the lawn.'

They went down in silence and stepped out of the castle. When they were out of earshot of the building, Dhavak spoke.

'Asma and Linda had a long chat with me last night,' he began. 'They seem to have a great amount of faith in you, and urged me to speak to you. They believe that you will correct the picture that has been painted.'

'In what way?'

'The picture is all wrong, Mr Athreya. The truth has been obfuscated. Who is a victim and who isn't is all top-sy-turvy. I want to tell you my version of what happened. I do so in the hope that you will ferret out the truth from this unholy mess.'

'Go on. I'm listening.'

'You have heard what the world has to say about Kumud Malakar. He is the molester, the pervert and the assailant of an innocent girl whom he verbally abused before trying to sexually assault her. Thanks to viral social media and the overzealous media coverage, he is now known as the depraved harasser of defenceless girls. These events took place four years ago, but let me begin my story a year be-fore that.

'Mrinal and I were once very good friends. She was twenty-seven and I was thirty-one. My line was music and she was struggling to set up a new business that was based on the internet. With the help of a young man named Aaron Mathew, she had set up a technology-driven business to teach kids English. The fledgling company was doing well despite his untimely death.

'Mrinal and I hit it off very well. Of course, I was not the shaggy, uncouth, bearded ape I now am. I was a neat and tidy, clean-shaven man who, by God's grace, was not unpopular with women. Mrinal and I got closer, and the relationship grew intimate. It was entirely consensual. We became more than just friends.

'That's when I made a suggestion to her, which she readily accepted. I suggested that she replicate what she was doing with teaching English to teaching music as well. We could use the same technology infrastructure that

Aaron had built and add another offering for kids. Only the content would be different. Instead of English, it would be music.

'Music is in my blood, Mr Athreya. It comes naturally to me. I can pick up a new instrument and start playing it proficiently within an hour. I am also gifted with a good voice. Not only am I good at singing and playing instruments, but I also understand the *structure* of music instinctively. I know its organization, its elements, the variations and everything else like the back of my hand. Actually better. There is nothing in this world I understand better than music.' He let out a harsh laugh. 'At any rate, I understand music better than I understand women.

'Because I knew music so well, I offered to create the content for the new initiative I had proposed to Mrinal. She was delighted, and we celebrated the decision with champagne.

'Over the next six months, I created everything needed. *Everything*. From introducing music to a three-year-old to training a young learner, to aiding a budding teenaged musician. Theory, notations, practice lessons, tests, sound clippings, videos, everything. They all went into a twelve-level course, each with multiple modules that could be self-learnt over the internet.

'But where I erred was in not having our agreement in writing. We were so close, so intimate that I saw no need for it. Our word was our bond, and there was complete trust. Or so I thought.

'When the content was complete and the testing successful, Mrinal changed. Abruptly, she grew cold and detached. She changed the entry codes to her flat and her office to keep me out. All of a sudden, we became strangers. The love that she had professed evaporated.

'Now, everything I had created was under the brand name of *her* business. She insisted that it was now *her* intellectual property. The company had paid me a notional honorarium for legal purposes and to avoid tax. That pittance, she now claimed, was the legal payment for the content. Consequently, the content that I had put my heart and soul into was the property of her company. I had no right to it. I was livid. She had used me like a paper napkin and discarded me. She had robbed me of my creation and cheated me out of my fair share of its success and credit. What you now see in her music app is entirely my creation. The business that has spread to five countries is, by rights, partly mine.

'Naturally, I confronted her. But unknown to me, she had planned for this. On a Saturday evening, when the office was empty, she left the front door open so that I could enter. The confrontation ensued. I was angry and demanded my rightful share. Never mind my broken heart and her calculated betrayal. At least, I should own a part of the business that had been my idea and my creation and get proper credit.

'But she was smart, very smart. She knew me well. She knew *exactly* how I would react to certain words and expressions. She fed me those words and showed me those expressions on her face. I grew furious and threatened her. How many photos she clicked, I don't know. She had muted the camera sound in her phone so that I wouldn't realize what she was doing. She went on clicking after taunting me. Taunt—click—taunt—click! She was nothing if not brave and cunning.

'Once she had enough photos, she turned and ran out to give the impression that she was fleeing from me. This too, she had planned for by wearing running shoes. She just left the office door open and ran. Being the fool I was, I hesitated to leave the office empty and unlocked. One minute's hesitation was enough for her to disappear. I know that she didn't return to her flat because I went there in search of her. I returned home realizing how I had been taken advantage of. I began contemplating legal action, even though

I knew that I didn't have a leg to stand on. Eventually, I drank myself to sleep.

'The next thing I know is that her Facebook post has gone viral. Photos of my angry face, of me shouting and threatening her were prominent. In addition there were two photos that showed her shirt ripped. After she had left, she ripped it herself. I hadn't touched her.

'The post went viral within hours, and the police came for me. The media was quick to pass judgement and to label me a pervert and a molester. Mrinal shot to fame for standing up to a harasser. The chief minister congratulated her on Twitter and the police commissioner announced a cash award for her. Thanks to viral social media, lakhs of people recognized me as a molester.'

They had reached the far end of the lawn. They stopped and watched the mist rolling into Peter Dann from the woods.

'As you have probably guessed,' Dhavak went on, 'I have a short temper. After the infliction of this gross injustice, when the policemen in the lock-up mocked, taunted and slapped me, I went berserk. I broke a few bones before they broke a few of mine.

'That ensured that nobody—the media, the police, the government—heard my side of the affair. They just refused to acknowledge that there was a version of the events that was different from what "poor, vulnerable and brave" Mrinal had put out. My father pulled strings to save my life and whisked me away to the tea estate for me to recover. Meanwhile, having achieved what she had sought, Mrinal grandly "forgave" me. I had suffered enough, she said. She hoped that I had learnt my lesson.

'My father and I discussed the matter for many weeks. Several lawyers were involved too. When we saw no recourse, we made a decision. Kumud Malakar disappeared and Dhavak Strummer—a hirsute ape—was born.

'That is my side of the story, Mr Athreya. I was betrayed

in every way you can imagine; betrayed by the innocent and vulnerable-looking angel. You would have noticed that Mrinal had a certain charm about her that worked very well with men. She could look vulnerable and lost when she wanted, and could evoke a feeling of protection in us. Sometimes avuncular, sometimes brotherly. We felt so sorry for her that we rushed to her aid. In doing so, we implicitly began trusting her. She used to play the "babe in the woods" act to perfection. If I am not mistaken, you, Javed and Dave fell for it too. Women didn't fall for it.

'But the fact of the matter is that she felt for nobody but herself. She was completely self-centred. She was incapable of feeling love and affection, but was an expert at faking it. My suspicion is that something was wrong up here.' He touched his temple.

'Well,' he went on after a long sigh, 'as far as my being a suspect is concerned, what I told you doesn't let me off the hook. If anything, it has only gone deeper. The reason I am telling you this is simple. I have been smashed once by Mrinal and I was quiet then. I have been hit again by her. I need to make sure that the world hears my version this time, even if I go down fighting. The last time, I had no one to speak for me. I hope it will be different this time. Good day, Mr Athreya.'

* * *

Hardly had Dhavak left Athreya than a slight figure appeared in the dissolving mist. It was apparent that she had watched Dhavak's conversation with Athreya, and had waited for them to finish. She and Dhavak crossed each other wordlessly at the centre of the lawn. Athreya knew that he was going to hear another story. He waited for her to come close.

'Hello, Linda,' he greeted. 'Up early? Or did you too skip sleeping?'

'Good morning, Mr Athreya. I slept, but not too well. May I walk with you?'

'But of course! What do you want to talk about?'

'I came to put my fate in your hands, sir,' she declared a shade dramatically. Her voice quivered with pent-up tension, matching the trembling of her fingers. 'Asma is someone I'd trust with my life, and she has a great regard for you. Her father backs her up unreservedly. I need your help, sir. I did not kill Mrinal.'

'Easy, Linda.' He put a hand on her shoulder. 'Don't get agitated. Get a hold of yourself and tell me what you came to tell me. It's about Aaron, isn't it?'

'Yes!' she whispered. 'Yes. Poor Aaron. How wonderful he was! I couldn't have asked for a nicer brother.' Her voice cracked. 'She killed him, Mr Athreya. Mrinal killed him.'

'How?'

'She drove him to suicide. She pretended to love him and extracted everything she wanted from him. Every single drop! The poor silly boy believed her, and she betrayed him. He was so sensitive and caring that he couldn't handle the shock. He jumped from twelve floors high, Mr Athreya! His body was shattered! How it must have hurt!'

She broke into sobs and clutched Athreya's arm. She buried her face in his sleeve and wept bitterly for a couple of minutes. He remained still and silent. At length, she let go and straightened.

'But I'm feeling better now: what goes around, comes around. The Lord ensured that. This chapter is closed except that I no longer have my dear Aaron.'

'Come, Linda,' Athreya said. 'Walk with me. Take your time and pull yourself together. When you are ready, start from the beginning and tell me what you came to tell me.'

She nodded and began walking close to him as if needing his protection. They completed half a round of the massive lawn in silence before she was ready to talk. She lifted her silver cross to her lips and kissed it.

'Aaron was a complete nerd,' she began with an odd tinkle of a laugh. 'But the nicest, most loveable nerd you'd ever meet. He was a brilliant software engineer, and he was excellent in English. He must have read every book there is to read. He topped the university both in his bachelor's and master's in English Literature. And he took to software development like a fish to water.

'It was six or seven years ago that he met Mrinal. I think he liked her right from the start, but didn't tell her because of his shyness. But she must have sensed it, and they grew closer. Aaron didn't tell Dad and Mum. Nor did he tell me for a long time. When he finally let his "little sister" into the secret, he described her vividly. "She's so simple and defenceless," I remember he told me. "So vulnerable! You'll like her, Linda. She is the nicest person I've ever met. She needs someone to take care of her, and that's going to be me." Aaron felt proud. I still remember his words and the images they conjured up in my mind.'

Athreya noted the similarity between Aaron's and Dhavak's descriptions of Mrinal, and how they aligned with his own impression of her when he had first met her at Clarksons. Dhavak had described it well as a 'babe in the woods'.

'That was when she was contemplating a start-up in education,' Linda went on. 'She wasn't sure what area in education she should begin with. She didn't know how to assemble the technology for it or how to write software. Of course, dear old Aaron volunteered. He would build the software for her and develop the content for English education.

'But she didn't have the money that would require, and no bank would give her a loan without collateral. Neither Mrinal nor Aaron had anything to offer as a collateral or a security. That's where matters stood until an elderly gentleman by the name of Sharif helped her out. He didn't have much money himself, but he had a sprawling house in the suburbs. He spoke to a banker friend of his and arranged for a loan. He stood guarantor and offered his house as the collateral.'

Athreya wondered who Sharif was and why he lent money to Mrinal. He hadn't heard the name mentioned by anyone at Peter Dann.

'Once the loan came through,' Linda said, 'Aaron went to work, building the software and hiring a data centre. He had already been working on creating the content for teaching kids English over the internet. He hired five programmers and the project was in full swing. Six months later, Mrinal launched her website.

'It was very hard work. Mrinal worked day and night on the business aspects while Aaron got the technology up and running. Lots of presentations and business meetings were needed to convince teachers and parents to subscribe to their service. Since Mrinal was not particularly strong in English, Aaron would go along with her to convince prospective customers with his wizardry in literature.

'At the end of it all, they pulled it off. Simultaneously, love blossomed between Aaron and Mrinal. They got engaged and were to get married the next year, once the business completed its first profitable year.'

Athreya glanced at Linda. He thought he knew where this was going. Dhavak had been betrayed. Was that Aaron's fate too?

'Two months before the imminent wedding, Mrinal walked out on him. Just like that!' Linda snapped her fingers. 'She offered no explanation or even an excuse. The love she had professed for him stopped abruptly as if a tap had been turned off. Aaron didn't know what hit him. He blamed himself, saying that it must have been something he had done that caused the break. He called her a hundred times, but she wouldn't answer. All of a sudden, she had become a stranger.

'Aaron followed her around, hoping to see her face to

face and ask why she had broken the engagement. One of those days when he was following her, he saw something that shattered him even more. Mrinal was seeing someone else. Want to guess who that someone was, Mr Athreya?'

'Dhavak?' he asked. 'Or rather, Kumud Malakar.'

'Bullseye! Yes, see, Mr Athreya, Aaron was the first napkin she had used and discarded. Dhavak—or Kumud, rather—was to be the second, although he didn't know it at that time. Nobody knew, except maybe Mrinal. You see what she had done? She got poor Aaron to build a system for her and develop content—which, by the way, is still being used on her app and website. Then, once she had got what she wanted from him, she ditched him.'

Linda's voice trembled. She paused and wiped her eyes with the small handkerchief she pulled out of a pocket. Athreya waited. This was indeed difficult for her.

'Poor Aaron was in a daze for two days after seeing Mrinal with Kumud,' she went on in a softer voice laced with sorrow. 'He came and told me what had happened. I assured him that he would find another girl, a better one. Told him that he was too good a person to let this devious woman destroy him. But what I said didn't stick. That night, he left me a goodbye note and another for Mum and Dad. In the wee hours, he left home and never returned. The next morning we heard that he had jumped off the tall office complex in which Mrinal had her office.

'So you see what I meant, Mr Athreya. Aaron fell two-hundred feet to his death. Mrinal fell fifty feet more. What goes around, comes around.'

Athreya cleared his throat and turned to Linda.

'Thank you for confiding in me, Linda,' he said gently. 'I don't want to respond now. I have to assimilate and mull over what you and Dhavak have told me.' He paused for a moment and looked into her eyes. 'But there is more that you haven't told me.'

'I have told you what I am free to tell. What I want you

to understand now, Mr Athreya, is that Mrinal was a bad person. An evil woman who was obsessed with herself. The Lord had given her a certain appeal, a charm that worked like magic on men. They went to her aid unquestioningly. In trying to protect and aid her, they ended up destroying themselves. Aaron and Kumud were not the only ones she destroyed.'

Athreya was sure that he would be hearing more about the people Mrinal had destroyed. Only Dhavak and Linda had spoken to him. The others hadn't—yet.

'You know what I call her, Mr Athreya?' Linda asked. 'A praying mantis. Just as the female mantis kills and eats the male while mating, Mrinal too devoured her men once they had served their purpose. The female sucks out the lifeblood and nutrients from the male—just as Mrinal sucked out every drop from Aaron.'

'Praying mantis,' Athreya mused. 'An apt description.'

'It fits her like a glove.'

Athreya nodded. 'And it conjures up vivid images.'

'Let me offer you an even more vivid image—that of a hand. A bloodied hand. Mrinal had blood on her hands.'

* * *

Athreya hastened to his room and locked the door behind him. He pulled out his suitcase and unlocked it to access the things he had put there out of reach of the castle staff and guests. From a large envelope, he drew out the photograph Negi had brought—the one with the bloodied hand that had been hounding Mrinal. He had seen it yesterday after sunset in the study where the lights were not particularly bright. He now took it to the window and held it up against the sunlight streaming in.

In view of what he had just heard, the image felt more ominous than before. And in the light of the morning sun, it looked disturbingly real. He stared at it for a long moment, studying the fingers and the blood dripping from the palm in the three rivulets. Then, something caught his attention; something he had not noticed the previous evening in artificial light.

At the centre of the palm, among the vivid red patches, were some letters in grey. They looked like a watermark on paper. He focused his eyes on the letters:

{centre}RRRAS

Five letters and five fingers. What had Linda said? '*Aaron and Kumud were not the only ones she destroyed.*'

Could the 'A' stand for Aaron?

If so, shouldn't there be a 'K' for Kumud or 'D' for Dhavak? Why was neither letter there? There must be a reason. What was the difference between Aaron and Kumud?

Athreya froze as the answer hit him: Aaron had died but Kumud was still alive!

Then, did this bloodied hand represent deaths?

'*Aaron and Kumud were not the ones she destroyed*'…
'*Mrinal had blood on her hands.*'

What did that mean? Were there four more deaths for which the five held Mrinal responsible? He looked at the letters again—RRRAS. Linda had mentioned another name—Sharif, the man who had lent money to Mrinal to start her business. It began with an 'S'! Did the last letter stand for Sharif? Whom did the three 'R's represent?

There was only one way to find out. Athreya picked up his mobile and called Shivali.

Twenty minutes later, freshly showered and with the photograph safely locked away again in his suitcase, Athreya went down for breakfast. As he reached the ground floor, a constable approached him.

'*Koi guest aaya hai, sir,*' he said. '*Aap ke liya pooch raha hai.*'

A guest has come, sir. He is asking for you.

Curious, Athreya followed the constable to the gate. Javed was already there and Negi was talking to a short, slim stranger with straight black hair. When Athreya reached them, the man's brown eyes turned to him. They seemed vaguely familiar.

'Mr Athreya?' he asked in a cultured voice.

'Yes. I'm Athreya.'

'Good morning, sir. My name is Pralay Shome.'

'Please come in, Pralay,' Athreya said, gesturing to Negi to let the newcomer enter. 'I am very sorry about your sister.'

Pralay nodded silently as he came forward. Athreya noticed Javed staring at the newcomer's shoes.

'How did you learn about Mrinal?' Athreya asked.

'Ipshita called me yesterday.'

'It's good that you have come. Have you had breakfast?'

Pralay shook his head.

'Other things can wait,' Athreya said. 'Will you join me for breakfast?'

'Thank you, sir.'

As they entered the dining room, Athreya felt a tug on his sleeve. He looked back to see that it was Javed. He wanted to have a word in private. Athreya fell behind and let Pralay enter the dining room where the women already sat. Ipshita rose and came straight to Pralay.

'Athreya,' Javed whispered into his ear. 'I know those shoes! Pralay was the sixth person in Nainital.'

21

'Mrinal always had problems with her emotions,' Pralay said.

He, Javed and Athreya were seated in the study. The young man was neatly dressed and spoke in mellow tones in a cultured manner. Athreya saw no evidence of the 'weirdo' that Kinshuk had compared him to.

'To the extent,' Pralay went on, 'that she was peculiar right from childhood. Most people experience the entire spectrum of emotions—from love to hate, from joy to grief, from fear to anger. But Mrinal couldn't feel some emotions like love, affection and gratitude. Even in our childhood, she used to be clinical and coldly objective. Let me give you a couple of examples.

'We used to have dogs at home when we were kids. My mother loved them, and my father too was fond of them. Having grown up with dogs around me, I too developed a love for them. Only Mrinal was different. She couldn't understand why my mother and I felt so much affection for our pets. She would ask us to explain, but when we did, she still couldn't understand. It's not that she disliked or feared dogs. She would give them a bath or feed them when my father or mother told her to do so. She would do it without resentment or reluctance, but with zero affection. She treated it as a task that needed to be done; as a part of the family, she did her bit. But, unlike the rest of us, she took no joy in it. Just as tables need dusting, dogs need bathing. Neither held emotion for her.

'I was seven years old when our first dog died. It was as if a member of the family was gone. I was shattered. I wept for days. So did my mother. In my father's generation, crying was not common among men, but I saw tears in his eyes. But Mrinal was unmoved. Entirely unaffected. When I came running and told her that the dog had just died, she was reading a book. She came out, looked at it lying lifeless, returned to the house and resumed her reading. Later, she told me that she was curious to see how a dead dog looked. That's why she had come out. Not out of sorrow or love.'

Athreya glanced at Javed. The big man was listening intently with an encouraging expression on his face that was not judgemental. It reminded Athreya of his police career when Javed the psychologist was listening to a witness or a patient.

'Similarly,' Pralay said, 'when my mother broke her hand in a scooter accident, Mrinal's only reaction was that of curiosity. She neither felt sorry for my mother, nor did she sympathize with her. We were shocked that she showed no concern at all. There were several such incidents in my early childhood. My parents were so concerned that they took Mrinal to a doctor. The doctor counselled her and assured my parents that she would become "normal" with time. Adolescence, he said, would fix her.

'He was right to the extent that she began exhibiting emotions. She began showing concern when one of the family fell ill. She would smile and congratulate me if I did well at school—something she had not done before. She began doing the kinds of things we all do. My father was relieved.

'But my mother was a very sharp lady. She saw through the charade. She realized that Mrinal had realized why it was necessary to *display* the kind of emotions others did depending on the situation. She learnt acceptable social behaviour very quickly. Soon, she became a master at it. To the extent that her display of emotions was perfectly timed and rang true every time. In short, she had become an accomplished actor. But in her heart, Mrinal hadn't changed.'

'But she was not *entirely* bereft of emotions, right?' Javed asked.

'That's right,' Pralay replied, 'She was not an automaton. She was human, but was incapable of feeling a certain set of emotions that included love and affection. It was selective. The one emotion that always moved her, often to tears, was self-pity. If she felt slighted or discriminated against, she would become angry or weepy. She was a very self-absorbed person.

'But that came with a very useful side effect. Whenever she took up something for herself, she would do it with single-minded determination. And more often than not, she would excel at it because, by nature, Mrinal was very intelligent and highly competent. More importantly, she was hugely effective—she knew *how* to get things done, even if it required being manipulative. When she wanted something, nothing else mattered.'

Javed shifted in his chair. Athreya saw that his expression had changed. From long experience of working with him, Athreya recognized the new look—a penny had dropped in the psychologist's mind—he had diagnosed Mrinal's condition.

'It was therefore no surprise to me that she succeeded so brilliantly in her start-up.' Pralay paused for a moment and dropped his eyes. When he continued, his voice was softer. 'Nor was it a surprise that she chose unusual ways to succeed. I believe you already know about Aaron and Kumud. What she did to them was entirely consistent with her nature. She felt nothing for either of them—no love, no affection, no gratitude and no loyalty. She led them down the garden path until she had obtained what she had sought. Once that was achieved, she discarded them.'

'Did you know them?' Athreya asked.

'Yes, but not very well. They were more like acquaintances.'

'Despite the fact that each of them, at different times, were in serious relationships with your sister?'

Pralay nodded. 'You see, Mrinal and I had moved apart by then. We didn't see each other and didn't speak. After my eighteenth birthday, I led my own life. Mrinal had transferred my share of our inheritance to me, and said that I was to manage it henceforth. After that, our worlds hardly overlapped.'

'Fair enough,' Athreya said. 'That gives us picture of your sister's mental make-up. However, there is another matter on which we need to speak to you urgently.'

'The burning down of our house in North 24 Parganas?'

'Yes.' Athreya eyed Pralay with curiosity. 'How did you guess?'

'The police have been making enquiries. I've received some phone calls from former neighbours. The police seem to have talked to everyone on that street who was there in 2010. I figured that you would want to hear my version too.'

'That's right. There are rumours that it was not the rioters who set it on fire.'

'It's no rumour, Mr Athreya. It is true. It was a deliberate act. I saw some things that convinced me. I don't have proof to offer, but that's an entirely different story.'

'I'd like to hear it. Tell me what you saw.'

Pralay rose from his chair and walked over to the window. For a minute, he stood there looking out through the glass pane. Athreya and Javed waited for him to prepare himself to talk about the night when his parents were killed. His anguish was understandable. At length, he turned and faced them, choosing to stand to speak.

'Let me start with the house itself,' he began in a voice laced with grief. 'It was an old, two-storey building that was getting to a stage where further repair was pointless.

Nevertheless, it had ample utility, and most important of all, it was home. The upper floor was a three-bedroom flat where we lived. We occupied the entire upper floor except for the landing at the stairwell.

'Downstairs was divided into two halves with the stairway separating them. The front half had been rented out to a trader by the name of Galani. He was from Mumbai, and he opened a shop. The funny thing is that my father knew very little about Galani. But as he offered a good rent—more than what others were willing to pay—my father let it out to him. The rear portion of the ground floor was a one-bedroom flat rented to a young couple by the name of Chakradhar. They had a one-year-old baby girl. There isn't much I need to say about them. They became victims just like us—they lost the baby due to the fire.'

Athreya rose and picked up a teapot that had just been delivered to the room. He looked enquiringly at Pralay, who shook his head. Seeing Javed nod, Athreya poured out tea for the two of them.

'Coming back to Galani,' Pralay said, 'let me describe the shop. All the doors and windows were rickety and warped. The front door opened out into the courtyard and the rear door opened into the hall and the staircase. Galani had the front door fixed, but he let the rear door remain as it was.

'That rear door was warped in such a way that it would never close completely. A gap remained between its two halves. Even when the door was latched from the inside, you could insert a pencil or a screwdriver through the gap and slide the latch open.

'Under the staircase, Galani stored big buckets and drums of paint, thinner and that sort of thing. This was illegal as he didn't have permission for flammables. It didn't occur to Dad that it could be dangerous in case of a fire. Since Galani had used up every inch of the shop and needed more space, he asked if he could take the rear portion too. But my father did not want to evict the Chakradhars. An argument ensued between Galani and my father.

'The next day, Galani offered to buy the ground floor for a price that was clearly above market. Then, evicting the Chakradhars would be his job, which he would do in a jiffy. My father refused to sell. He had realized that sharing the land with a man like Galani would be a disaster. Another row ensued, and my father served notice on Galani to vacate. But he refused to leave. Tenancy laws, being what they are, made evicting an unwilling tenant easier said than done. Because Galani needed more space, as I said he had begun using the space under the staircase. That's how the combustible liquids came to be stored there.'

'An extremely dangerous situation,' Athreya said. 'I wish the authorities had intervened. But do go on, Pralay.'

'Against this background,' he continued, 'let me go to the night of the fire. In preparation for the coming riot, Galani had shut up shop, double-locked the front door and gone away, presumably to his house. That was the last we saw or heard of him. He never returned after the fire, and is suspected to have fled to Mumbai. Not surprising, as it was his illegally stored flammables that razed the house and killed my parents.

'Mrinal and I were at my music class in the block of flats opposite our house. My music teacher's flat was on the second floor, facing the street. A small group of us kids were to have our usual class. But because of the riots and approaching noise, we were all frightened—which was why my mother had sent Mrinal to escort me.

'None of us could sing properly as we were scared. Every couple of minutes, one of us would go to the window and peep out to see if the riots were coming our way. Being closest to the window, I was the one who looked out most often. That was when I saw the figure darting into our building and then rushing out a couple of minutes later.

'It didn't occur to me then to connect what I had seen

with the subsequent fire. I didn't realize that someone other than the rioters had set the house on fire. The destruction of my house and the death of my parents scrambled my brain, and it remained muddled for more than a year. It was terribly traumatic. Besides, the official version was that the rioters had burned it down and none of the neighbours let us hear rumours to the contrary. Imagine how it would have been to be told that your parents had been murdered. We had already suffered a huge, huge shock. The neighbours shielded us.'

'It is amazing that you remember so much from a time when you were just thirteen,' Javed rumbled. 'So many details.'

'The events of that day are burned into my mind, sir. I don't know how many times I have relived them.'

'I can imagine. Please go on.'

'It was only after a couple of years that I put two and two together. What I think happened is this: somebody opened the rear door of the shop and started a fire inside. You remember my telling you that it could be opened by a pencil or a screwdriver? That's what was done.

'I then recalled what I had chanced upon a couple of days before the fire. On two occasions, the rear door had been opened surreptitiously. And on the afternoon before the fire, the same thing had been done, and someone had punctured a couple of plastic drums of something that smelled like turpentine or kerosene. I remember the smell as I passed the rear door on my way to the music class.

'Which meant that preparations had been done in advance. The shop was primed for a blaze. All that was needed to start the inferno was a small naked flame. Entering through the rear door, starting a small flame and exiting wouldn't take more than a minute or two. That's what the killer did.'

'You saw him enter your building?' Javed asked.

Pralay nodded without looking up. 'But by the time I

pieced together what had happened, it was too late. Four years too late.'

'Did you recognize him?'

Pralay nodded again. His eyes were staring at the carpet.

'Who was it?'

Pralay looked up. His eyes were brimming with tears.

'Not a "he", Mr Javed. It was a "she"... Mrinal.'

* * *

A stunned silence greeted the declaration. Javed was speechless with his mouth hanging half-open. The intensity in his eyes showed that his mind was racing.

'You smelled the turpentine or kerosene on Mrinal when she came back, didn't you?' Athreya asked in a whisper. 'But you didn't recognize the smell until later.'

Pralay nodded mutely.

'And the trick of opening the rear door was a secret between you and your sister. Everything added up when you looked back three or four years later. You saw things very differently from what a befuddled thirteen-year-old boy had seen. And you didn't want to believe that it was your sister. It took you a year to do that. That's when you broke away from her.'

'What could I do, Mr Athreya?' Pralay sounded broken. 'How could I accuse my sister? Who would believe me? The grief she displayed was so, *so* convincing!'

'Why did she do it?'

'She was twenty-one and raring to go and prove herself. For that, she wanted money... she planned to set up a business. All Baba had was the house; no real cash. Galani's offer had showed her how valuable the property was. That big parcel of land was a prize commodity. Even if half the proceeds went to me, she would still have more than enough.

'Remember what I said? When she wanted something,

nothing else mattered. She felt no love for her parents. She just saw them as a source of money that she wanted so badly. She figured out a way to get it. But this is conjecture, Mr Athreya. We will never know now.'

'She sold the property, did she?'

'The very next month. Claimed that she could no longer stay there after the tragedy.'

A sudden insight seared Athreya's mind.

'Pralay,' he asked, 'what were your parents' names?'

A bewildered look came on the young man's face. 'Shome,' he said.

'No, no! Their *first* names.'

'Ranjan and Rani.'

Two 'R's! Did they stand for two of the 'R's in 'RR-RAS'?

'And the name of the baby who died in the fire?' he asked. 'The Chakradhars' baby?'

'Rimi.'

Three 'R's! 'RRRAS' stood for Ranjan, Rani, Rimi, Aaron and Sharif! That meant that the man who offered his house as the collateral for Mrinal's loan must also be dead. He hoped that Shivali would soon find out about him.

Another thought flashed across his mind as he recalled Purbhi's surname.

'Chakradhar! Was Baby Rimi Purbhi's niece?' he asked.

Pralay nodded miserably. 'Brother's daughter.'

It all fit in now. It was clear why the five guests had hounded Mrinal. The bloodied hand represented the five deaths Mrinal had caused. Directly or indirectly.

'Sharif,' Athreya whispered. 'Tell me about him.'

Pralay shook his head. 'I don't know much. Except that Mrinal defaulted on the loan and Mr Sharif lost his house. He ended up in a dirty old-age home where he died a very broken man.'

* * *

'Sounds like a type of personality disorder,' Javed said. 'Of course, we can't ever be sure as Mrinal is no longer around to talk to. But everything you have described, Pralay, suggests a type of antisocial personality. People who suffer from this are unable to feel empathy, affection, loyalty, and those sorts of emotions. It's not deliberate— they just can't help it. That's how they are wired. Therapy sometimes helps, but it often doesn't.'

'Why was it not diagnosed?' Pralay asked. 'My parents took her to a psychiatrist.'

'Difficult for me to say, Pralay. Human behaviour, as you can imagine, is very complex. Often, there is no visible boundary between "normal" behaviour and a disorder. In some cases such as psychosis, the disorder is very apparent. But the personality disorder Mrinal seems to have suffered from is subtle. She also learnt to fake emotions very convincingly. Tell me, did she also have difficulty feeling guilt or remorse?'

'Yes!' Pralay exclaimed. 'I didn't mention that, but when she did offend or hurt someone, she wouldn't feel sorry. It's happened *many* times. At times, she felt *so* cold-hearted.'

'That's typical of this malady. The sufferers lack what we loosely call a "conscience". A hundred or two hundred years ago, this condition used to be called "moral insanity". Far more expressive than today's sanitized terminology. Everything these people do or don't do is driven by their own desires and wants. Depending on the intelligence of the person, the desire could range from the immediate and short-term to long-term.'

'That can be dangerous, Javed,' Athreya remarked. 'Very dangerous if accompanied by a lack of conscience.'

'Indeed. Their actions range from living normally to mere irresponsibility to serious criminal behaviour. Sometimes when the patient is intelligent and articulate as Mrinal clearly was, they can be dangerous.'

'Mrinal was charming too,' Athreya added. 'As Dhavak

said, men fell for her "babe in the woods" act. I am not ashamed to admit that I too felt sorry for her. She seemed so vulnerable and lost that I felt an avuncular protectiveness rise within me. I saw the same thing reflected in Dave.'

'You were not the first to experience it, Mr Athreya,' Pralay whispered. 'Fortunately, you are among the last.'

'Intelligence, charm and remorselessness,' Javed rumbled, 'when combined with the inability to feel empathy, affection and loyalty, can become a potent combination in a person who is driven entirely by her desires. You see how she gained the trust of her friends, especially men? A praying mantis, Linda called her. Very apt, indeed. Just like the female mantis devours her mate, Mrinal consumes her men.'

Athreya frowned. Something was tugging at the back of his mind.

'All this sounds vaguely familiar, Javed. Haven't we seen this before? The combination of brilliance and moral insanity?'

Javed nodded his large head. 'The Shimla school murders case. It was a good twenty years ago, but I'm sure you will recall it if you try—the supremely intelligent mathematics teacher who blamed his colleagues for his misfortunes. Very similar features.'

'Yes, I remember. If I am not mistaken, we cracked the case primarily due to your diagnosis. You had recognized the disorder in him. But you didn't recognize it when you met Mrinal.'

'I had very little time, Athreya. I must have spoken to her all of fifteen minutes. Five minutes at Clarkson's and ten minutes in the lounge. Then too, I met her socially along with three or more people. But I do remember wondering why such a successful and charming young lady exhibited unusual diffidence and visible vulnerability. They didn't seem to fit, and I wondered if some of what she displayed was put on. But you are right—I never imagined that I was looking at such an extreme case of the personality disorder.'

Javed turned to Pralay.

'I truly regret it has come to this, Pralay. And that too at Peter Dann. My deepest condolences. But I hope my explanation helps you understand your sister's condition.'

'I hope so too, sir, but I am still trying to get my head around it. A part of me says that it was not her fault if she could not help it. But she *actively* killed my parents. They had given her nothing but love and support, and she killed them in cold blood.'

'Perhaps,' Athreya said, 'time will help. Speaking of time, how did you get here so quickly? Ipshita couldn't have called you before lunchtime yesterday. You didn't come from Kolkata, did you?'

'I may as well say it myself, Mr Athreya, and not wait for the police lady to discover it. I have been staying at a homestay less than four kilometres from here. A place called Oakvale. I've been there for a few days. I arrived the day Mrinal died.'

* * *

'This is not the only disorder that we've seen recently at Peter Dann,' Athreya said once Pralay had stepped out of the study. Athreya had asked him to send Purbhi in. 'There is one more, which is by way of a minor mystery.'

'Purbhi?' Javed asked, as a knock sounded on the door and it opened.

'Come in, Purbhi,' Athreya said. 'Sit down.'

She took a seat warily and watched the two men.

'Pralay told us about your niece Baby Rimi,' Athreya went on in a gentle voice. 'We are very sorry to hear about it. Our condolences.'

Purbhi nodded and wiped a tear from her eye. She still said nothing as she fidgeted with the mobile phone in her hand. Athreya changed the topic.

'That mobile is very dear to you, isn't it?' he asked her. 'It's central to your life.'

Her face jerked up and she stared at him wordlessly.

'If you need help, Javed can help you,' Athreya went on softly. 'He is an experienced psychologist who can tell you how exactly to get rid of the addiction with minimal pain.'

Her eyes flickered to Javed and back.

'You know?' she whispered.

Athreya nodded. 'I've seen internet addiction before, and I've seen it cured in a matter of weeks. You don't have to be a slave to the internet, Purbhi.'

'Really?' Her eyes lit up. 'I can ditch it?'

'Without doubt. And it doesn't need you to trek to a place where there is no connectivity. Such disruptive measures result in nasty withdrawal symptoms. You've suffered enough. Yes, it was a bad idea for you to go on the hike.'

'How did you know? Did Ipshita tell you?'

Athreya shook his head.

'I overheard you and Ipshita the day after I arrived here. You spoke outside my door, not realizing that the room was occupied. Then, when I saw you on the trek, I grew surer. The event that removed any remaining doubt was your putting my power bank into Asma's bag.'

Purbhi buried her face in her hands and bent over. The ponytail at the top of her head fell forward over her forehead. A minute passed. Then, without lifting her face, she spoke.

'I am so ashamed!' she said from between her fingers. 'I am so ashamed that I stole.'

'Borrowed, Purbhi, not stole. Don't beat up yourself over it. It's a common outcome of addiction. The fear of not having connectivity for four days must have been overpowering. You knew that you couldn't help but search for a mobile signal against all hope, and that would drain your battery. Your own power pack might not last for four days.

So, you needed a supplementary one. And as there were no shops here, you borrowed mine.

'But when you got no signal, you borrowed Asma's phone when she was asleep. Hers was the only BSNL phone in the women's tent. You surfed the web and deleted the browsing history. That left her battery low on power. That's how I figured it out.'

Purbhi lifted her face and stole glances at their faces.

'It's okay, Purbhi,' Javed rumbled. 'Nobody else knows. I myself came to know just now. The important thing is to not let this condition continue. We'll have you cured in a couple of weeks, don't worry. All you need is a regime that gradually phases out your dependence. No drugs are necessary. Let's talk about it later—just you and I. Nobody else needs to know.'

'Thank you, sir. I would be very grateful for your help. Please call me whenever you get free.'

She rose. 'Thank you, Mr Athreya. Thank you for keeping my secret.'

Purbhi left the room and closed the door behind her. Athreya also rose. But before he could go to the door, Javed waved him back to the chair.

'I have something to tell you,' he said as Athreya sat down. 'You may as well hear it from me rather than Shivali.'

Athreya watched his friend silently. Javed was ill at ease. Athreya wondered if it had anything to do with the enquiry thread that Shivali was yet to speak about.

'It's about Sharif,' Javed said, confirming Athreya's suspicions. 'The man who lost everything when Mrinal defaulted on the loan. I had known that he had been cheated by someone, but I hadn't known who it was. It was only when you and Pralay spoke about him today that I made the connection.'

'Is it true that he lost everything?' Athreya asked.

Javed nodded. 'The bank repossessed the only asset he had—his house. That left him on the street. But Sharif was too proud to accept our help.'

'How did you know him?'

'He was Naira's cousin. They were very close even though he was much older. She was shattered when he died in penury. It worsened her condition. She never emerged from it.'

Javed looked up and met Athreya's eyes with a stoic gaze.

'So you see Athreya, that gives me a motive… a powerful motive.'

22

Athreya and Asma stepped onto the rooftop terrace a little after 10 a.m. All the others, including Javed and Maazin, had already gathered there. Athreya had just spent half an hour with Asma, discussing a number of matters including those related to Sharif and Naira. He was now about to confront the guests.

'This is an informal meeting,' he began. 'ACP Suyal is in Nainital, finding out who stayed at which hotel six weeks ago. She is also collating the results of multiple tests. Negi, her sub-inspector, has gone to Oakvale, which is where Pralay has been staying. I wanted us to meet here so that nobody else overhears what we say. I am going to put on the table much of what I know about this affair. Also understand that I will tell the ACP *most* of what I know.'

He paused for the emphasis on 'most' to sink in before continuing.

'First of all, let's do away with a needless pretence that is fooling no one. The ACP has already identified the hotels where three of you stayed at Nainital. She will have the remaining names soon. There is no point in carrying on with this fiction any longer. Let us acknowledge that the five of you and two others met at the Naini Retreat six weeks ago and planned something. We now know that the sixth person was Pralay. Before we leave the terrace this morning, I will name the seventh.'

The six looked at each other, not knowing how to respond. At length, Dhavak and Pralay simultaneously took the lead. They nodded to the others.

'Yes, Mr Athreya,' Ipshita said in a clear and calm voice. 'We accept that for now. However, we reserve what we want to say to the police.'

'Fair enough!' Athreya rubbed his hands. 'We have passed one hurdle. We also know that you made fake bookings at Peter Dann to ensure that there were no other guests here when you came. Other than Mrinal, of course. The police are already tracing the credit card numbers given when the bookings were made. They are also tracing phone calls and emails. We will soon know the outcome.

'Unfortunately, I landed up here unexpectedly, and you had to get me out of the way. So, you drugged me so that I could not interfere. You dealt with Kinshuk the same way. I don't ask you to confirm or deny this. Now, let me come to the crux of the matter.

'As I had said during our first dinner, I am not obliged to share my views with the police as I am not the official investigator. I may not suppress evidence, but my perspectives and theories are my own. Which means that now is a good time for you to say the things you have withheld.'

'Withheld?' Kinshuk exclaimed. 'They better not withhold. This is a—'

'Kinshuk!' Athreya cut him off sharply. 'I have withheld from them the contents of your discussion with the ACP last evening. If you do not wish that to become public knowledge, I suggest you reconsider what you were about to say.'

Without giving him a chance to respond, Athreya turned to the five guests and Pralay, who were sitting together.

'When I went to bed last night, the picture of Mrinal that had been painted was that of a serial victim. In a few hours this morning, that has completely changed. She is now a serial offender. This is what represents Mrinal now.'

He pulled out the photograph of the bloodied hand and held it up for all to see.

'This bloodied hand… this is the picture of Mrinal now. The five fingers represent the five deaths she was responsible for—some directly, some indirectly. In the palm of this bloodied hand are five etched letters—RRRAS. Each letter stands for one victim—Ranjan, Rani, Rimi, Aaron and Sharif.

'The deaths of Ranjan and Rani Shome gave Pralay and Ipshita a very strong motive to kill Mrinal. Baby Rimi's death did likewise to Purbhi. Aaron's death is Linda's motive. That leaves Sharif… I will come back to him later.'

He turned to Sarosh and went on.

'The ACP has been gathering details of your business dealings with Mrinal,' he said. 'I don't have them yet, but I don't think I need them. You have already given that to me.'

'Me?' Sarosh asked in confusion.

'You told me the story about two persons by the fictional names of Amit and Rahul. Amit and Rahul had entered into a deal worth twenty crores. You had wanted my help in nailing Rahul. Remember?'

Sarosh nodded. He had gone pale.

'Amit is you and Rahul was Mrinal. You believe that she cheated you in a twenty-crore deal.'

'*Believe?*' Sarosh fumed in indignation. The tips of his magnificent moustache quivered and his mismatched earrings shook. 'It's a fact! She cheated me!'

'And that gave you a motive. That's why you became a part of the five.'

'So, all five had motives to kill Mrinal,' Kinshuk snarled. 'Which of them did it is the question. Or did all of them do it?'

Athreya turned upon him in a flash.

'I will not go into the details of *your* motive, Kinshuk,' he snapped, 'except to say that you and Mrinal had a massive fight the night before she died. The cause was something that was utterly unacceptable to her. She had made up her mind to break off the engagement. In fact, the two of you were to return to Mumbai separately.'

All heads turned to Kinshuk.

'You don't need to tell us, Mr Athreya,' Sarosh said, his fiery gaze on Kinshuk. 'We can guess it—infidelity! All of Mumbai knows about him. Except Mrinal. Kinshuk must have been unfaithful to his fiancée.'

Kinshuk rose as if to assault Sarosh but stopped when he found a towering Dhavak in the way. He sat down, his eyes smouldering like coals.

'So, that's what it was!' a small voice exclaimed. Athreya turned towards it. Linda continued, 'You see, Mr Athreya? What goes around, comes around. What Mrinal did to poor Aaron, Kinshuk did to her.'

'Yes, Linda,' Athreya replied. 'But let's go on, if you don't mind. Let's return to two things. First, what was the connection between Sharif and the group that met in Nainital? Second, who was the seventh person?'

Athreya paused and surveyed the faces. The five guests and Pralay were watching him unblinkingly. Kinshuk was still seething. Javed was stoic as ever. Asma was close to tears. Maazin was uncertain. After scanning all the faces, Athreya's eyes came to rest on one person.

Maazin.

'You were the seventh person. Were you not, Maazin?'

Maazin drew a couple of deep breaths before responding. He nodded.

'Yes, Mr Athreya. It was I. I rode down on my bike from here. When I saw Mr Rais at the restaurant, I hid behind a pillar.'

'Thank you, Maazin. That makes it so much easier. The reason for your participation in the group was Sharif. Correct?'

Maazin nodded again.

'Tell us, Maazin'—Athreya's voice had gone soft—'what was Sharif to you?'

'Technically, Mr Sharif was my grand-uncle. But in reality, he was more like my father. I come from a poor family, Mr Athreya. We lived hand-to-mouth. Mr Sharif allowed us to live, rent-free, in an outhouse on his plot. Before I came here, it was he who had given me everything I had. He had taught me everything I knew before coming to Peter Dann.

'He was a man with a golden heart, Mr Athreya. A generous and loving man who gave far more than he ever took. A very, *very* kind man, he was. Mrinal, with her charms, ran rings around him. She got him to approach a banker friend to grant her a loan. And she convinced him to offer his house as the collateral for the loan. When she defaulted, the bank repossessed Mr Sharif's house. That destroyed him. Both he and my family were on the streets after that.'

Athreya glanced at Javed. He was staring at Maazin aghast. His mouth was half-open. Rarely had Athreya seen his friend so stumped.

'Maazin,' Javed croaked, 'why didn't you tell me?'

'What good would it do, Uncle? You had enough grief in your heart after Aunty died. Why add more? What happened was the past that couldn't be changed.'

'Let's move on,' Athreya said gently. 'Shall we, Javed?'

He nodded, his sorrowful gaze still on Maazin.

'It's now apparent that all of you had motives to kill Mrinal,' Athreya resumed. 'Have no illusions about how the police will view this. All of you are suspects. We also *know* that Mrinal was killed. It was *not* suicide. I will not go into the reasons, but be assured that it was murder.'

Seven agitated faces seemed to plead silently with him. Some opened their mouths to speak, but Athreya raised a hand and silenced them.

'I know that you thought otherwise,' he continued. 'But that is not true. Something happened between 11:20 p.m. that night and 12:30 a.m. Between Asma seeing Mrinal and Maazin locking up the terrace. Something happened in those seventy minutes of which you have not spoken. Something that made you believe that Mrinal had committed suicide. You were quite certain of that. That's why Linda has kept insisting that she had leapt to her death.

'You already knew of Mrinal's death when you started your trek the next morning. That's why you weren't surprised when I told you that she had died. You assumed—for whatever reason—that she had committed suicide. The only time you showed surprise was when I said that it could be murder.'

A gasp sounded. Athreya turned. Maazin was staring at the other trekkers with his mouth open. Athreya couldn't help feeling that his astonishment was genuine. From Maazin's reaction at Top Camp, Athreya already was sure that he had not known of Mrinal's death. Which meant that only the five guests had known. And that they had kept that news from Maazin.

'I will stop now and allow you to consider your options,' Athreya concluded. 'I *must* know what happened in those seventy minutes. If I don't, ACP Suyal will draw her own conclusions. I urge you to speak to me before she returns. It is in your interest to do so unless one or all of you murdered Mrinal.

'Realize one more thing. Now that it is certain that it was murder and not suicide, you are free of an abetment of suicide charge. Unless you killed Mrinal, you have nothing to fear. I will be in the study if any of you need me.'

He turned to go.

'Mr Athreya,' Linda called. Again, her fingers were touching the silver cross that hung from her neck 'Are you *absolutely* certain that Mrinal was murdered?'

'Yes, Linda. There is no doubt whatsoever. And the murderer is here on the terrace now.'

* * *

Within half an hour, the expected knock sounded at the study door. It was Maazin, looking wretched and pale. With him was Asma. Athreya and Javed gazed at him silently as the former waved him to a chair. Asma went to a corner of the study and sat down without a word.

'I've come to make a full confession of what I have concealed,' Maazin began in a quavering voice. 'I don't know whether it will help your investigation, Mr Athreya, but I dearly hope it does. I asked Asma to join us as she deserves to know the truth. I will begin my story six months before today.

'You already know how I felt about Mr Sharif's death and about what Mrinal did to him. I also felt that the way Mr Sharif died affected Naira Aunty very badly. It deepened her misery, from which she didn't recover. In my mind, it contributed to her death.'

'Are you saying that Naira jumped from the terrace?' Javed asked.

'No, Uncle. Aunty was very strong-willed, as we all know. She would never have done that. She told me many times that she would never take her own life despite the burdens she bore. What I am saying, Uncle, is this.

'When her condition worsened after Mr Sharif's death, Dr Farha increased the dosages of Aunty's medicines. We all saw how unsteady she became after that. Dr Farha had told us not to let Aunty go to the terrace. But that was the high point of Aunty's day—the one thing she used to look forward to when she woke up every morning. She liked to see the open sky and loved watching the sunrise on the peak. They lifted her spirits as no medicine could.

'But the increased dosages made her more unsteady. The movement of her limbs was affected. And she had become *so* thin. I think that she lost her balance and fell through the crenellation. That was because of her unsteadiness which was due to the increased dosage. That, in turn, was because of Mr Sharif's death which was caused by Mrinal.

'So, Mrinal not only caused Mr Sharif's death, she was also responsible for Naira Aunty's demise. I hated her for that, Mr Athreya. I still do. Naira Aunty was such a wonderful person! She looked after me like her own son.'

He thrust out his hand and showed it to Athreya. Tears shone in his eyes.

'See this ring, sir?' he croaked though a constricted throat. 'Naira Aunty gave it to me. She said that it was too big for Asma to wear and that I needed one. She said that a young man had to show the world subtle signs of prosperity, and the ring would do just that.'

Maazin reached up and wiped away the tears with the back of his hand.

'I understand the motivation, Maazin,' Athreya said. 'I understand what drove you. But what did you do?'

'When someone called Pralay Shome contacted me six months ago and told me how his sister had ruined many lives, I heard him out. He told me about his parents and Baby Rimi, about Aaron and Dhavak. About Mr Sharif. He said that they were planning to get back at her and asked if I would like to be a part of it. I agreed, although I didn't know what it would entail. They began planning, and when it reached a certain stage, they felt that we needed to meet. We decided to meet in Nainital, with each person staying at a different hotel. Except me, as I would ride to Nainital on my bike.

'We decided to make Peter Dann the place where we would confront Mrinal with her sins. I began sending her and Kinshuk promotional emails and messages, telling them about Peter Dann and the treks we offered. And as it was not yet the holiday season, we were offering attractive discounts. Earlier, Sarosh had begun sending her the bloodied-hand photographs.

'When Mrinal made a booking, the others followed. They made other fake bookings to ensure that no other guests would be here at that time. But she cancelled the trip, forcing the others to do likewise. When Mrinal made a booking the second time, she didn't cancel, and all the others made their bookings too. We decided that Pralay shouldn't stay here as that would complicate matters.'

'No other guests were to be here,' Athreya guessed. 'But Javed unexpectedly brought me from Nainital. Your five guests were surprised to see me and learn that I too was a guest.'

'Yes, sir. To make it appear as if all of them came together at Peter Dann by chance, they pretended to be strangers. Of course, we hadn't bargained for Javed Uncle's sharp eye and excellent memory. So, this is how it all happened, Mr Athreya.'

'This explains the premonitions I had,' Javed growled. 'Now that I think back, I overheard you cancel genuine guest bookings and shift their dates without an apparent reason. You must have moved other guests so that these five had a clear field to confront Mrinal. But at the same time, I think you encouraged Kinshuk to come here on those days. But I did not think much about it as you usually handle bookings very well. I might have overheard other conversations too. But it stuck in my subconscious mind and bothered me.'

'I'm sorry, Uncle,' Maazin said. 'But I ensured that I only shifted dates. We didn't lose any guests or revenue.'

'The bloodied hand,' Athreya mused, 'were you the one who enlisted the Cochhas to drop a copy of the photo into Mrinal's room?'

Maazin nodded miserably. 'They also slipped it into her room at Clarkson's and put the marks of the bloodied hand there and here too.'

'Was the attack on Asma your doing too?'

'No, sir. It was Dhavak's. He felt that a physical threat was necessary to convince Mrinal that she was in danger. I was not aware that he too had spoken to the Cochha.' He threw a pitiful glance at Asma.

'What did you hope to achieve by bringing Mrinal here and confronting her?'

'The hope was that two months of receiving letters, messages and bloodied-hand photos would wear her down. The attack by a stranger would push her close to the edge.

'After having done what she had done, after having caused so many deaths, she couldn't confide in anyone. The fear of discovery or death would be very real for her, and she would have to deal with the pressure all by herself. That would be enough to crack anyone.

'On top of that, if she were confronted in the middle of the night by six people in a lonely, out-of-the-way place, the pressure would be unbearable. She was sure to crack and say something that could be used against her. She might or might not make a confession, but we hoped that she would say things that we could go to the police with. To gather evidence, we recorded the confrontation on two phones—Ipshita's and Purbhi's.'

'But Mrinal didn't crack,' Athreya said. 'She was too strong. She weathered your two-month harassment and the confrontation.'

Maazin nodded.

'She said nothing that could be used against her,' he said. 'She was remarkably strong-willed.'

'You better give the recordings to the police, Maazin,' Javed said.

'Unfortunately, we can't.' The young man shook his head. 'Ipshita and Purbhi have deleted it and reformatted their memory cards. It can't be retrieved.'

'Anyway, I'm glad that you told us this, Maazin,' Javed rumbled. 'I am not happy at what you did, but it clarifies how the atmosphere was set up and it solves the puzzle of the five guests. But it doesn't tell us how Mrinal died or what you did between 11:20 p.m. and 12:30 a.m.'

Maazin nodded and shifted in his chair.

'This is what happened after Asma went down... '

23

The party was over. The lounge was empty except for the six—three men and three women. Asma had bid them goodnight and gone down twenty minutes ago. Her father had preceded her. Athreya and Kinshuk had long retired to their respective rooms, and were presumably sinking deep into drug-induced sleep. They had been yawning uncontrollably since 10:45 p.m. There was no danger of their interfering. Maazin had instructed the staff not to come up to the lounge. The six had waited for ten minutes to make sure that the coast was indeed clear. It was, and Mrinal was still on the terrace.

The time for the confrontation they had been planning six weeks for was finally here. It was 11:40 p.m.

The six of them went up the front stairway and stepped onto the terrace. Maazin closed the door behind him, but didn't lock it. They went to where Mrinal was sitting, staring into the darkness of the night over the southern parapet wall. She didn't seem to have heard them.

She gave a start when Dhavak threw down a copy of the bloodied-hand photograph on the table before her, face up. Simultaneously, Ipshita had switched on the light in her mobile phone and shone it on the photograph. Mrinal stared at it, but didn't look up at them. Perhaps, she knew who they were.

'Five people!' Dhavak hissed. 'You killed five people. Not counting what your slander did to me. Not counting the crores you swindled from Sarosh and Sharif. Not counting the death of Asma's mother that Sharif's death caused. Not counting the terrible grief endured by multiple families. There aren't enough fingers in your bloodied hand to count the number of lives you've ruined. We were alone the last time I confronted you. There were no witnesses. Now, there are five. You can't frame me *this* time.'

At last, Mrinal looked up and scanned the faces. She said nothing.

'What kind of a monster are you?' Ipshita hissed. 'You killed your own parents for money! Your mother who brought you into this world. Your father who gave everything for you. There can be no crime more heinous than what you did. Murderer!'

'And the baby!' Purbhi added. 'An innocent one-year-old baby. What did she do to you? You killed her because you wanted money to set up a business. How her mother cried! For years! How you snatched the happiness away from her and my brother. And from all of us. No punishment is too much for you.'

'You are the Devil himself,' Linda sobbed. 'Aaron gave everything to you. *Everything!* You just discarded him as if he were an old sock. Even today, you shamelessly use what he built.'

Mrinal shook her head.

'It is my intellectual property,' she said in a measured voice. 'Be it what your brother did or what Kumud did. The legal position is *very* clear. As far as your brother is concerned, I hold no ill will against him. It was a phase. People come together, people move apart. I can't help it if he chose to take his own life.'

'He fell two hundred feet,' Dhavak cut in. 'If I throw you over this wall, you'll fall two-hundred-and-fifty.'

'But you won't,' Mrinal countered. 'You've never had it in you.'

'This is where Asma's mother fell from,' Maazin interjected. 'You are sitting not five feet from the spot. Mr Sharif's death affected her so badly that she stumbled and fell.'

'So, that's your angle.' Mrinal threw a glance at him. 'I was wondering how you came to be with this lot. Sorry, but I am not likely to leap over the wall.'

'Of course not!' Ipshita retorted. 'You are too much in love with yourself.'

Mrinal ignored her and turned to Sarosh.

'And you, Sarosh? You made a bad business deal and are now whining. I am not the only one you have thrown your family's money at. Maybe you've learnt a valuable lesson.'

Sarosh said nothing. No words would come. He had gone red and his chest was heaving. The usually garrulous investor was speechless with fury. His fists were clenched, as was his jaw. Hatred oozed from his eyes.

'Your accusations that I have siphoned off money are ridiculous,' she went on. 'The money is still parked in liquid mutual funds. I sent you the account statements as recently as last week.'

'Fake!' Sarosh managed. 'The statements are fake.'

'Do you even know to read those statements?'

Mrinal dismissed him and turned her attention to Ipshita.

'I know what *you* are after,' she said over Linda's sobs. 'You want Pralay to get my money. You are trying to make me take my own life by jumping over the wall. If I die, my wealth goes to Pralay. You are a leech like any other. You will suck away the money and leave him. I know your kind. Kolkata sees many leeches during the rainy season.'

For once, Ipshita was struck speechless.

'So, Kumud,' Mrinal went on calmly. 'Did you come up here to throw me over the wall? Or did you come to make me feel so sorry that I would do it myself?'

'You freak!' Dhavak thundered. 'I have a good mind to throw you over and face the consequences. The world would be free of a snake!'

'You never did have the guts, Kumud.'

'You—!' Dhavak lunged forward, only to be restrained by Maazin.

'It's not worth it, Dhavak,' Maazin pleaded, as he struggled to hold back the stronger man. 'She is not worth it.'

'Maazin's right!' Linda beseeched, coming between Dhavak and Mrinal. 'What goes around, will come around. The Lord will ensure that that this praying mantis gets her due.'

'Lord?' Mrinal chuckled. 'You'll have to wait all eternity, sweetie. The praying mantis is God's creation too.'

For the next fifteen minutes, the back and forth continued, but Mrinal ran out of things to say. Under the relentless verbal assault, she gradually cracked. Six against one was an uneven battle that began rattling her. Halfway through, she stopped responding and covered her ears. At the stroke of midnight, the six turned away and returned to the lounge.

They had failed.

They left a thoroughly unnerved Mrinal on the terrace with her face buried in her hands.

* * *

'Mrinal was alive when you left the terrace at midnight?' Javed demanded, breaking the silence that followed Maazin's confession. 'Are you *absolutely* sure of that?'

'Yes, Uncle.' Maazin was looking wretched. 'I swear to God. I'll swear on my mother's name if you wish. Mrinal *was* alive when we came down. I remember the scene very well— her face was buried in her hands and her hair had fallen over her hands. But she was not crying—she just wanted to tune us out of her world.'

'Was she depressed?' Athreya asked.

Maazin shook his head. 'I know depression, sir. I've seen it at close quarters. Let me assure you that she was not depressed in any way.'

'In any case,' Javed added, 'there is no way she would have committed suicide. From what she said to the six, it is clear that she was in no frame of mind to take her life. Quite the opposite.'

'Then, there is only one possibility,' Athreya said. 'Someone went back upstairs and killed her. Her confronters expected Mrinal to crack and say things that could be taken to the police. Even if it wasn't a confession, she might have said something that incriminated her. But when Mrinal didn't crack, when she gave them no ammunition against her, the whole purpose of this elaborate deception came to naught. The endeavour had failed. She would go free the next morning, and there was nothing they could do about it.'

'Nothing, except take the law into their hands,' Javed added. 'So, one or more of them went back to the terrace and killed her.'

A pregnant silence followed this pronouncement. Maazin and Asma looked terrified. Javed himself was grim-faced. Athreya was pensive as his right index finger furiously traced words on his knee.

'Maazin,' Athreya said, breaking the silence, 'I want you to recall—as accurately as you can—what each of the five was wearing. Down to the details of how the women wore their hair.'

Maazin closed his eyes and recalled as much as he could. It tallied with Athreya's recollection of seeing them in the lounge. Which meant that none of them had changed their clothes before going up to the terrace. All the three women, as far as Maazin remembered, wore ponytails.

'Except Linda,' Asma interrupted, correcting him. 'She broke her elastic band and had let her hair loose.'

'Yes,' Maazin nodded. 'That's right.'

'What did you do after you came down to the lounge?' Athreya asked.

'I went downstairs to the kitchen. There was still work to do. I came back up at 12:30 a.m. and checked the terrace before locking it. Mrinal wasn't there. She had told about Ravi ten minutes earlier that she would be going to her room shortly. I assumed that she had returned there.'

'And you went on the trek the next morning.'

Maazin nodded.

'You saw or heard nothing more of Mrinal that morning?'

'No, sir.'

'Nothing that might have suggested that she had committed suicide?'

Maazin shook his head. 'Nothing. That's why I was stunned when you told us about it at Top Camp.'

'Then,' Athreya asked in a near whisper, 'how did the other five know that Mrinal was dead? They showed no surprise at Top Camp. They believed that she had committed suicide.'

'I... I don't know, sir,' Maazin stammered. 'I really don't.'

'Maazin!' Javed thundered like an angry lion.

'Uncle, I swear! I don't know.' He was in tears. 'Ask Asma and Mr Athreya. Ask Chetan. I was stunned when Mr Athreya told us that Mrinal had fallen from the same spot Naira Aunty had. I don't know how the others knew.'

'I think he is telling the truth, Javed,' Athreya whispered.

'Maybe,' Javed fumed. 'But the fact remains that the other five knew about Mrinal's death *before* they left on the trek.'

'Which means that someone went back to the terrace between midnight and 12:30 a.m.'

* * *

Javed watched over Athreya's shoulder as the latter took a sheet of paper and wrote down the timeline of events as indicated by the multiple testimonies they had heard. They were alone in the study.

09:45	— Mrinal goes to terrace
10:15	— Dinner announced
10:15–10:20	— Athreya's and Kinshuk's drinks drugged
10:45	— Athreya and Kinshuk start yawning; drowsy
11:05–11:10	— Athreya, Javed & Kinshuk retire
11:20	— Asma retires after talking to Mrinal
11:40–12:00	— The six confront Mrinal on terrace
12:01	— The six return to the lounge
12:02	— Maazin goes downstairs
12:03	— The women go to their room
12:15	— Dhavak & Sarosh go down to lawn
12:22–12:23	— Ravi checks on Mrinal on terrace
12:30	— Maazin locks up terrace

'If all that we've been told is true,' Javed said, 'there is only a very small window when Mrinal could have been killed. It's barely enough for the killer to go up to the terrace, kill her, tip her over the parapet wall and come down.'

'Not only that,' Athreya replied. 'The killer also had to dump Mrinal's phone and the murder weapon into the pond. Too little time. Too risky.'

'Of course, this would be the case only if *all* of them are telling the truth. Someone might be lying.'

'We saw the events with our own eyes till 11:10 p.m. There is no ambiguity till then. And I take it for granted that Asma's testimony is true as well. Mrinal was alive at 11:20 p.m. The uncertainty begins after that.'

'Maazin,' Javed growled. 'His testimony is the one after Asma's. It begins at 11:40 p.m.'

'I'd wager that Maazin spoke the truth, Javed,' Athreya said. 'Of course, I could be mistaken. You know him better.'

Javed nodded. 'I tend to agree with you. Maazin is a good boy—'

The ringing of Athreya's phone interrupted him. It was Shivali calling from Nainital. Her trip there had been eminently successful.

'I have the names of the hotels where each of the five stayed,' she began. 'We also found that a person by the name of Pralay Shome was involved. I suspect he is Mrinal's brother.'

'He was and he is,' Athreya confirmed. 'Good work! And what of the test results?'

'They have come in too. It is now confirmed that the dregs at the bottom of Kinshuk's glass were a sleeping drug. The analysis of the blood sample the GP took shows the same drug. When zaleplon and alcohol are mixed, the effect can be over-powering, and can induce blackouts.'

'Kinshuk did black out when he was woken up the next morning.'

'Yes, sir. And, as you suspected, there is gin in Mrinal's hair at the back of the head where she had been struck with the bottle.'

'Aha! Then you have confirmed the murder weapon too.'

'We have. It was the bottle you found in the lily pond. Microscopic analysis shows that the sliver of glass and the piece of yellow paper found in Mrinal's scalp came from the bottle. And the discolouration on the label is blood.'

'Excellent work, Shivali! Congratulations on making such rapid progress. The case is all but solved. All we need is one confirmation. I heard something this morning that we need to confirm right away. Remember the venture that Sarosh had set up with Mrinal? The one about which you heard whispers of financial misappropriation?'

'Yes.'

'Mrinal apparently said that Sarosh's money is parked in mutual funds. But he claims that she siphoned off the money and faked the mutual fund statement that shows that the funds are still there. We need to get to the truth. All we need to do is to get a copy of the statement and show it to the mutual fund company. We will know at once who is telling the truth.'

'I'll have it done right away. Someone is already looking into the financials. But, sir, you said that the case is all but solved! Do you know how Mrinal was killed and by whom?'

'I think so, Shivali.'

'I'm returning to Peter Dann right away!'

'Do come, Shivali. We'll have a showdown this evening. Be prepared to make an arrest.'

24

Twelve people sat in the lounge, facing Athreya. The time was 7 p.m. The five guests and Pralay sat close together at the centre of the lounge. Kinshuk occupied a single chair some distance away. Between them were Javed, Asma and Maazin, sitting as a group. Shivali and Negi had taken seats between the others and the stairways.

'It's time to bring this affair to a close,' Athreya began. 'This morning, I had asked you to give me an account of what had happened that night between 11:20 p.m. and 12:30 a.m. Maazin has come forward to tell us, and Linda has confirmed it. Mrinal was alive when the six of you left her on the terrace after confronting her.

'On the table were Mrinal's mobile, an empty dinner plate, half a glass of orange juice, a half-full bottle of gin, an empty can of tonic, an ice bucket, some napkins and a hair clip. That was at midnight.

'Mrinal was alive at midnight, but when Maazin went up to lock the terrace at 12:30, she wasn't there. She was killed sometime between midnight and 12:30.'

'But, Uncle,' Asma interrupted, 'Ravi saw Mrinal after Maazin went down. He spoke to her.'

'Indeed, he did, Asma,' Athreya agreed. 'That was at 12:23, by my reckoning. Which suggests that Mrinal was killed in the remaining seven minutes between 12:23 and 12:30. Correct?'

Asma nodded.

'So, the killer went up to the terrace, took the bottle of gin from the table *in front of* Mrinal, hit her at the *back of her head*, threw her over the wall, hid the bottle and Mrinal's phone inside the lily pond and came down. That's a lot to accomplish in seven minutes! And remember, the killer had to pick up the bottle that was in front of Mrinal in order to hit her. Would she let the killer do that? Especially after the confrontation that had just taken place? She would have been on her guard. Unlikely.

'We must therefore seek another solution. To do that, let me quote to you some of the things you yourselves have said.

'Maazin said this about Mrinal when you left her on the terrace at midnight: "*I remember the scene very well—her face was buried in her hands and her hair had fallen over her hands.*" Right, Maazin?'

He nodded.

'Further, these are Asma's words about Mrinal when she visited her on the terrace at 11:20 p.m.: "*She buried her face in her hands a couple of times, making her hair fall over her face and obscure it.*" Correct, Asma?'

'Yes.'

'So, what is common between these two statements? That when Mrinal buried her face in her hands, her hair fell over her hands.'

Athreya scanned the faces around him. Confusion reigned on them.

'Here's another clue.' He turned to Asma. 'Did you examine Mrinal's hair clip that was on the table on the terrace?'

Asma nodded.

'What did you find?'

'It was broken.'

He surveyed the faces once again.

'Got it?' he asked. 'Mrinal's hair was falling over her hands and face whenever she leaned forward. And her hair clip was lying broken on the table. That means that Mrinal's hair was *not* in a ponytail when she died.'

'Yes, Uncle,' Asma said. 'Why is that relevant?'

'To answer that, let me quote from Ravi's testimony. This is what he said when I asked him if Mrinal had been wearing a shawl: "*Yes, sir. It was wrapped around her shoulders and arms. Her hair was hanging in a ponytail outside the shawl.*"'

'She was wearing a ponytail?' Javed almost bellowed. 'Mrinal was wearing a *ponytail* at 12:23 p.m.? How is that possible?'

'It's possible because of the simple fact that the woman Ravi saw at 12:23 p.m. was *not* Mrinal.'

A stunned silence gripped the lounge. Most faces wore a perplexed look. Three had paled.

'Who was it that Ravi saw and spoke to at 12:23 p.m.?' Athreya asked, breaking the silence. 'Remember, Mrinal had checked in only that evening. Ravi would not have had a chance to become familiar with her voice. When Maazin sent him to talk to Mrinal, he assumed that the woman in the chair on the terrace must be Mrinal. He only saw her from behind and didn't see her face. Besides, he saw nobody else on the terrace. Somebody impersonated her when Ravi went up to the terrace. This somebody had to impersonate her because, at that time, *Mrinal was already dead.*'

'Who?' Shivali snapped. 'Who was it?'

'There are three possible candidates—Ipshita, Purbhi and Linda. I rule out Purbhi for two reasons. First, her ponytail is very distinctive—it sprouts from almost the top of her head. Ravi would have recognized it, as she had already stayed here for several days. Second, her voice is unique and cannot be mistaken for someone else's. That leaves Ipshita and Linda. The elastic band that Linda used to tie her ponytail had broken late that evening. Both Asma and Maazin confirmed that. Is that right, Linda?'

'Yes,' she whispered in relief. 'It broke a few minutes before we went up to the terrace. I was tense and kept pulling at it. It broke.'

'That leaves only one candidate,' Athreya concluded.

* * *

All faces turned to Ipshita, who had gone white as a sheet. Purbhi too had blanched. Linda was trembling.

'I didn't kill her,' Ipshita whispered. 'Honest!' She glanced at Pralay. 'I didn't kill her.' She turned back to Athreya and pleaded, 'It's not the way you think. I didn't—oh God!'

'I did not say that you killed her,' Athreya said.

Ipshita's head jerked up. She searched his face for hope. 'No?' she croaked.

'No. But you haven't told me the whole truth. I told you repeatedly that if you did not kill Mrinal, you had nothing to fear. I meant it. But you didn't take my advice. You could have spared me all this drama, had you listened to me.' He smiled wryly. 'However, to make it easier for you, I will tell you what happened.

'Immediately after Dhavak and Sarosh went down to the lawn, you and Purbhi went to the terrace. Why you did that, I don't know, but you left Linda in the room and went up there again. Later, you bullied Linda into not telling about it.'

He glanced at Asma. 'That was the argument Ipshita and Purbhi had with Linda in the women's tent at Top Camp. Linda was terrified of suppressing evidence, but the other two brow-beat her into maintaining silence. Correct, Linda?'

She looked fearfully at Ipshita but didn't speak.

'I will answer that, Mr Athreya,' Ipshita said. 'I've bullied Linda enough. What you said is true. I coerced Linda into keeping quiet. I will now tell you what we have withheld so far.

'As soon as Dhavak and Sarosh went down to the lawn, Purbhi and I went back up to the terrace. I had something more to say to Mrinal, and this was probably the last chance I would get. I took Purbhi with me to watch out for anyone else coming up.

'But Mrinal was not there. We knew that she had not come down because Dhavak and Sarosh had been in the lounge all the time, and they hadn't seen her. And as soon as they went down the stairs, Purbhi and I came out of our room. We were puzzled to find that she wasn't on the terrace. We looked around and couldn't find her.

'As we thought about it, we decided that it could mean only one thing—that Mrinal had leapt over the parapet wall and taken her own life. We were terrified. If our confrontation with Mrinal came to light, we would be charged with abetment of suicide. Our brains froze at the thought, and we didn't know what to do. We just stood there like two stupid statues. That's when, we heard footsteps.'

'Footsteps?' Athreya echoed.

Ipshita and Purbhi nodded in unison.

'Someone was coming up by the rear stairway. We ran to the lily pond and crouched behind it. The person went to where Mrinal had been sitting and did something at the table that we couldn't see. From the way he grunted and cleared his throat, it was apparent that it was a man. His movements were very quick.

'He glanced over the parapet wall. Then, to our dismay, he came towards us. He came around the wall of the pond as if he knew where we were. We crouched down further and slunk the other way, hoping and praying that he wouldn't hear us.

'He didn't. Shortly, we heard the sound of the water in the pond moving, and half a minute later, he left the terrace by the rear stairway.'

'You didn't see who he was?' Shivali asked.

'No, ma'am, we didn't. We were afraid to look.'

'Go on.'

'After he left, we went to where Mrinal had been sitting. We peered over the parapet wall, but could see nothing. We were about to go down when we heard footsteps again. This time, they sounded different. It was Ravi... we were trapped on the terrace near the table. I quickly sat down in the chair Mrinal had used. And to hide my clothes, I wrapped the shawl around me. By force of habit, I put my ponytail outside the shawl.

'Ravi didn't come near. He just spoke from a distance, and I answered him with minimal words. My voice is not very different from Mrinal's. Once he left the terrace by the rear stairway,

Purbhi and I waited for thirty seconds and went down to our room by the front stairway. We reached our room at 12:24 p.m.

'As I said earlier, we assumed that Mrinal had committed suicide. The man peering over the wall reinforced it. On the trek the next morning, we told Dhavak and Sarosh about what had happened. But we didn't tell Maazin because we didn't know how he would react to the news of another suicide at Peter Dann.'

'Another?' Javed thundered. 'Another? There has *never* been a suicide at Peter Dann!'

'I'm sorry, sir,' Ipshita replied immediately. She was contrite. 'I said that without thinking. Please forgive me.'

'So, that is how you knew that Mrinal was dead even before Mr Athreya told you,' Shivali said. 'A fine mess you've stirred up, but the main question remains—which of you killed Mrinal? It's apparent that she was killed between midnight and 12:22 p.m. All of you had the opportunity.'

* * *

'Before we answer that,' Athreya purred, 'let us digress a little bit and talk about gin.'

'Gin?' Javed demanded. 'What gin?'

'Gordon's Gin, to be specific. That was the brand Mrinal drank. How many bottles did you have, Maazin?'

'None, sir. It's a difficult brand to find in these parts and we are currently out of stock.'

'Mrinal was particular about what she drank. Right, Kinshuk?'

He nodded.

'Particular enough to carry her preferred brand with her when she came to these foothills. She couldn't be sure that she would be able to get it here.

'On the night of the murder, when Mrinal went up to the terrace, Maazin took up her bottle of Gordon's Gin and a can of tonic. How much gin was in the bottle, Maazin?'

'About half-full,' Maazin said.

'But when I went up the next day, the bottle was nearly full! The obvious inference was that she had finished the old bottle and had opened a new one. But when I asked Maazin and Asma, both said that Mrinal hadn't drunk a drop of alcohol after going to the terrace. Then, how did the bottle fill up? Had someone added water to it? Worse, had someone poisoned it? I asked the ACP to have the bottle analysed.'

'And we found that there was nothing wrong with the gin,' Shivali piped up. 'No dilution, no poison, nothing.'

'Which meant that the bottle we saw in the morning was *not* the bottle that went up the previous night. Why was that? Gordon's Gin comes in a heavy bottle. Heavy enough to be used as a cudgel. To stun... or even to kill.

'The next question was whether the bottle had left any sign on Mrinal's head. It had: a sliver of glass and a tiny piece of paper that was yellow. Gordon's Gin's label is primarily yellow. Further, there was a discolouration on the label that turned out to be blood.'

'So, that's how you predicted the colour of the paper!' Shivali exclaimed.

'Coming back to the murder,' Athreya went on, 'when was the second bottle of Gordon's Gin taken to the terrace? By whom?'

He turned and looked at Maazin.

'I don't know, sir,' the young man stammered. 'There were no bottles of Gordon's Gin at the castle.'

'Except in one man's possession. The man who bought several bottles for Mrinal before they left Mumbai for Peter Dann... Kinshuk.'

'I couldn't have killed her!' Kinshuk protested. 'I was drugged senseless. Just like you were.'

'Yes, you were,' Athreya agreed. 'There is no doubt of that. Both of us were heavily drugged.' He turned to the five guests. 'Which of you drugged us?' he asked with disconcerting mildness.

They remained silent.

'Did you supply the Nitrosun, Maazin? It was a medicine Naira used to take.'

'Yes, sir,' he whispered. 'I know Nitrosun well. I knew that it does no harm. It induces sleep quickly. But I didn't drug you, sir. I refused to… you are a guest here.'

'Then who did?'

'I did.'

Athreya turned to regard Sarosh with a slight smile.

'Tell us what you did,' he said.

'Before the party began, I dissolved the tablets in water and removed as much of the white sediment as possible. But I couldn't remove all of it. I then kept the Nitrosun solution in a small bottle.'

'When did you drug us?'

'When dinner was announced. Everyone was keen to see what was on the menu. Both of you left your glasses unattended and went to look at the buffet. That's when I did it.'

'And you saw it take effect very quickly, didn't you?'

Sarosh nodded.

'Speaking for myself,' Athreya went on, 'I was completely knocked out that night. It took sustained knocking on my door to wake me up the next morning. I believe nitrazepam's and alcohol's effects are additive. I was woozy for much of the next day too. What about you, Kinshuk?'

'You saw me,' Kinshuk exclaimed. 'I was floored! I even blacked out on the sofa downstairs.'

'Yes, you did. I am certain that you couldn't have faked that. It was far too real, including the drool when you dozed off on the sofa with your mouth open. And the dilation of your pupils.'

Athreya paused dramatically and held up a sheet of paper. It was a lab test report.

'But there is an inconsistency,' he said. 'The drug in your brandy was not nitrazepam. It was zaleplon—a very different drug from what Sarosh had laced our drinks. Incidentally, the police have discovered that Mrinal was using zaleplon.'

Kinshuk said nothing. He stared aghast at Athreya.

'You drugged yourself later,' Athreya went on. '*Much later,* after Mrinal had died. You saw Sarosh spike your drink and knew that they were up to something that night. You went up to the terrace and emptied your glass into the pond.

'On your return to the lounge, you began feigning drowsiness. As the others expected you to be drowsy, your masquerade worked perfectly. They decided that you wouldn't wake up that night.

'But you stayed awake, listening at your door. A couple of minutes after the six went up to the terrace by the *front* stairway, you went up by the *rear* stairway, which is right outside your room. You hid behind the lily pond and witnessed the entire confrontation. As you listened, an opportunity presented itself to you.

'Immediately after the six went down, you went to Mrinal, offering sympathy. In the state she was in, she would have ignored you. You picked up the bottle of Gordon's Gin and hit her at the back of the head. She collapsed. You picked her up and threw her over the wall. I suspect you killed her sometime between 12:05 and 12:10.

'You had little doubt that the two-hundred-and-fifty-foot fall would obliterate the signs of the blow you had inflicted on her. Therefore, chances were that it would be assumed to be suicide. To encourage that belief, you misdirected the police by talking repeatedly about the bloodied-hand photo and the persecution Mrinal had faced. What you were suggesting was that she had been hounded to death.

'When Javed told you that Mrinal had *fallen* off the terrace, you said: "*No... she didn't... she didn't actually do it!*" You tried to make us think that it was suicide. In the worst case, you would leak some of what you had overheard during the confrontation on the terrace. The five would be booked for abetment of suicide. You would have gotten away with it had we not been specifically looking for signs on the victim's scalp.

'After you threw Mrinal down, you realized that the bottle had cracked and the label had blood on it. If it was left on the table, suspicions of murder would arise. Questions would also crop up if the bottle went missing. Had you thrown it into the woods below, it would probably be found and the bloodied label would show that it was the murder weapon. So, you went down again by the rear stairway. You picked another bottle of Gordon's Gin from your room and returned to the terrace to place it on the table. That's when Ipshita and Purbhi saw you. You then dropped the old bottle and Mrinal's phone into the pond before going down again.

'You must have returned to your room around 12:20 p.m., just a minute or two before Ravi came up. You then waited for everything to quieten down, and when all noise and movement ceased, you went to Room 2 where the rucksacks were kept. You took a hammer, rope, gloves and pegs and threw them through the window, into the woods where Mrinal had fallen. You did that for no reason other than to create a red herring.

'Just in case the police decided that it was murder, these items would raise misleading questions such as "was the hammer the murder weapon?" and "were the rope and gloves used to scale the southern wall?" In short, they would create confusion, and direct attention away from you.

'After that, you went to your room and drugged yourself silly. You *had* to, if you were to convince the police the next morning. But you didn't have nitrazepam. You used zaleplon instead.'

Athreya sat down. Kinshuk had frozen in his chair with a haunted expression on his face. All eyes were on him.

'Gotcha!' Javed rumbled after a minute. 'Good job, Athreya! What was the motive?'

'I'm done, Javed. The ACP will tell you.'

'Money, Mr Javed,' Shivali said as she and Negi rose. 'Eight out of ten times, it is that. Kinshuk had forged Mrinal's signature and redeemed funds invested in a mutual fund. He had siphoned away about eight crores without Mrinal's knowledge.

He prepared fake mutual fund statements to cover his embezzlement.

'After Mrinal discovered his infidelity, the engagement was broken off, so it was only a matter of time before she discovered the theft as well. Also, he had just heard Sarosh mention fake mutual fund statements. When he saw the opportunity to get rid of Mrinal, he took it with both hands.'

'Thank you, Shivali,' Javed rumbled, as he rose and pulled out his pipe. 'Peter Dann continues to live up to its reputation. Whatever happens here, happens for the best. The world is a better place now.'

'You were right, Linda,' Athreya said with a trace of a smile. 'Aaron fell two-hundred feet. Mrinal fell two-hundred-and-fifty. For being unfaithful in love to Aaron, her fiancé cheated on her. And for having swindled Sharif, Kinshuk swindled her.'

'Yes, Mr Athreya,' Linda whispered. 'The Lord never lets down the faithful. What goes around, comes around.'

EPILOGUE

Several people were on the rooftop terrace again, watching the Nanda Devi spectacle at sunset. Athreya had not brought his camera this time, preferring to watch nature's show uninterrupted. He had taken enough photographs the last time. While he was sipping cider, Javed and Dhavak had already moved on to the more potent drinks. Tonight, they were having a party on the terrace that would stretch to a late open-air dinner.

Asma had decided that they would have enjoyable and memorable events on the terrace from now on. The unfortunate incidents that had happened here needed to be overshadowed by pleasant ones. It was time to move on and leave the past behind. This was the second night after the case had been solved.

Pralay had returned to Kolkata with his sister's remains to have her cremated and perform the customary last rites. Ipshita had wanted to go with him, but Pralay wouldn't hear of it. He preferred her to, at last, have a good time at Peter Dann before returning to Kolkata. The last few days had brought all the guests at Peter Dann closer to each other. It was time for them to let their hair down.

When the Nanda Devi show ended, Dhavak strummed his guitar, triggering a round of anticipatory applause from the expectant gathering. He had promised to sing as much as they wanted, and had also drawn up a list of duets to sing with Ipshita. He began with an old, fast-paced Hindi song—'Main Hoon Jhumroo'—to set the tone for the evening. At once, Chetan and Maazin joined in, with the former breaking into an impromptu dance, making his hair fly all over as he grinned showing his yellowed teeth. The women began clapping in rhythm, ushering in a festive atmosphere that touched everyone.

Athreya made a video call to Veni and broadcast it to her. While Veni was an exponent of classical music—both Carnatic and Hindustani—she was also extremely fond of old film songs like this one. When the song ended all too soon, Dhavak moved on to 'Aaja Aaja Main Hoon Pyar Tera', a very popular Hindi duet, and Ipshita leapt up and joined him. The rest of the younger group joined Chetan on the dance floor, making Veni wail in envy. Had the roly-poly lady been here, she would surely have danced.

An hour later, taking a break from the first instalment of singing and dancing, they flopped into chairs, tired but elated. Stronger liquor was now flowing, including a couple of single malts that Javed had brought from his personal stock. Dhavak stuck to his local whisky, saying that expensive single malt was wasted on someone like him who couldn't appreciate the delicate flavours. He sat down beside Athreya with his bottle in one hand and a cigarette in another. Having been a smoker in his younger days, Athreya didn't mind the smoke.

'I don't know how to thank you, sir,' Dhavak said for the umpteenth time. His attitude towards Athreya had undergone a complete reversal. He now almost worshipped the investigator. 'Nor does my father. My mother is absolutely elated that the cloud has lifted from me.'

'There is no need to thank me, Dhavak,' Athreya replied, 'as I've told you repeatedly. Javed brought me here to solve a riddle, and I did what I like doing. All's well that ends well.'

'True, but I still want to show my gratitude. It's difficult for another person to fathom what this release means to me.'

'You already have, Dhavak. Many times over.'

'Words, Mr Athreya… they were mere words. I don't have my chequebook with me, but once I get back home… I'll take your address. No amount of money can show my gratitude, but a token will be in order.'

'Your choice, Dhavak,' Athreya smiled, knowing full well that people in Dhavak's position felt a very strong urge to thank him in a serious way. 'But please don't feel compelled.'

'Thank you, sir. I think it will be in order… you see, Pralay has said that he will be giving me a fair share of Mrinal's firm that he will inherit. He feels that I deserve it.'

'What are you two talking about?' Linda asked, coming up to them.

'I was just telling Mr Athreya that he should visit one of my family's tea gardens,' Dhavak lied smoothly as the others joined them. You too, Linda. All of us! Let's have a get-together sometime soon.'

He turned to Athreya and continued, 'Seriously, sir. You should come with your wife. Give me a chance to play host and to give Maazin and Asma a break. Will you, sir?'

'Yes, Dhavak,' Athreya laughed. 'I will certainly make it one of these days. Now, why don't you sing us some more songs—say, classics from the last millennium.'

Dhavak leapt up, took a long swig from his bottle and picked up his guitar. He strummed it a couple of times and began a Beatles number: 'Ob-La-Di, Ob-La-Da'.

While the others began clapping in unison, Athreya found that Purbhi had stayed back beside him.

'I just wanted to tell you that I've begun my therapy,' she said softly. 'Mr Javed is *so* good! *So* understanding! I'm already feeling better. I'm happy that I came to Peter Dann. I'm going to stay here for another couple of weeks or until I'm cured.'

'How wonderful!' Athreya responded. 'Excellent decision! As a freelancer, I guess you can work from anywhere as long as you have connectivity.'

She nodded and reached out figuratively to squeeze his hand.

'I'm not good with words, sir,' she said gruffly. 'I can't really express what I feel. But you have given me and my brother closure on Little Rimi, my niece. God bless you, sir.'

Athreya smiled and said nothing. This was the reward for his work. By the time Dhavak was done with singing, all the five guests had thanked him personally and profusely. As had Maazin.

Javed, who had been observing from a distance, came up to him.

'Popular, aren't we?' he asked with a smile.

'Goes with the territory, my friend,' Athreya replied.

'It does. I hope you'll be staying for a few weeks. At least a couple.'

'Veni is away for a couple of months, and I have nothing to do. I haven't taken an extended break for years.'

'Good!' Javed nodded. 'Nothing like the present. Make full use of it. Who knows what the future holds.'

Little did Javed know how prophetic his words were.

About the Author

RV Raman is the author of the Harith Athreya mysteries, a series Agatha Christie-esque whodunits, published by Agora Books, as well as the Inspector Ranade and Inspector Dhruvi thrillers, published in India. Having travelled extensively in India and abroad, Raman takes his readers to real-life locations through his mysteries – each is set in a different picturesque location in the vast Indian countryside. The first Harith Athreya mystery, *A Will to Kill*, was named a New York Times Editor's Pick.

Find him at www.rvraman.com and at @RVRaman_

CPSIA information can be obtained
at www.ICGtesting.com
Printed in the USA
JSHW021505060523
41350JS00004B/5/J